SPARK

SPA

RK

BY

SARAH BETH DURST

CLARION BOOKS
HOUGHTON MIFFLIN HARCOURT
BOSTON   NEW YORK

CLARION BOOKS

3 Park Avenue, New York, New York 10016

Copyright © 2019 by Sarah Beth Durst

Clarion Books is an imprint of
Houghton Mifflin Harcourt Publishing Company.

hmhbooks.com

The text was set in Electra LT Std.

Library of Congress Cataloging-in-Publication Data
Names: Durst, Sarah Beth, author.
Title: Spark / Sarah Beth Durst.
Description: Boston ; New York : Clarion Books, Houghton Mifflin Harcourt,
[2019] | Summary: Naturally quiet since birth, Mina and her stormbeast,
Pixit, lead others like themselves in defying authority and attempting to
spread the truth that Alorria's idyllic weather comes at a steep cost.
Identifiers: LCCN 2018035180 | ISBN 9781328973429 (hardback)
Subjects: | CYAC: Quietude — Fiction. | Dragons — Fiction. | Weather — Fiction.
| Fantasy. | BISAC: JUVENILE FICTION / Fantasy & Magic. | JUVENILE FICTION
/ Girls & Women. | JUVENILE FICTION / Animals / Mythical. | JUVENILE
FICTION / Action & Adventure / General.
Classification: LCC PZ7.D93436 Sp 2019 | DDC [Fic] — dc23
LC record available at https://lccn.loc.gov/2018035180

Printed in the United States of America
DOC 10 9 8 7 6 5 4 3 2 1
4500753497

For Alyssa, Adam, Jonah, and Brianna

⟞CHAPTER⟝
ONE

MINA was quiet.

Every morning, she liked to tuck herself into the corner of their farmhouse kitchen and watch her family storm through: Papa singing off-key as he poured sugar into the pot of oats, Mother yelling at him to add less sugar, Papa yelling back cheerfully that he could add *more* but not *less* because he was just that sweet, her older brother, Gaton, stomping in to say he couldn't find his socks, Papa joking that he'd added them to the morning oats, and the twins waddling in with Gaton's socks on their hands like puppets.

And every morning, after her family had whirled tornado-like into the kitchen, Papa would bellow, "Mina! Mina? Is Mina awake? Anyone seen Mina?"

Giggling, the twins would wave their sock puppets at the corner where she perched quietly on her favorite chair.

He'd clap his hands to his bearded cheeks dramatically, making the twins giggle even harder. "I thought that was a shadow! No one eats until my little shadow eats." And then Papa would scoop the biggest, sugariest, best scoop of oatmeal into a bowl and give it to Mina before Gaton could inhale the rest and before the twins could spill any of it on the floor.

"Love you, Papa," she'd say.

"Love you, Mina," he'd say, and wink.

She'd always been quiet. She'd been born without a cry on a peaceful night when the stars over their family farm sparkled brighter than usual, or so her mother liked to say. Mina didn't think that was very likely. She'd been in the next room when the twins were born, and she knew babies were *not* quiet. Ever. Even when they slept, they made cute, gurgling chirps. But she let Mother tell the story how she wanted. It was probably close enough to true.

Most mornings, Mina would eat in her favorite corner and listen to her family chatter and laugh. She liked the way the sounds flowed around her. It felt warm, as though her family were tucking a cozy blanket of babble around her, and she loved that they never pushed her to add to the noise.

But this morning, Mina had news.

So she finished her oats, carried her bowl to the sink, and stood in front of the table. This was unusual enough that Mother shushed Gaton, the twins quit smearing their breakfast on their cheeks, and Papa scraped his chair across the wood floor as he turned to look at her.

She liked to think this was one of the secrets about being quiet: when you finally speak, everyone assumes you have something important to say. *And I do*, she thought.

"I think my egg is going to hatch soon," Mina said.

It was as if she'd dropped a teaspoon of water into a skillet of boiling oil. Everyone popped up and began jabbering at once. From Mother: "Are you sure?" From Gaton: "Are you nervous? Don't be nervous!" From the twins: "Yay! Yay! Yay, Mina!" From Papa: "We're so proud of you!"

She grinned at them all.

Mina had a storm-beast egg. One in four kids in Alorria was awarded care of one of the country's precious eggs and tasked with bonding to the unborn creature. For two years, she had devoted three hours a day to her egg, being sure to touch its shell so the growing beast could absorb her thoughts and feelings. If she'd done this correctly, then when it hatched, it would come out as a perfect match for her, and they'd be bonded mind-to-mind and heart-to-heart. She'd be its storm guardian, and it would be her storm beast.

Storm beasts and their guardians were responsible for making Alorria as perfect as it was. Every day in Alorria, you woke to a blue sky. You felt warm air and a soft breeze. Sometimes you saw a rainbow, but only when the farmers asked for rain on their fields. Wind gusted over the sea, but only when the sailors needed it to sail their boats. Snow fell on the mountain peaks, but never below the tree line. Lightning never struck the ground and was instead harvested from the clouds to power the city's magnificent machines. And there had never been a tornado or a hurricane. All thanks to the storm beasts and their guardians.

Soon I'll be one of them, a real storm guardian! Just thinking that made Mina want to do a little dance. Quietly, of course. She'd been anticipating this day for two years. Longer, really. Long before Gaton got *his* egg, as soon as Mina had been old enough to read stories about storm guardians, she'd wanted to be one of them — to be out there, making the world more wonderful.

She felt as if she'd been waiting for this all twelve years of her life.

"She's going to hatch a sun beast," Gaton declared. He pounded his fist on the breakfast table for emphasis. The bowls rattled, causing the twins to giggle again.

"Are you willing to bet on that?" Mother asked, a twinkle in her eye. "Three weeks of cleaning the chicken coop *without* complaining if I win?"

"And three weeks of *not* milking the goats if I win," Gaton countered.

"Deal." Mother held out her hand.

"Deal!" Gaton said. They shook to seal the bet.

Maybe I shouldn't hope for a sun beast, just to see Gaton clean the coop. Mina made a soft clucking sound, which one of the twins, Rinna, immediately imitated, twice as loud.

"Mina isn't half as lazy as you are," Mother teased Gaton, as soon as they'd shaken. "She'll hatch a rain beast for certain."

The other twin, Beon, clapped his pudgy hands. "Wind beast! Wind! Wind!"

All of them turned to study Mina, and Mina tried to not squirm under their gazes. She didn't like being stared at, even by her family. Even if it was kindly meant, it made her feel like a bug about to be squished. Sensing her discomfort, Beon wrapped his arms around her leg and squeezed. Mina ruffled his hair in thanks.

"Not wind," Papa said thoughtfully. "She's too steady."

"Exactly!" Gaton said. "She's dependable. Her beast will be a sun beast."

I do want a sun beast. Sun beasts and their guardians were responsible for maintaining the endless summery temperature in Alorria and for beaming any excess sunlight onto crops to make them grow faster. Gaton had hatched a sun beast three years ago. His beast's power would be fading soon — once a storm beast finished growing to full size, it lost its ability to control the weather — and he'd said several times that he wanted his little sister to take over his work in the local fields.

Sometimes Mina thought she'd like spending her days the way Gaton did, out in the fields, drawing in and dispersing the sun's energy over the crops. Because of the storm beasts and their guardians, everyone in Alorria always had enough to eat. *But I also want a rain beast. Or a wind beast. Flying on a wind beast would be amazing!* She'd spent hours imagining herself with different kinds of beasts. All of them had a role in making Alorria great. "I'll be happy with any kind of beast," Mina said.

"I wanna snow beast," Rinna announced. "So I can throw snowballs at Beon all the time."

Mina smiled as Beon and Rinna stuck their tongues out at each other. Neither of them had ever so much as seen a snowball, but lately Mother and Papa had been telling the twins lots of tales about the different kinds of storm beasts, in preparation for Mina's egg hatching.

Altogether, there were five kinds of storm beasts: sun, rain, wind, snow, and lightning. Any egg could hatch any kind of beast — how the creature developed depended on the personality of the girl or boy who'd taken care of its egg. What it absorbed from them shaped how it grew. Years ago, Papa had hatched a rain beast, and Gaton had his sun beast.

Mina thought of her egg upstairs. *I can't wait to meet you!* Soon she'd see which of her daydreams were going to come true. Lately, she'd been hoping for a wind beast, because she loved wind days so much — in fact, today was a wind day: "Shouldn't we be getting ready?" she asked when they paused for breath.

"Yes, we should! Good of you to remember," Papa said, jolted out of his contemplation of Mina's future. "The wind should start in about twenty minutes."

"See?" Gaton said. "She's responsible. Sun beast."

"You do look out for everyone," Papa said to Mina with a proud smile. "You're going to be a wonderful guardian."

"I hope so," Mina said softly. *With all my heart, I hope he's right!*

Mother clapped her hands. "Okay, let's move!"

Everyone sprang up from the breakfast table and scurried

to help clean, chattering all the while about what kind of beast would hatch, how wonderful it all was, and how, regardless of the bet, her brother would have to take over all Mina's chores, including the chicken coop, once she started training. Groaning, Gaton said, "Maybe it would be better if your egg *didn't* hatch soon."

Mina laughed. She left her bowl on the rack to dry, nestled against the other bowls, and then went outside. The screen door banged behind her as Mother called, "Mina, get the kites!"

Mina waved so Mother would know she'd heard.

The farm sparkled in the morning sun. The fields stretching out before her shimmered with dewy leaves that waved in the soft breeze. As always, it was a beautiful day.

Orli, Papa's old rain beast, was flying above the farmhouse, her wings stretched wide. She was dragon-shaped, like all storm beasts, but had the beautiful blue color that marked her as a rain beast. Her chest was covered in shimmering blue scales, and her wings were blue feathers, every kind of blue in the sky from pale morning yellow-blue to deep storm blue-gray.

Mina imagined herself flying on a rain beast, guiding the water that would soak the fields or fill the reservoirs. *It must feel amazing to bring the rain!*

"Gaton!" Mother called, sticking her head out the kitchen window. "Have you secured the wheat seeds? We can't let the wind blow them away!"

Gaton called back from within the corn, close to the house but not visible behind the stalks. "Already done, Mother!"

Standing up on her tiptoes, Mina looked for her brother and saw the sunset-red glow of his beast, Arde, between the rows. A fat dragon, Arde didn't fly often. He spent most of his days with Gaton out in the fields, soaking up the sun's rays and then distributing them to whatever farm needed them the most. He also liked to chirp at passing birds. He had the silliest chirp for a beast his size. *Not that I'd ever tell Gaton that,* Mina thought. Gaton adored his beast.

"You'll adore yours, too," he'd told her once. "You'll see. You can't help it. Your beast will hatch, and it will feel like you've always known each other."

She wanted that so badly that it sometimes felt like an ache. *Hatch soon!* She'd always thought of herself as patient — Papa called her "steady" — but now all her dreams were so close . . .

"Mina!" Mother again. "Stop daydreaming, and get the kites!"

Quickly Mina retrieved the kites from the shed and hurried around the house to where Papa was already hooking the twins up to the posts. If you wanted to be outside on a day when the wind guardians and their beasts swept across the farmlands, you had to secure yourself. It wasn't strictly necessary, since the winds were never truly dangerous — not the way they were beyond the mountains — but if you weren't used to feeling any wind, you could get knocked off your feet.

The twins were giggling and squirming as Papa tried to attach their harnesses. "Rinna, stop that!" Papa was saying. "Beon, don't chew on the rope. You're not a puppy."

"Arf! Arf! Arf!" Beon barked.

Joining Papa, Mina handed the twins their kites, and they clutched them to their chests. She tied the ends of their kite strings to the posts. Papa at last clicked the harnesses into place and heaved a sigh of relief.

"Papa, I have to go pee," Rinna announced.

Mina smothered a grin. *I should have bet Gaton she'd say that.*

Papa's shoulders slumped, and he banged his forehead lightly on the post. "Can you hold it?"

Mother breezed past on her way to the porch. "No, she can't. She's too excited. Unhook her, take her in, and hook her back up. Beon, stop eating the rope. You'll ruin your supper."

"Arf!" he said to her.

"Woof! Woof!" Mother barked back.

Mina whispered to Beon, "Meow."

Beon giggled so hard that he stopped chewing on the rope.

"I'll watch him," Mina told Papa.

Papa kissed her on the head. "You're my sweet girl. Don't forget to secure yourself. I heard from the message balloon that this one's going to be spectacular." He quickly freed Rinna and shepherded her into the house.

Beon laughed and meowed as Mina clipped on her own harness and then showed him how to unravel the end of his kite string. Before today, the twins had been too little to be outside for a wind day, and now Papa had made the twins' first kites — simple diamond shapes, decorated with the symbol for their family's farm. Hers was more elaborate — on both sides she'd painted pictures of the mountains that bordered Alorria, as well as their family's sign.

The wind guardians used the kites to help them navigate. Every wind day, all the farmers flew kites so the fast-flying guardians could distinguish one farm from another. It was tradition. *Also, it's fun,* Mina thought.

A few minutes later, Papa rushed back with Rinna in his arms and attached her harness.

"Papa," Beon said, "I have to —"

Papa leveled a finger at his nose. "No. You don't."

Beon giggled again.

From the kitchen window, Mother called, "Mina, did you shut your window? You don't want the wind blowing dirt on your egg!"

Of course she had. "Yes, it's shut," Mina said.

Mother leaned farther out, trying to see Mina's window. "What did you say? Speak louder!"

Bells began to ring, a cascade of notes that reverberated over the hills. The wind guardians would be here soon! "It's almost time!" Papa called. "Where's Gaton?"

Emerging from the cornfields, Gaton jogged toward them. "Right here, and I can see Mina's window — it's definitely closed! Tornadoes take us if anything were to happen to her unborn sun beast." But he winked at Mina so she'd know he wasn't serious.

"It will be a *rain* beast!" Mother called as she disappeared from the window, closing the shutters behind her.

"Snow beast!" Rinna cried.

Looking up at her bedroom window, Mina thought, *I'll love you whatever you are! Just hatch soon!*

Mother emerged outside and hurried across the yard. "It won't be a snow beast. Mina isn't creative enough. Not that there's anything wrong with that, Mina. You've plenty of strengths. You're responsible, mature, thoughtful."

Not creative? "I love to draw," Mina said softly.

"And you're very good at it," Papa said to her.

She beamed.

He grumped at Mother, "Mina's plenty creative! Look at what a pretty kite she made."

"I wanna pretty kite," Rinna said. "Mina, make me a pretty kite! Papa, tell Mina to make me a pretty kite! Please, please, please!"

"Me too!" Beon shouted.

"I'm sure Mina will help you both make pretty kites for the next wind day, if you ask her nicely," Papa said, and Mina saw his pleading expression. She hid a smile and looked sternly at the twins as if she thought they were incapable of asking for anything nicely.

Rinna yelped, "I said please!"

Mina opened her mouth to say yes, but Mother was already talking. "Of course she'll help you, but you must promise to help her with her chores whenever she asks. And you mustn't bother her when she's with her egg. You understand why? Beast and guardian need to bond."

Beon and Rinna chorused, "Yes, Mother."

The bells tolled louder, chiming all together now in a mess of notes. Giggling, the twins clapped their hands over their ears. Mina held tightly to her kite. Beneath the bells, she could hear it: the wind. It had its own voice, a roar that steadily grew louder.

Before them, the cornstalks swayed, gently at first and then harder, until they were pitched at an angle. Mina felt the wind lift her hair, and she heard the twins squeal excitedly.

"Ready?" Papa shouted.

Ready, Mina thought.

"Ready!" her family shouted.

Each of them unspooled their kite string. As the wind blew, it lifted their kites into the air. Mina released her string faster and faster, and her kite rose. The ribbon tail flapped in the breeze.

The kites danced in the sky, and the twins shrieked with delight. Mina laughed out loud as hers dodged and swooped. The colors were brilliant against the blue, and she felt the tug on the string as if the sky wanted to run away with her kite. Beside her, Papa was twisting the two strings that held his kite so it would dive beneath the others, then rise up above them. Gaton's kite was wobbling in the air, and he unspooled more string. Mina guided hers higher and higher.

Soon she heard voices carried on the wind: the wind guardians on their beasts. Holding her kite steady, Mina watched the sky.

And there they were!

The wind beasts were silver dragons with white feathery

wings and brilliant, sparkling antlers like deer. They flew in loops and spirals through the air between Mina's family's kites, while their guardians called to one another, shouting and laughing. Dozens of them flew overhead, flocking like shimmering birds, and Mina knew that hundreds of them were spread all across the farmlands, on their way to the bay to carry the fishing boats out into the deeper ocean. They'd remain with the boats for the rest of the fishing season. *But today is our wind day!* Mina thought as she flew her kite higher. With her free hand, she waved to the wind guardians.

Very soon, I'll be flying too.

~CHAPTER~
TWO

AFTER the wind passed, Mina drew her string in and rolled it up carefully. Less careful, Gaton tossed his kite aside and squirmed out of his harness. Mother and Papa unhooked themselves and the twins. "Excellent wind day," Papa said.

Mother agreed, and the twins squealed.

"Remember Gaton's first wind day, when he lost his grip on his kite —"

Mother laughed. "And it flew up and smacked that wind guardian in the face!"

Mina grinned at Gaton. She'd been too young to remember, but her parents brought it up every wind day, to Gaton's dismay. At fifteen, Gaton liked to think of himself as all grown up, the mature storm guardian who knew everything, who'd never been a silly kid. *He is still a kid, though,* Mina thought. *Even if he thinks he has all the answers.*

She wondered if she'd feel that way too, once she had her beast.

"The kite didn't hurt the guardian," Papa quickly reassured the twins.

"Surprised him, though," Mother said with relish. "And made him colorful. The ribbons got tangled around his wind beast's antlers —"

"Hey, it wasn't my fault!" Gaton protested. "I was four."

They continued teasing Gaton as they tromped up to the house, and Mina reached to free herself. But the hook didn't budge. "Mother? Papa? Could you help me —"

The farmhouse door banged shut behind them, even though their chatter continued to spill out the windows. Frowning, Mina wiggled the hook. She raised her voice. "Gaton? Papa? I'm stuck."

They didn't hear her.

She continued to try to free herself. *If I force it . . . No, that doesn't work.* Mina's fingertips started to ache as she pushed at the clip. The harness wasn't budging. She shouted for her family again: "Help!" But when no one heard her, she gave up calling for them and concentrated on wiggling the clip and squirming out of the ropes.

At last the hook snapped open. *Free!* Quickly she shucked off the ropes and ran into the house.

Inside, the twins were shrieking — one of them had a spoon that the other one wanted. Papa was trying to cajole them into accepting a second spoon, but no, they both wanted *that one, right now*. Upstairs, Gaton was calling down that he needed his hammer — who'd taken it? Scrubbing the oatmeal spatter off the twins' chairs, Mother was still reminiscing about past wind days. Mina stood in the doorway, her kite clutched in her arms, and opened her mouth to say something, anything, about how they'd left her and hadn't heard her calling for them . . .

But there was no point now. She'd freed herself, and it would only make her family feel bad. *Real storm guardians solve problems*, she reminded herself. *They don't cause them.*

"Ah, Mina, there you are!" Mother said. "You should go bond with your egg. Remember: skin to shell."

"Yes, Mother." She fled past Papa and the twins, up the stairs to her room, and shut the door behind her.

In the corner of her room, tucked between her bed and the bookshelf, was her storm-beast egg. It wasn't anything like an egg from one of the chickens in the coop. For one thing, it was enormous, larger than either Beon or Rinna. For another, it was a swirl of colors: reds and purples and golds. She'd cushioned it in its own nest of quilts.

It didn't look any closer to hatching.

She swallowed back the taste of disappointment. She'd hoped she'd been outside long enough that when she came back in, she'd see a noticeable difference.

After dropping her kite on her bed, she examined the egg, checking for any new signs that it was about to hatch. The hairline crack she'd seen that morning was still there, no wider or longer than before.

Maybe I was wrong. Maybe it wasn't time for her future to begin yet.

Curling up against the cushion of quilts, Mina laid her cheek against the shell — skin to shell, as Mother had said. Speaking softly, she told the egg all about her morning: her painted kite and how proud she was of it, seeing the wind guardians and their beasts and how glorious they were, and then struggling to free herself of the harness and how frustrating it had felt when no one had heard her.

"When you hatch, we'll be the kind of beast and guardian who listen when people need help," Mina promised. "We're going to make a difference."

She picked up the book she'd been reading to the egg: the story of the group of rain guardians who'd created the lake district. Some kids used their three hours with their egg to nap or knit or play solitaire — there were dozens of solo games invented for kids to entertain themselves with while their beasts developed, shaped by the thoughts from the kids' heads — but Mina liked to read aloud, so her unborn beast could hear her favorite tales of adventures and righting wrongs and of people who lived exciting lives beyond her family's little patch of farmland.

As she read, she wondered when her beast was going to come out and tell her what it thought of the two years' worth of stories Mina had read. Gaton had told her what it felt like to be linked mind-to-mind to a storm beast: he couldn't hear all of Arde's thoughts the way he heard his own, and Arde couldn't always hear his, but he could always *feel* his beast, Arde's emotions like a constant hum in the back of his mind. Gaton said it was like hearing a distant song: he couldn't quite make out all the words, but he felt the tempo and bits of the tune. And when he wanted to talk to Arde, all he had to do was concentrate on both the words and his beast. It was like shouting. But quietly. She thought she'd like that.

Mina read until the end of the book, closed it, and then pressed her lips to the shell. "Looking forward to meeting you."

Crack.

Jumping to her feet, Mina stared at the egg. Was it . . . ? Had it . . . ? But she didn't hear another sound. She circled around it again, examining every inch of its iridescence. No new cracks. She ran her hands over the hard, smooth shell, and it felt like it always did.

Maybe I want it so badly I imagined it.

She could easily believe that.

Laying her cheek against the shell again, she whispered, "Come on. I know you have things you want to tell me, too." She pressed her hand against the smooth rainbow surface. "You can do it. Break free." *Whenever you're ready, I'm here,* she thought at it.

But the egg was silent.

Sighing, she curled up against the egg and pulled out her sketchbook and began to draw the egg with its crack. She then drew more cracks, as if that would make it hatch faster. Drawing always made her feel better. It was soothing, the way her pencil whispered on the paper. You could capture a past moment with a pencil, or imagine a future one.

She heard footsteps thump up the stairs and her mother call, "Mina? Is it hatching?"

"Not yet," Mina said. She kept drawing, adding more cracks, which branched in thin lines like veins in a leaf.

The door swung open, and Mother popped her head in. "Mina? Anything?" She hadn't heard Mina's answer.

Mina shook her head.

"All right. Remember: when you've put in your bonding hours, you still have your chores."

Mina nodded.

From the other side of the house, Gaton hollered, "Mother? Have you seen the garden shears? I left them in my boots, but they're not there now."

Sighing, Mother backed out, shutting the door behind her. "Why would you put scissors inside your boots?" Her footsteps thudded back down the stairs. "And have you taken Arde out in the north field yet?"

Crackle-crackle-crack!

Jumping up, Mina dropped her sketchbook. "Mother, it's hatching!"

But Mother had already gone downstairs and been swallowed by the calls of the twins, demanding her attention, and of Gaton searching for his shears and now his boots. She didn't know if he'd ever found his hammer, which he'd been missing at breakfast, but she didn't care. Mina took a step toward her egg and forgot about everything else.

After two whole years, it was happening! Right now!

Thin cracks ran through the rainbow shell. Awed, she laid her hand on the cracks, her fingertips touching several at once. "Come on," she whispered. "You can do it."

Her heart was beating so hard that she thought she'd crack out of her own skin. *It's really happening! My beast is coming!* "Hatch!" she cheered it on. She traced the veins — they radiated from one spot on the shell. She hadn't drawn them exactly right. Some cracks were longer, and some connected like edges of a puzzle piece.

Crack!

She felt it! The shell bulged under her hand.

Crack! A shard popped out. She saw a claw poke through and then scramble at the hole, widening it. Digging her fingers in, she helped, yanking away bits of shell. More claws poked through. Chunks of shell fell to the floor. And then a scaly yellow arm burst out of the hole.

Claws opened and closed on air.

Mina felt herself smiling so hard that her cheeks hurt. She broke the hole open wider, and then she reached inside and helped her beast climb out.

The beast spilled onto the quilts around the egg, lifted his head, and turned toward Mina. He looked like a small dragon with a serpent-like body and stocky arms and legs. He had brilliant yellow scales. His face was like a lizard crossed with a puppy, and Mina thought it was the most adorable face she'd ever seen.

«*Hello, Mina. I am Pixit.*»

Mina heard her beast's voice inside her head like a cascade of bells. *Gaton didn't tell me how beautiful he'd sound.* She felt tears prick her eyes. "Hello, Pixit," she whispered.

His purple eyes were streaked with zigzags of bright white, and he was gazing at her as if she were the heart of the world. «*I hear you, and you hear me,*» Pixit said inside Mina's head, and with the words came a warm rush of love and joy.

Mina had never felt anything this *right*. It felt as though she were half a puzzle, and Pixit were the other half — there was the wonderful sense that she was finally complete. She hadn't even known she was incomplete before. But now that Pixit was here . . . His emotions spilled into her along with his thoughts, and she felt his joy bubbling in her throat as Pixit said, «*I am yours, and you are mine. And we will always be together!*»

"Together we're going to do great things," Mina told him. Then she tried sending her words from her mind to his silently, as Gaton had described. *Just like in the tales.*

«*Yes, we are! Together we're going to set the world on fire! We'll right every wrong and have adventures and — ooh, I have wings!*» Pixit stretched out two yellow dragon wings and twisted his head right, left, and upside down, trying to admire them from all angles.

She laughed, feeling so full of bubbling joy — both Pixit's and her own — that she wanted to cry. *Go on. Try them. Fly!* She jumped up, hurried to the window, and threw open the shutters. Sunlight poured inside, and Pixit flapped his wings enthusiastically. *You can do it!*

Wobbling, he rose into the air. And then, with a happy shriek, he flew out the window. «*Wheeeeeeeeeeeeeeeeeeeeeeeeee eeeeeeeeeeeeee!*»

"Yay! Go, Pixit!" she cheered him on.

Her beast sailed shakily over their yard, then swooped up, clipping a line of fresh laundry with his clawed foot. The rope twanged back, and the shirts catapulted off it onto the ground, landing in the dirt. Mina winced.

"You can do it, Pixit! Flap harder!"

«*I can flyyyyyyyyyyyyyyyyyyyyy!*»

Pixit wobbled in the air, his tail dipping into the cornstalks. Sparks danced over his scales, and several sparks jumped from him onto the leaves and the tufts of corn silk below. *Uh-oh,* Mina thought.

«*Why 'uh-oh'?*» And then: «*Oh no. Uh-oh.*»

Losing control, the young storm beast dropped lower into the cornstalks, disappearing for a moment. When he rose up, flapping harder, the field beneath him was on fire.

«*I'm sorry, Mina!*»

She felt his chagrin like a spurt of scalding oil — the feeling came with his words. It tasted sour in her mouth.

Mina ran across her room, yanked open the door, and raced

downstairs. "Fire in the field!" she yelled. She didn't stop — she kept running out the back door of the farmhouse.

Behind her, she heard Mother. "What did she say?"

And Gaton said, "But we haven't been cleared for a burn —"

Outside, Pixit was circling the fire, his wings flapping furiously, trying to put out the flames, but fanning them only caused them to grow.

Pixit, you're making it worse! Fly higher!

He obeyed her, spiraling up into the air.

Mina ran for the well. A bucket, brimming with water, hung from a rope. Hefting the bucket up, Mina turned to the field.

It's too far! I won't reach it before it spreads!

A shadow passed over her, and she looked up. It wasn't a cloud — clouds were never allowed to drift over the farms of Alorria, except when the fields needed rain. It was Papa's rain beast. She had a sudden idea. "Orli! Orli, put out the fire!"

Papa's old rain beast circled her once and flicked her tail.

"I know you don't have rain power anymore, but you can carry this." Mina held the bucket up to her, and Orli understood. She swooped down and, with her delicate talons, lifted the bucket by the handle out of Mina's arms.

Behind her, she heard Gaton. "Great idea, Mina!" He began hauling another bucket up out of the well, preparing it for Orli. By now, Mother and Papa had run out of the house and were shouting to each other to fetch more water.

On the porch, the twins were shrieking.

"Beon and Rinna, go inside right now!" Mother called as

she rushed to Gaton's side, helping at the well. Papa ran to the shed for more buckets.

«*I did bad? I'm bad.*» High above the fields, Pixit was spewing sparks in all directions. His dragon-like body twisted as he flew in circles above the fire. The more upset he was, the more he seemed to spark.

No, she told him firmly, as if he were Beon saying something ridiculous. *It was an accident. You didn't mean to.*

«*I'll make it better. I can help!*» He swooped down.

No! Stay high, at least until you stop sparking. They needed a way to quash the fire, not fuel it. The buckets from Orli weren't enough — the flames sizzled and smoke rose in dirty wisps, but the fire was spreading faster than they could quench it.

«*But Mina, I want to help.*»

Mina had another idea. "Gaton, send Arde out to stop the fire."

He didn't hear her.

Yanking another bucketful of water out of the well, Gaton shouted, "Orli, next one's ready!" He held the bucket over his head. The rain beast swooped down and plucked the bucket out of his hands. Gaton went for the next empty bucket.

Mina tugged on his arm. "Gaton, the heat won't hurt Arde. Have him lie on the flames!"

"Stop, Mina — Orli needs more water!" He shrugged her away and turned back to the well, and Mina stumbled backward. Tripping over a root from the apple tree, she fell, landing on her rear end.

«*Mina!*» Pixit shrieked as she fell. Mina saw him streak through the sky, flying to her rescue. Bits of electricity shed from his tail as he dived toward their yard.

Pixit, no! You'll spread the fire!

"What's he doing?" Gaton cried.

Orli flew to stop Pixit, and Arde barreled out of the fields, huffing and snorting, coming to protect Gaton from whatever was upsetting him. Mother and Papa ran across the yard.

Pixit, stop sparking! Mina cried.

«*I don't know how!*»

Then fly higher!

But Pixit got so flustered with Orli flying toward him and everyone shouting at him that he lost control of his newly discovered wings. He landed in a tumble. In Mina's head, she heard him babbling, «*I'm so sorry — very, very sorry — I didn't mean . . . I wanted to help!*»

Mina ran to Pixit and threw her arms around his neck. She felt his electricity skitter over her skin. It felt like a tickle of grass on bare feet. Everyone was yelling. At Orli. At Pixit. At Mina.

"Arde, go sit on the fire," Mina said, but no one heard her.

Pixit's voice echoed in her head, but in a funny, distant kind of way, as if he wasn't talking to her. «*Arde, do as Mina said! Go sit on the fire! Please!*»

Hearing him, the sun beast, Arde, skidded to a halt in front of them. He plowed up dirt and grass with his front paws with the force of his stop. He looked at Pixit, then at the fire in the field, then at Gaton. And then he bounded through the field.

They all watched as he trampled the cornstalks and leaped, his massive body lurching into the air, and landed with a *whomp* on top of the flames.

He smothered the fire.

Closing her eyes, Mina sagged against Pixit, and Pixit leaned into her. Pixit's tail curled around Mina. It continued to give off sparks that crackled and popped.

For one glorious moment, everyone was silent.

And then they exploded into even more shouting.

"What is that thing?" "Is that a lightning beast?" "Did your egg hatch?" "Did it start that fire?" "This has to be a mistake! You can't have gotten a lightning beast!" "Whose beast is it?" "Where did it come from?" "It can't be Mina's! How could it be Mina's?" "Mina, what happened?" "Mina, how can this be your beast? This can't be right!" "Mina, answer us!"

«*It's loud outside my egg,*» Pixit observed.

Yeah, Mina agreed. *Maybe we can both go back in it.*

⟞CHAPTER⟝
THREE

MINA leaned against the wall of the well with Pixit curled up in her lap. Her new storm beast was snoring lightly, which was zero help with facing her family. *It must be exhausting to be born and set a field on fire all in the same day,* Mina thought, but she couldn't help smiling down at his puppy face. *And exhausting to be this cute.*

As Pixit snored, his tongue stuck out between two teeth, causing him to whistle with each breath. Mina stroked between his wide ears. His yellow scales were soft as velvet, covered in a fine fur, and he had feathers sprouting like antlers from his forehead.

Outside of pictures, Mina had never seen a lightning beast before, but there was no question that Pixit was one. If the sparks that had set the fire hadn't given it away, his brilliant yellow color would have. Rain beasts were blue, sun beasts were red, wind beasts were silver, snow beasts were white, and lightning beasts were yellow.

He's beautiful.

Papa crouched beside her. "Mina, did you really hatch a lightning beast? You couldn't have. There must have been some kind of mistake. Were you out of the room while it hatched? Maybe there was a switch?"

Gaton snorted. "Worst practical joke ever. Who would do that? And how? We were all home. I didn't see a stranger sneak in a lightning beast and sneak out Mina's."

"You do know what the word 'sneak' means, don't you?" Mother said as she leaned over to peer at the sleeping Pixit. She then mollified her tone. "But I agree with you, Gaton. There's no reason for someone to switch beasts."

Mina smiled gratefully at her mother.

But Mother wasn't done. "There must have been something wrong with the egg."

Mina's smile vanished. *There's nothing wrong with you,* she thought at Pixit, even though he was sleeping too soundly to hear. "He didn't mean to set the fire. He's sorry." Lightning beasts were supposed to absorb electric charge from the world around them and store it, like living capacitors, but new ones didn't know how to store it perfectly — that was why he sparked so much. *He'll outgrow it. I think. And to be fair, he did say we'd set the world on fire, even if he didn't mean it quite so literally. He meant we'd be like the guardians and beasts in the tales I read him, who changed the world with their heroics, not their flammability.*

"We know, sweetheart," Papa said. He patted Mina's shoulder, careful not to touch any part of Pixit, even though he wasn't sparking anymore. At least not much. "But you couldn't have hatched a lightning beast! Lightning guardians are brash and loud and brave. You're not . . . Well, it doesn't suit you. You and your beast are supposed to be perfectly matched in temperament."

Mother corralled Beon and Rinna, who both wanted to get a look at the "sparkly puppy with wings." "Super sparkly!" Beon cried, making grabby hands at Pixit.

Scooping up Beon and bouncing him on her hip, Mother snapped, "This needs to be fixed! Maybe he can be . . . I don't know . . . *changed* somehow, to something more appropriate."

Papa was nodding. "There must be something that can be done, a way to undo this —"

But I don't want anything done or undone! Mina wanted to say. *He's my Pixit!* She could feel the swirl of his dreams in the back of her mind, like a whispered tune. She thought that he was dreaming about flying.

Gaton snorted. "You can't 'change' a beast. What are you going to do? Stuff him back into his egg and glue the shell together? When they're born, that's it. You have to love them as they are." He tossed his arm around Arde, who had shuffled in from the field. The sun beast didn't look any worse for wear after his fire-quenching adventure. If anything, he glowed a little brighter. He stuck his snout in one of the buckets and drank, spilling water on the grass.

As Mother and Papa debated how to fix this "mess," Mina hugged Pixit closer to her. He barely fit in Mina's lap, his serpent-like body spilling onto the grass. "I don't want him changed, even if he could be. Not a single scale. Not a single spark."

No one heard her, of course. So Mina repeated herself. "He's not a mistake. He's my storm beast, and I'm his guardian." She was shaking as she said it. She rarely ever tried to make them listen to her when they were all riled up like this. Usually she bided her time until they were ready to listen. But this was too important for waiting.

Gaton stared at her, as did the twins.

"He's my storm beast," Mina said. "We're meant to be together." She felt as if she was flushed bright red. She hated speaking up and hated being the center of attention.

"Sparkly?" Rinna said.

"That's right. My sparkly," Mina said. "Mother? Papa? There isn't anything to fix. Pixit hatched, and we're bonded." She tried to say it firmly, the way Mother spoke when she needed them to do their chores. Mina didn't want to argue. *And I'm not arguing,* she thought. *I'm just telling them the way it is. He hatched, and that's that. He's mine, and I'm his.*

Mother and Papa were both staring at Mina now too, and Mina wished she could swallow back the words. This wasn't how she'd pictured this moment. Her family was supposed to be happy. Her egg had hatched! She had a storm beast! She wished she could think of what to say that would make them see everything was all right.

"Mina, sweetie, we just don't want you to be unhappy," Papa said.

Why wouldn't they listen to her? "But I'm not —"

Before she could finish, Rinna, who didn't understand what was happening except that everyone was upset, began to wail. "I don't want Mina to be sad! That makes *me* sad!"

And that set Beon off wailing too. Great, fat tears rolled down his cheeks, and he screamed even louder than his sister, which was impressively loud. In Mina's lap, Pixit stirred. «*Loud sound.*»

Sorry, Mina thought at him.

«*They don't like me?*»

They don't know you. You just surprised them, that's all.

«*Do you like me?*» He sounded so forlorn.

"Like" wasn't even the right word. Mina felt as tangled up with Pixit as a kite string. She'd known him only a handful of minutes, but it felt like a lifetime. *Yes*, she told him, and she tried to put every ounce of her love into that word. *But it's more than just "like" or "love." We belong together. Two pieces of a whole.*

He purred, his eyes wide. The white zigzags in his pupils shimmered as if they held bits of lightning.

Looking up, Mina noticed that her family was still talking. ". . . send a message balloon to the capital, and let them sort the mess out. It has to have happened before," Mother was saying. "She can't be the first with an unsuitable beast. Surely they won't punish us for a faulty egg. Let another child endanger herself, playing in thunderstorms far away from home. Not mine."

Mina gaped at her. A message to the capital! But she *wanted* this! She wanted to train and be a guardian — it was what she'd wanted her entire life! She might not have known she'd hatch a lightning beast, but that didn't matter. She and Pixit belonged together! They were going to do great things!

Mother and Papa think they know what's best for me, Mina thought. *But Pixit is what's best!* Her family continued to argue, none of them listening to or paying any attention to Mina.

Taking Pixit's face in her hands, cupping his cheeks, she looked him in the eyes and said, both out loud and in her mind, "Whatever anyone says, you are *not* a mistake. You are not a mess to be fixed. You are Pixit, and you are mine and I am yours, forever and ever."

He purred. «*Forever and ever.*»

⚡

By late afternoon, Mina still hadn't thought of how to convince her family that there wasn't anything wrong with Pixit. Ignoring everything she'd tried to say, they'd sent a message balloon to the capital with the morning mail, asking for advice, and they were waiting for a reply.

Watching Pixit eat on the porch, Mina tried not to let any hint of her worry seep out. The trick seemed to be to avoid focusing on anything in particular for long. He heard thoughts that she lingered over, but anything she flitted past was no more than a buzzy whisper.

«*You buzz a lot. But it's okay. Especially if you keep feeding me crunchies.*»

They're called potatoes, she told him. *We usually cook them.*

«*That's a terrible idea.*»

She smiled. *Sometimes people like terrible ideas.*

He'd already eaten twelve.

Opening behind them, the kitchen door squeaked. "Here, try this," Mother said to Pixit. She carried a bowl, which she set down on the porch floor. "It's sugar water. Lightning beasts are supposed to like it."

He stuck his tongue in. «*Mmmmm!*» And then he plunged his entire face into the bowl and began slurping up the sugar water, splashing it everywhere.

Laughing, Mina scooted back as water sprayed all over her.

Pixit raised his head out of the bowl. «*What did I — oops.*» His fur was sopping wet, and his ears drooped and dripped on the grass.

Also sprayed with sticky sugar water, Mother sighed and then returned to the house, muttering as she went, "This shouldn't be happening. All wrong."

Pixit looked sadly after her.

Drink as much as you want as messily as you want, Mina told him, determined to make him feel better. *You should have seen the mess Rinna and Beon made when they first started eating.* She played through the memories in her mind for him so he could see how they'd spattered oatmeal everywhere. Literally everywhere. Every window had been sprayed with clumps. Every person had

had it in their hair. Every pot and pan hanging from the ceiling, every bundle of dried herbs, every jar of applesauce, every pair of boots by the door. Years later, Mother and Papa were still finding chunks of it wedged in between the floorboards in rooms that were nowhere near the kitchen.

Pixit giggled, then snorted as he laughed harder, and it was so infectious that Mina started laughing too.

It felt amazing to be talking with Pixit and feeling all his responses. His delight spilled into her, as sweet as ice cream sliding down her throat. She'd never felt this way before, as if someone heard every word she said — and every word she didn't — and understood. He was tickled by the same things that tickled her, and she could feel that he loved her crazy, loud family just as much as she did.

She replayed even more memories of meals gone terribly wrong, like the chicken that Mother had prepared to cook by chopping its head off — only to have the headless chicken, its nerves still alive, promptly run under the house. Gross but hilarious. And the time that Papa had cooked an entire stew, simmering it for hours, before discovering that Beon had dropped not one, not two, but *six* pairs of shoes into the pot. Now every time they had stew, they asked first if it was "shoe stew."

«*I want to try shoe stew!*»

Someday, she promised. *We'll both try everything, now that you're out of your egg.*

«*And see everywhere?*»

Mina felt a twinge, thinking of the worry in her parents' eyes. But she couldn't stop the wave of excitement. *Yes.*

«We'll see the whole world. Like you've always wanted to.»

That was something she'd never said out loud to anyone. Except to Pixit. She'd whispered it to him plenty of times. She wanted to see beyond the farmlands — to see the raised rivers, the sparkling city, the hills, the lakes, the mountains . . . even beyond the mountains. A frivolous dream, Mother would have said. Who cared about the other side of the mountains — it was full of outsiders! Besides, everything they needed was right here. But ever since Mina had read her first tale of snow guardians exploring the peaks, she'd wondered what, and who, lay on the other side.

How am I going to tell my family that I want more than a life on the farm? They'll never understand.

Glancing up at the perfect blue sky again, she saw it: high above, a stream of red balloons, each with a basket dangling underneath. From this distance, they looked like polka dots against the blue. A wind guardian led the line, pulling the bit of breeze that propelled the mail across the farmlands. Mina felt as if her heart had leaped into her throat. *It's here!*

«Mina, what's here?»

The afternoon mail!

And maybe the reply from the capital.

She jumped up and ran into the yard. The balloons bobbed above the line of trees that marked the edge of their farm.

Shielding her eyes from the sun, Mina watched them dip and rise.

A second wind guardian darted forward and sent a gust of wind toward one balloon. It split from the others and drifted toward the neighboring farm. Mina waited, trying to be patient, as the line of balloons drifted closer.

It was very, very hard to be patient when one of those balloons could be holding the fate of her dreams.

Shoved by its own stream of wind, a single balloon drifted over their fields, across the newly seeded third-harvest wheat, above the shoulder-high cornstalks, bobbing and weaving in its one finger of wind, and then dipping to land ever so gently in their yard, by a swing that hung from a tall oak tree. The balloon was made of cotton, bright red to stand out against the sky, and it carried a pouch beneath it. Mina ran to it.

Dropping to her knees in the grass beside it, Mina began to untie the pouch. Her fingers were shaking so hard that it took her two tries. She then lifted the balloon above her head as she'd seen her parents do.

A little dancing breeze scooped the balloon out of her hands, and she watched it fly up, back into the stream of messages with the two wind guardians. She waved to them, and they waved back.

As they flew out of sight, she dared at last to look down at the pouch in her hand. Her mouth felt dry, and she swallowed hard.

She *should* take it in to her parents and let them open it.

But it's about me. My future. My life. And Pixit's! And sure enough, her name was on the outside: Mina Yellowfield, Farm 283, East Islin, Alorria, written in neat gold letters.

«*Open it,*» Pixit encouraged her, loud in her head.

Jumping, she glanced over her shoulder. He'd come up to her silently, his cheeks bulging with unchewed potatoes. *But they're waiting for this.*

«*It's about us and our future and our dreams, right?*»

Mina wondered how hard she'd been thinking that thought.

«*Very hard.*» He stuck his nose over her shoulder. «*Go on.*» He chewed loudly.

Hands shaking, she took the letter out. It was sealed with a dot of resin. She ran her fingertips over the bump. What if it said her parents were right and she shouldn't be bonded to Pixit? What if it said she'd done something wrong while he was in his egg?

«*We belong together. Never doubt that.*»

She didn't! Not for a second! But her family . . .

«*Just open it, Mina.*»

Sitting on the grass, Mina broke the resin seal and unfolded the letter. Two other pieces of paper fell out of the folds: tickets. River-ship tickets. Did that mean . . . ? Her heart was pounding, and she heard roaring in her ears.

«*Mina? Are you okay?*» Pixit nuzzled her hair with his snout. «*What's wrong? Your thoughts are all jumbly. I can't tell if you're happy or sad.*»

She read the letter aloud:

"'Congratulations on the birth of your storm beast! Your storm beast has been registered in the records of Alorria.'" She skimmed through. It was all official language, stilted and impersonal, from the office of the prime minister — welcoming her storm beast, discussing what a great honor it was to be guardian to an Alorrian storm beast, a rare creature of great importance to their country's safety and prosperity, the reason their country was superior to those beyond the mountains, blah, blah, blah. It was the kind of letter copied hundreds of times.

And then: "'You and your storm beast are officially enrolled in Mytris Lightning School in the Northwest Barrens. Two river-ship tickets are enclosed.'"

Yes!

She felt relief so sharply that tears popped into her eyes. No one was going to separate them! She was going to become a storm guardian with Pixit!

«*See? Nothing to worry about.*»

Except her family. And how they weren't going to understand.

She read the letter again, reassuring herself that she hadn't imagined it. At the bottom, the letter was embossed with a quote from one of the first storm guardians of Alorria: "'A true heart is never a mistake.'"

«*I like that,*» Pixit said.

I like that too. Even though she'd heard the famous quote before, it felt as if that long-gone guardian were talking directly to her. Pixit had been shaped by her mind and heart, and it couldn't be a mistake that he was what he was. He was meant to be a lightning beast, and she was meant to be his guardian.

She knew that. He knew that. And soon everyone else would too.

Pixit pressed his furry forehead against hers, and she knew he could tell what she was feeling even before she put it into words. She threw her arms around his neck. Sparks skipped over his scales and across her skin.

We're going, she thought firmly. *Together.*

Now she just had to figure out a way to tell her family. Releasing Pixit's neck, she looked down at the letter on her lap — in time to see a flame eating away a corner.

Mina yelped, threw it on the ground, and jumped up to stomp the flame out. She then picked up the slightly-charred-around-the-edges letter. «Sorry.» At least the two tickets were unscathed. She tucked them into her pocket and stared at the house.

There was going to be more yelling. She wasn't sure how to make them hear her.

«*I wish I could talk for you.*»

Me too.

With Pixit beside her, she went into the house. Mother was wrestling Beon into his highchair, and Papa was feeding Rinna. "Mina," Mother said without turning around, "your beast stays outside. Or on the hearth."

"But . . ." Mina began. She'd planned on having him in her

39

room just like when he was in the egg. Gaton had had Arde sleep at the foot of his bed until he grew too big to fit through the bedroom doors. And Orli still sometimes took naps in the living room, especially in the winter, to be closer to Papa. She hogged the whole couch.

"He's not an indoor beast," Mother said.

"Then I'll sleep outside with him," Mina said. New guardians were supposed to be with their beasts as much as possible. It was good for their bond.

"You'll sleep in your bed," Mother said firmly. "You need your rest."

"And besides, sweetie, we don't want you getting too attached," Papa said.

That made no sense. She'd been bonding to Pixit for two years, talking to his egg for at least three hours a day, creating this telepathic link. She didn't think it was possible to be *more* attached than they already were. But she didn't argue. *Pixit?*

Tucking his tail between his legs, Pixit slunk to the hearth and curled up on the flagstones. Only a few sparks popped into the fireplace.

Sorry, Pixit. One battle at a time, okay? When you were quiet, you had to choose your battles carefully, or else you wouldn't win any. And Mother did have a point. Certainly her family wouldn't like Pixit more if he accidentally set the house on fire. *Maybe when you can control the sparks better, they'll let you stay in my room.*

Out loud, she said, "Um, Mother? Papa?"

Mother waved an applesauce-encrusted spoon toward Mina. "We'll talk in a bit, after the afternoon mail comes." She'd finally gotten Beon to sit and was trying to feed him before escape attempt number three hundred forty-seven.

Mina looked at the letter, then at Mother and Papa feeding the twins.

Then she looked at Pixit, his shining eyes full of hope and trust.

She felt her resolve harden. There wasn't anything to discuss. *I don't have to tell them,* she realized, *not with my own words.* The letter was clear. She had already won this battle. Her parents just didn't know it yet. *Starting tomorrow, we won't be apart,* she promised Pixit.

Happy, he thumped his tail on the hearth, scattering sparks.

Mina positioned the letter on the table where her parents were certain to see it, and she hurried upstairs to pack. Since her family wasn't listening to her, the letter would speak for her.

She met Gaton on the stairs. He was carrying an armload of shell bits, cradled in quilts. "Your room looks different without the egg," he told her.

"Oh. Thanks." She hadn't asked him to clean it. She'd thought that was something she should do herself, since she'd been there for the birth. But no one had asked her how she felt about it. *And I never said.*

They assume they know me and what I want, but they don't.

I want to be a lightning guardian. Even if I didn't know it before I met Pixit.

"Just wait until you see how different everything will look when you get back from training," Gaton said cheerfully. "Home will seem much smaller, after you've been out in the world."

Mina glanced back down toward the kitchen. They hadn't seen the letter. Yet.

«*They will,*» Pixit said. «*Your little brother just vomited, though. I think he did it on purpose. He really doesn't like applesauce.*»

"Hey, Mina, don't be scared, okay?" Gaton said, misreading her expression. "I know how it feels — you're not ready for everything to change. I felt the same way."

That wasn't how she felt. Still, it was nice of him to say. "Thanks, Gaton." As he continued down, she ran up the final steps to her room.

Without the shell and its nest of quilts, her room looked oddly bare. Pixit's egg had been there for so long that its absence felt like it altered the shape of the room. *Gaton was right. It doesn't even look like my room anymore. It's changed.*

Everything's changed.

Except for me.

She felt the same, with only one major difference: she wasn't waiting anymore. Pixit was here! And no matter what her parents thought, Mina knew they belonged together.

She found a bag in her closet and opened it. She didn't know what to bring to Mytris Lightning School. She wished the letter had included more information, but it hadn't, so she stuck to the basics: clothes, a hairbrush, a sketchbook with a bunch of blank pages. She also packed a handful of nice pencils.

Through the floorboards, she heard the moment that Mother and Papa discovered the letter. The yelling started almost immediately, which wasn't a surprise. Mina wished she'd told Pixit to go outside. Certainly she wasn't going back down there, though.

Pixit, are you all right?

«*Are you all right, Mina? Your thoughts feel swirly again.*»

I feel swirly. Like I'm in a mixing bowl. So much had happened so quickly. She didn't know whether to be excited or nervous or happy or scared.

Glancing around the room, she tried to think of anything she'd forgotten. She'd pack her toothbrush in the morning, before she left to meet the ship. *Maybe by then Mother and Papa will be used to the idea that I'm going to be a lightning guardian.*

Eventually, Mother and Papa would realize they had no choice. The law was clear: storm guardians and their beasts served Alorria in whatever way they were needed until their power faded. It was the deal you made when you accepted an egg. And it was an honor to serve. Without the storm guardians and their beasts performing their duty, Alorria would be like the world beyond the mountains, wild and dangerous.

The storm guardians and their beasts were what made Alorria great. Over the last century, with the weather under perfect control, Alorria had become the most peaceful, prosperous, safest, happiest country in the world. Everyone knew that, and everyone knew that the guardians *had* to serve to maintain that greatness.

But even if Mina did have a choice, she knew what she'd choose. She loved her home, her family, and their farm, but there was a whisper inside her, and if she listened hard enough, she could hear it. *This is it!* it said. Looking at her packed bag, she told herself she could do this. She could make all her dreams happen.

The shell had cracked.

A new adventure had begun.

FOUR

MINA perched next to Papa on the cart. He held the horses' reins in his hands, though the horses didn't need any direction beyond "trot straight." All the roads in Alorria ran in straight lines, even in the hills. She wasn't sure about in the mountains. *Maybe I'll see the mountains from Mytris Lightning School!*

Pixit popped his head up between Mina and Papa. «*I can see mountains right now. Are your eyes okay?*» He was riding in the back of the cart with the carrots and the onions. The feel of his concern tasted like a puff of too-sweet cotton candy.

The country of Alorria was nestled between mountains to the north, south, and west and an ocean to the east. You could see at least a few mountains from anywhere, protecting Alorria from the world beyond. The peaks looked like white-and-gray shadows against the blue sky. Mina had sketched them plenty of times, but only as distant smudges. *You know I meant close-up.*

He giggled in her head.

And then: «*Um, Mina, would it be bad if I ate all the onions?*»

It wouldn't be good. I have to travel with your breath.

He was silent, and she twisted around in her seat. Looking innocent, Pixit kicked the empty onion bag behind him with a clawed foot, and then he sat on it. Mina smothered a laugh.

Beside her, Papa said, "You know if you don't like being a lightning guardian, you can always come home."

"Papa . . ." She wasn't going to quit — she was meant for this!

"If you get there and decide you don't belong . . . Just know that we love you, no matter what. We want you to be happy, Mina."

"I'll be happy," she promised. She kept her tone as light as she could, trying to cheer him up. He seemed so certain that she was going to be miserable. It was hard not to let that worry her. "I get to ride on a river ship!"

She thought she saw the corner of his mouth twitch into an almost smile. "You have a joyful spirit, my little minnow. You remember that. The other lightning guardians might look like they spark bright, but you sparkle inside, where it counts."

She didn't know what to say to that, though it was very nice.

«*Was it something you ate?*» Pixit asked curiously.

Was what?

«*Is that why your insides are sparkly?*»

Reaching back, she scratched Pixit behind his ears. He flopped sideways so she could reach his neck better. The cart continued to roll forward, and they rode in silence. Behind them, she could no longer see their farm — it was hidden by the gently rolling hills. On either side of the road grew waist-high wheat. As their horses clopped by, startled birds burst out of the grass and, squawking, fled to the sky. She watched them until they settled in another part of the field, vanishing from view.

Mina felt a bit like those birds — Pixit's birth had roused her from where she'd hidden, in the safe, warm shelter of home, and now she was in the air, wondering where she'd land and hoping it would be as wonderful as she dreamed. She touched the ship tickets in her pocket, reassuring herself that they were still there, still real.

We're really going! All her dreams about going on adventures and seeing the world and doing great things and righting wrongs . . . It was all finally beginning!

They traveled for half the day, until the great raised rivers were visible. Aqueducts built on vast stone arches, the rivers were wide and deep enough for ships with triple masts and billowing sails to travel along them. For the first half of every week, the rain guardians led water down from the mountain lakes, through the farmlands and orchards, and to the sea, while the wind guardians filled the ships' sails. For the second half of each week, the rivers flowed salty, away from the sea.

Today the rivers were salty.

She'd sail northwest, first toward the capital city, then on to the barren lands. And the lightning school — Mytris!

She felt a bit of nervousness curl inside her, and she wasn't sure if it was her emotion or Pixit's. It had a taste: like stale bread that crumbled in your mouth, inedible.

47

"Have you ever sailed the rivers, Papa?" Mina asked. The rain-guardian training school was in the farmlands — he would have taken the roads, rather than the rivers, when he was her age.

"Once, a long time ago, when I married your mother." He had a wistful look on his face, as if remembering. *He wouldn't look wistful if he'd crashed,* she thought. *It must have gone well.* She wanted to ask more: Was it scary? Did the ships ever crash? Did any ever sail off the arches and smash to the ground far below? Or was it just as glorious as she'd always imagined? But she waited, in case he continued on his own. And he did. "Your mother wanted to see the city, and our families had saved up in secret — it was their gift to us. Our first hour on the ship, she climbed to the top of the middle mast to look out at the mountains. She was the first to see the city and all its lightning-powered wonders when we approached it."

Mina couldn't imagine Mother doing anything so reckless as climbing that high. Mother always kept her feet flat on the ground. A thought occurred to her: *Maybe there are pieces of her I don't know, just like there are parts of me my family doesn't see.* "Did you like the city?"

"Very much." He smiled at her, and Mina could tell it was forced from the way his cheeks strained. But she appreciated that he was trying. "You're going to have a grand time, and when you get back, you'll tell us all about it, every detail."

"I will," she promised.

Reaching the river station, Papa parked the cart and tied

the horse reins to a post by a water trough. He then helped Mina climb down from the bench. Behind her, Pixit jumped up onto the side wall of the cart and then to the ground. He shook out his feathery scales and stretched his legs and tail. Already she thought he might have grown, even in just a day, but it could have been her imagination.

Papa handed Mina her pack and then a smaller sack. "Lunch for the trip. I know they'll feed you, but Mother said . . ." He swallowed as if it was suddenly hard for him to talk. "She wanted you to have a bit of home in your belly, to start you off. It's your favorites."

Honey cake and peach jelly? She peeked inside the sack. It was! "I'll miss you all."

"Remember we love you." Papa hugged her so hard that she nearly chirped. But she didn't try to pull away. She stood on her tiptoes and buried her face in his neck and breathed in his familiar smell: fresh soil and garden herbs.

"I love you too," Mina said.

Suddenly she didn't want to leave. This was already farther from home than she'd ever been. She wasn't like the heroes in her books — how could she think she could do this? She tried to push the doubt away and focus on the fact that she was about to start living her dreams.

Wistfully, Pixit asked, «*Can I hug him goodbye too? You told me so much about him when I was in my shell. He's my papa too, in a way.*»

It felt strange having to be someone else's voice, when she so rarely used her own. Mina looked down at Pixit, who had tiny sparks arcing on the top of his head from feather to feather. "He wants to hug you too," she told Papa.

Papa eyed the sparks. "How about a wave?"

She felt Pixit's disappointment — it tasted like peppery lemon. *Maybe after you learn to control your sparks better,* she comforted Pixit. She felt a stab of guilt for not defending him more, but she didn't want to leave Papa with an argument. It was already harder than she'd thought it would be to say goodbye.

«*He still thinks we don't fit. He doesn't want to get too attached.*»

He'll see he's wrong, she told him.

Releasing her father, Mina took out the two tickets. "I'll send a message by balloon after we arrive," she promised.

Papa nodded. His eyes were wet.

Above, from the river station, a bell rang — the next ship would be arriving soon. She turned to face the raised river. In front of her were stairs, carved into the stone, worn from the feet of hundreds of people who had climbed them before her. They zigzagged twice up the side, higher than the tallest tree on the farm. Taking a deep breath, she began to climb, with Pixit following behind her. She knew Papa was watching her and knew he'd stay until she was out of sight in the station above, and probably until she boarded the ship and sailed away.

She kept close to the stone wall as she climbed — the steps had a rope railing, but it looked flimsy. "Pixit, please don't set the rope on fire," she said, speaking out loud so she could be sure he didn't miss her warning. "Other people need it."

He didn't reply.

Pixit?

«*It's only charred.*» He was flattened against the stone wall, inching up step by step with his body pressed as close to the stone as he could manage, trying to keep from igniting the rope railing. Sparks kept leaping off him onto the stone, which couldn't burn, and onto the rope, which sizzled. «*Sorry!*»

She swallowed a laugh and climbed faster.

Don't worry. You'll learn control at Mytris.

Her legs were aching by the time she reached the top, and Pixit flopped down on the station platform. She looked back — Papa's cart was tiny down at the bottom, and she could see the farmlands beyond. *Maybe as far as home?* She couldn't be certain. The fields — dark green, pale green, brown, golden yellow — stretched for miles in every direction, and the houses were specks in the distance. Her fingers itched to sketch them.

Far to the north and west, impossibly far, were the mountains. Sometimes it was hard to believe that anything was beyond them. Mother would have said, "Nothing that concerns us anyway. Mind your chores instead."

The bell rang again, and Mina nudged Pixit back to his feet. *Look! It's beautiful!* The ship was coming closer. It was glorious: painted black wood, three wide white sails on each of three masts, a lookout platform at the top of the center mast, and red banners with the symbol of the sun embroidered on each one.

"Tickets, please," a man said.

Mina turned to the stationmaster, a man in a gray uniform

with the same Alorrian sun symbol on his chest. Wordlessly, she presented their tickets.

"Ah, the barren lands." He marked them and handed them back to her. "Funny — you don't seem the lightning type."

Startled, she stared at him.

"I see a lot of new lightning-guardians-to-be come through on their way to Mytris. Most are reckless, arrogant things who wouldn't care if their beast burned that rope. Yes, I watched you as you came up. Appreciated your carefulness."

She wasn't sure what to say to that. *Thank you,* maybe? Or *You're welcome?* "I'm bonded to a lightning beast. I am going to be a lightning guardian."

"Are you now?" The stationmaster humored her. "Well, when your ship sails through the city, you'll see what you'll do with your beast, once you finish your training." He tipped his hat to her. "Enjoy your journey."

"I will," Mina promised, but he was busy already preparing for the ship's arrival.

«*You're worrying again,*» Pixit said.

No, I'm not.

«*I can taste it.*»

As the ship drew closer, she saw its sailors scurrying over the deck. Shouting to the stationmaster, they called, "Ready the dock!"

"Ready the ship!" he called back.

A plank was laid between the ship and the dock, and the

sailors bustled back and forth. No one so much as glanced at her and Pixit, and she did her best to stay out of the way.

Crates were moved off.

Crates were moved on.

And, at last, the stationmaster turned to her and said in a kindly voice, "On you go, both of you. Quick now, before the wind picks up."

Only then did Mina notice that the steady wind had died down — long enough for the ship to stop, load, and unload. It would start again shortly.

This is it! We're really going!

Trying to shove every bit of worry away, she glanced back once at the stairs and waved, not sure whether Papa could see her or not, and she hurried over the plank onto the ship. The plank wobbled beneath her, and she felt Pixit's anxiousness like bubbles inside her as they walked onboard.

«*Setting out on our adventure sounded a lot easier when I was still in my egg. Are storm beasts really supposed to travel by boat?*»

Mina wondered if she should ask someone where she was supposed to go. She felt like she was the only one on the ship who didn't know exactly what she was supposed to be doing.

«*Mina?*» Pixit sounded nervous, a buzzy kind of feeling in her head. «*It's all made of wood.*» His tail was sparking harder, with embers boring themselves into the wooden deck.

"Excuse me, ma'am?" Mina asked one of the sailors.

But the sailor hurried past without hearing her and climbed

one of the masts. She released a hook, and a sail billowed out. Mina felt the wind blow harder, and the sail puffed like a shirt on the laundry line.

The captain called, "Watch the rigging! Careful now! Ease her into the stream! That's it — and someone get that lightning baby onto the rubber! What are you thinking, girl? Ships are flammable!"

Jumping, Mina realized he was shouting the last at her. *Onto the rubber?* What did that mean? She spun in the circle, hoping it would become clear.

"This way," a sailor barked at her — the one who had passed her a second ago, now down from the mast. Pixit and Mina trotted after her, across the deck to some steps. "Honestly, why don't they teach you how to travel before they expect you to journey?" She then gave them a smile and softened her voice. "Not your fault you don't know. You're a skittish one, aren't you? Especially for a lightning guardian. You sure you're with the right beast?" The sailor's voice was lightly teasing, but the words struck Mina right in the heart.

She was sure, but she couldn't seem to find the words to say it.

"Keep your sparky friend down there on the black, and he won't do any harm. It's safe for his kind. You'll be the second stop, after the city." She was back climbing the ropes to one of the crossbeams as soon as she finished her speech.

"Thank you," Mina said, albeit too softly for the sailor to hear. "And I'm sure."

The "black" was a sunken area of the deck lined with an odd shiny material. Mina followed Pixit down the steps onto whatever it was. The captain had called it rubber, she remembered. Squatting, Mina ran her hand over it. It felt smooth, a little sticky, and very hot. Pixit hopped down the steps, joining her. He was still sparking, but when his bits of lightning hit the rubber, they didn't burn or spread.

It wasn't a very large area, just room enough for Pixit and Mina and a few other items. A hammock-like chair was hanging from a hook. She stowed her bag in an empty crate near it. A bowl with water was in one corner — a pipe led to it, so maybe it was connected to more water?

«Do you think they have lightning-beast food?»

I can explore and see . . .

«Don't leave. Please.»

Kneeling, she put her arm around his shoulders. You don't have to be scared. We're exactly where we're supposed to be, doing exactly what we're supposed to do. She tried to sound more confident than she felt. It was disconcerting how both the stationmaster and the sailor had seen how un-lightning guardian she was. If it was so obvious after only a few seconds . . .

«I'm not scared! It's just . . . It's a nice view, isn't it? I don't want you to miss the view.»

Mina didn't point out that she could feel he was scared. And he was polite enough not to point out that she was scared too. She just looked out at the view, across the fields toward the mountains, and he laid his head against her shoulder.

Out loud, she asked, "What do you think is beyond them?"

To her surprise, one of the sailors answered her. "Heard tales," she said as she coiled a rope. "Terrible tales. Of storms with winds so fierce they rip trees from the earth. And rain so hard it washes away the roads and overflows the rivers."

"Hurricanes," another sailor, also a woman, said, taking the rope from the first sailor and hanging it on a hook. "That's what they call them. Heard you can survive the winds blowing, but you can't survive *what* the winds are blowing. Can't predict them, so can't protect against them."

"Tornadoes, too," another added, an older man with a braided beard. "Where the winds whip in a funnel, busting through everything in their path."

"Lightning storms that fry everything."

"Blizzards that freeze."

"That's why you have to train hard and learn fast, little guardian," the first sailor said seriously. "It's not right that so much depends on children, but it does. You're what makes Aloria great."

With that, they went about their work. Mina sat in the hammock, while Pixit curled up on the rubber beside her — both of them still thinking about the sailors' words. *It's okay to be nervous,* Mina thought, *when you're about to try to do something big and important.*

«*It's nicer to be nervous together.*»

After a while, Mina pulled out her sketchbook and began

to draw what lay before them. She wanted to remember every second of this, the start of their adventure.

From the river ship she saw the farms, golden in the afternoon light. White farmhouses were like jewels in the heart of the green. The distant mountains looked amber against the sky, as perfect as if they were painted. She felt as if all of Alorria were spread before them, bigger and more gloriously beautiful than she'd ever imagined.

And soon we'll be part of making it stay this way.

It didn't matter that she was different from other lightning guardians, did it?

⊸CHAPTER⊸
FIVE

SEVERAL hours later, they sailed through the city. Mina and Pixit leaned over the side of the ship, trying to see every-thing. She didn't want to blink for fear she'd miss seeing a marvel.

And the city was full of marvels!

She saw a waterfall flowing *up* the side of a skyscraper, spraying into a fountain at the top. A clock tower covered in gears chimed, announcing three-quarters after the hour, as they sailed past. A train zipped by on a single rail, parallel with the river ship. She waved at the passengers, and they waved back, their feathered hats fluttering in the wind. And then the train banked around a building and disappeared from view. Hundreds of towers — some as straight as a pine tree, others as curved as a ram's horn — fit together like pieces of a puzzle, squeezed tight to be as close as possible to the central power station. All were connected by bridges. Mina watched the city folk scurry across the bridges and climb into glass elevators that shot them high up the sides of the towers. In the streets below, carts ran without horses.

Everything was powered by lightning. *By kids like me*, she thought, *with beasts like Pixit*. Another train zoomed past, diving beneath a bridge.

«*We're going to do great things,*» Pixit said confidently. «*Just as soon as we learn how.*»

Reaching over, she scratched Pixit behind his ears.

One of the sailors passed by. "Going to dock soon. Got a pickup. New lightning guardian. Like you. You'd better make room on the rubber."

Mina and Pixit looked at each other, then at the already cramped area.

«*A new friend?*»

She wasn't sure she was ready to meet someone new. There was already so much "new" battering her senses that she didn't know if she'd be able to find the words to encapsulate it all. *Maybe they won't mind being quiet.*

She spent the next few minutes searching the ship for an extra hammock-chair. And then begging for another extra after Pixit fried the ropes on the first one she found. Mina strung the hammocks up on either side of the rubber area. She tucked the crate with her bag beneath her hammock and left an empty crate for the new passenger. With a borrowed broom, she swept the floor

— Pixit had dropped a few feathers and dribbled bits of half-chewed potato all around. (The sailors had given him a bowl of his favorite food.) She corralled all the debris into a single pile, then called to Pixit. *Could you please shed a few sparks over here?*

«*I don't know how to direct the electricity — according to those stories you always read me, that's what a guardian does. You're supposed to catch and guide it. I just absorb and store it.*»

She had no idea how to do that yet. *We don't need to direct it. You just need to do whatever you did when you set the cornfield on fire.*

He sounded embarrassed. «*That was an accident. I don't know how I did it. I can feel the electricity inside me — it kind of tickles — but that's all.*»

Just come closer and think of something exciting. Maybe that would set off his sparks. He'd been excited when he flew over the field. *Try watching that.* Mina pointed to the central clock tower. She'd heard that the city clocks performed every hour on the hour. It was nearly seven o'clock, and the sun was dipping between the buildings. Everything glowed a rosy orange.

The minute hand clicked up to twelve.

Celebrating the hour, lightning-powered fountains exploded into the air. Water splayed into fans, then fell, and then water shot straight up as high as the tops of the tower. Around the river ship, the sailors clapped and hooted and cheered. Mina spun in a circle, trying to see everything.

Reflected on the glassy walls, the water danced and played all around the city. It caught the orange-and-red light of the setting sun, holding its rays in its droplets. When the minute hand clicked again, it ended. Mina looked down at her feet and saw a tiny fire eating the dust, dirt, and potato bits. *Thanks, Pixit.*

«*I liked the sparkly water.*»

Me too. Maybe someday we'll be the ones to catch the lightning that makes it happen. The idea made her shiver — could she really learn to do that? Fly fearlessly into a storm and help Pixit absorb the electric charge? It sounded so impossible.

But so did waterfalls flowing upward and trains zooming by.

She wanted to believe in the impossible.

As the sailors docked the ship, Mina drew as much as she could in her sketchbook, determined to capture everything she saw before the sun set. Skyscrapers filled the paper. She drew the trains and the bridges and tried to sketch the fountains in mid-spray.

As the last rays of sunlight sank behind the city, electric lights blinked on, covering the towers in what looked like a blanket of stars. And then she saw them — the lightning beasts with their guardians, flying between their towers, sparking like fireworks.

All of them looked like Pixit: dragon bodies and dog faces, yellow scales and feathers. Out of the corner of her eye, she saw Pixit testing his still-tiny wings — they might have been strong enough to hold him, but he couldn't fly with her yet. *Soon*, she told him. She felt him yearning to soar, and she imagined how it would feel so high above the city, with the wind in their faces and lightning on their skin.

A girl's voice cut through her daydream. "Someday that will be us!"

Stuffing her sketchbook away quickly, Mina jumped out of the hammock. In front of her was a girl about her age with black hair cut to her ears, a heart-shaped scar on her chin, and a lightning beast by her side. The girl was wearing brown leather like a blacksmith would wear — *smart*, Mina thought approvingly, *fire-resistant* — and carried a small satchel.

"You must be the other new student," the girl said. She hopped down onto the rubber and stuck out her hand. "I'm Jyx. This is Chauda." Her voice was loud, as if she were proclaiming everything to the world. It made Mina want to shrink back.

"Mina. And Pixit." She shook Jyx's hand awkwardly. She'd never shaken another kid's hand before. It was a city-folk tradition, usually only for grownups.

Chauda waddled forward to the lip of the deck and then thumped down next to them in the black area. Both Pixit and Mina were crowded against the ship railing — Chauda was wider than Pixit but had the same-size wings perched on her broad back, which meant she was newly hatched too. She sniffed at Pixit as if saying hello. Mina couldn't hear her thoughts, but Pixit could.

«*Yes, I'm sure I'm a lightning beast,*» Mina heard him say, apparently in response to something Chauda had asked. «*And, yes, I came this size. Besides, your wings aren't any more mature than mine!*»

It's all right, Mina soothed him. She wasn't sure what the other beast had said, but she didn't like Pixit being upset. It made her feel as if she'd swallowed a thistle.

Jyx thumped Chauda on the back. "Be nice. Is this seriously all the space they gave us?" She didn't bother to lower her voice as she complained, nor did she give Mina a chance to reply, even if Mina had wanted to. "Not that I want to hang out belowdecks. You know it stinks like fish down there." She craned her neck, looking at the masts. "Up *there* looks perfect. Come on!" She jumped out of the rubber area and began climbing up the middle mast.

Her lightning beast lumbered after her.

«*I thought we were supposed to stay here so we don't set the ship on fire.*»

You're right. We are.

Mina didn't know if she should call up to the other girl, or if she should tell one of the sailors. She saw Jyx reach the crossbeam and swing herself up onto the platform. Legs spread wide, Jyx balanced on the platform, surveying the city with her hands on her hips. Her face was in shadow, but in the lights from the city, her silhouette was sharply visible. "Great view! Mina, Pixit, come up!"

Well, she's not quiet.

The lightning beast Chauda flew up to the platform and flopped onto it, then sat next to Jyx, also looking out at the city. Mina wondered how far they could see and if the electric lights looked any different from up high. But no, there was no reason to climb up there, and plenty of reasons not to.

I'm responsible and dependable and mature. I keep my feet on the ground. Literally.

«*I could fly up instead of climbing. Can't burn the ship from the air. I mean, I'll try not to.*»

You should stay here, where it's safe. It did *not* look safe that far up, even if Pixit could avoid burning the mast on his way.

«*But it looks nice up there. And Chauda is there.*»

She looked up again at the platform and didn't see Jyx. Her breath froze in her throat — *Did she fall?* But Jyx hadn't fallen. Mina spotted her a second later, her arms out for balance, walking down the crossbeam.

"Reckless," she remembered the stationmaster saying. *I'm not like that. And I don't want to be.* But would she have to be, in order to be a real lightning guardian?

We stay here, she told Pixit.

«*Okay.*»

They watched Jyx and Chauda.

Pixit fidgeted.

Stay.

«*I'm staying.*»

He flexed his wings.

Pixit?

«*Not staying. Sorry.*»

He flew up.

Oh no, she thought. She climbed out of the rubber area and looked around — there was a jug of water next to a sailor. "Can

I borrow this? Thank you." Mina scooped it up, slung the strap over her shoulder, and began to climb.

Stout nails stuck out on either side of the mast, making a ladder. She tried not to look down. She'd never climbed much — there wasn't much cause for it on the farm.

«*You can do it.*» Pixit encouraged her.

You shouldn't have done it, she told him. She pictured her mother shaking her head and telling Mina she had to train her beast, not the other way around. Pixit was newborn. He was trusting and vulnerable and . . .

«*But it's so pretty up here! And Chauda called me chicken.*»

Don't listen to Chauda.

«*She made clucking sounds in my head.*»

Then you moo right back at her. If she wants to make farm-animal noises, then give her farm-animal noises.

She sensed his delight at that idea.

Reaching the top, she tried to swing herself onto the platform. She felt Jyx grab her arms and yank her up. Ungracefully, Mina flopped at Jyx's feet. "This isn't safe," Mina said.

"You're a worrier, I can tell," Jyx said. "You know, people can die from too much worrying. You should worry about *that.*"

"I'm not a worrier," Mina said, but she said it softly, and Jyx didn't hear. She was already walking back out on the crossbeam, balancing.

Over her shoulder, Jyx called, "Come on, scaredy-cat. It's fun!"

Mina didn't move. "Meow."

«*Moo.*»

A flash of light caught her eye, and she forgot about Jyx and stared out. Jyx had been right — she could see so much farther from here! The sparkling lights covered the cluster of towers at the heart of the city. Beyond that, Alorria was a sea of darkness. It made the city look even more special: a glowing jewel in the middle of the black night. The river, stretching on ahead of them, was a shiny black ribbon. The distant mountains were indistinguishable from the night sky.

As they sailed beyond the city, the darkness closed around them, too, and Mina could at last see the stars. They'd been blotted out by the electric lights of the city.

Jyx plopped down next to her. "What kind of lightning guardian is afraid of heights?"

Mina shrugged. She wasn't afraid; she was sensible. But the question wormed its way inside her, joining her other worries.

"You're going to have to get over that, if you're going to fly into a storm cloud."

She didn't answer. It was true. But by then she'd be flying on Pixit, and she knew he wouldn't let her fall. And besides, they'd both be trained by experts. *So I don't have to worry, right?*

«*You don't have to worry about anything,*» Pixit said confidently. «*We're going to be great at this!*»

Mina wasn't so sure about that. She eyed Jyx, cataloging all the ways they were different. If Jyx was a typical lightning guardian and Mina was nothing like her . . .

"You don't talk much, do you? Or is it because you don't like me? I've been told I'm unlikable. That I'm pushy, selfish, and impetuous." Jyx said this as if it were a point of pride. Mina wondered who had called Jyx all those things. She didn't think it was anything to be proud of or happy about. "It's okay," Jyx said. "We don't have to be friends."

"I'd like to be," Mina said quietly.

That seemed to startle Jyx.

"But please ask your storm beast never to call Pixit a chicken again."

"Okay. I can do that." Jyx was silent for a moment. "Done. And Chauda apologizes. She says she was only teasing, and she knows he doesn't cluck or lay eggs."

"Thank you," Mina said.

"She does want to know why he's mooing at her, though."

Mina smiled. *Pixit?*

«*Sorry. I'll stop.*»

"Do you really think we can be friends?" The way Jyx asked made Mina think she didn't expect the answer to be yes. Her voice was small, like Beon's when he asked for a treat he knew he shouldn't have.

"Yes," Mina said. She could say more — that it would depend on whether Jyx was nice, whether she'd accept that Mina was never going to be chatty, and what she meant by "pushy" and "selfish" — but she didn't. "Who told you you were pushy?"

"My parents," Jyx said. "They don't like kids much. That's why I never really had friends. Glad to have met you, though."

"Me too."

"I think we're going to be best friends!" Jyx announced.

"Maybe we should make sure we like each other first?"

"Oh. Right. Okay." Then Jyx grinned at her. "Hey, scaredy-cat, I'm sure I like you."

Despite herself, Mina couldn't help smiling back.

They sat side by side while the river ship sliced through the dark countryside. Mina was happy to see that Jyx was capable of being quiet. Not everyone was. And it was nice to sit next to someone who could possibly become a real friend. *This is a good sign*, Mina thought at Pixit. Maybe Pixit was right and she didn't have to worry. Maybe her family was wrong about who she was meant to be. She tried to put as much confidence and enthusiasm into her mental voice as possible. *I think we're going to do well at the lightning school!*

«*Um, Mina?*»

Sighing, Mina turned and dumped the jug of water on the small fire he'd started.

CHAPTER
SIX

THE letters had been seared into a brass plaque nailed to the river-ship station:

MYTRIS LIGHTNING SCHOOL

Mina stood on the plank that led from the ship to the dock and wasn't sure she wanted to step off. It was a lot easier to be confident and brave in daydreams, but now that she was really here . . . *I could really fail.* If she couldn't master the necessary skills, she couldn't become a lightning guardian.

That was a horrible thought.

She told herself firmly to quit being so dramatic. She didn't even know what the training was going to be like, much less whether or not she'd be able to do it. Maybe she'd be a natural.

Around her, sailors swarmed, loading and unloading crates

and shouting to one another. It was still dark. Beyond the lanterns that lit the station, the barren lands looked like swampy blackness. She couldn't see any school.

She heard a whoop above her and looked up to see Jyx swinging down from the crossbeam on one of the ship's ropes. Both Chauda and Pixit flew from the ship onto the station platform, landing at the same time as Jyx.

Pixit hopped from foot to foot. «*Mina, Mina, Mina, we're here!*» He ran in a tight circle, like a dog chasing his tail. His excitement felt like bubbles inside her. «*Here, here, here! Aren't you excited?*»

Of course I am, she told him.

She just happened to also be terrified.

She glanced at Jyx, wondering if she felt the same kind of doubts and fears. But Jyx was bouncing up and down like an overexuberant rabbit.

"This is going to be awesome," Jyx cried. "Wait for it!"

"Wait for what?"

On tiptoes, Jyx was peering out into the darkness beyond the station. Mina stared too, wondering what she was supposed to be looking for —

A streak of light shot through the blackness.

And then another.

Beside her, Jyx jumped up and down, clapping her hands. "Yes!" She punched the air as another streak flew and then was met by what looked like a ball of electricity.

The streak began to zigzag through the sky, so bright that

when Mina blinked, she still saw its light, lingering behind her eyelids. She heard shouts and cheers in the distance.

"What's going on?" Mina asked.

"They're playing lightning relay! Don't you know anything about Mytris? It's how they train us!" Jyx jogged forward toward the stairs. "Come on, I want a better view!" She jumped up onto the railing with Chauda, balancing with one hand on the station gutter and one on her lightning beast.

Pixit hopped up beside them, but Mina stayed on the ground. She thought about telling Jyx to be careful, but decided that that would be like telling a sun beast not to shine. Instead Mina just watched the sky, trying to see what had excited Jyx so much.

And then she saw them: the storm guardians riding their beasts, lit up by sparks of electricity, pulling streaks of lightning behind them, as if they were glorious comets. She gasped as they sparkled brighter than the stars.

"Really simple rules. Really hard to play," Jyx said. "You have to get a bolt of lightning to your team's goal. Each bolt is a point." She pointed to a streak of lightning between two sparking beasts. "The other team has its own goal, and they can steal your bolt. There are three fifteen-minute rounds. Most points wins."

«*Fun!*» Pixit cried.

"It's awesome!" Jyx said, leaning forward, stretching both arms to hold on to the gutter and Chauda. "My parents were in the top team their year. Told me I'd better be too."

Mina watched one of the beasts plummet and then right

itself. She knew what *her* parents would say watching this: that it was a ridiculous waste to play games with storm beasts, that they should be doing something practical to help the farm, that it was too dangerous, that Mina of course wanted both her feet on the ground, safe and sound. "It looks dangerous."

Jyx nodded. "Totally is."

Mina sensed Pixit laughing in her head. *What?*

«*You think it looks fun, too.*»

Do not. It looks absurd.

«*You want to do it.*»

No.

«*Mina.*»

I don't.

«*I can read your mind.*»

Oh.

He laid a paw on her arm. «*Mina, you aren't your family. And you aren't who your family thinks you are. You're you. And I love you exactly as you are.*»

I love you too, Pixit.

Trying to quiet the imagined voices of her family, Mina watched the storm beasts and their guardians chase through the sky. Her heart began to thump faster. Her fingers tapped on the railing. She shifted from foot to foot, rising up on her tiptoes as the streak of lightning shot across the sky, illuminated a tower with a rod, and then sizzled down the rod.

"A point!" Jyx yelled.

«*What do you think of that, Mina?*»

Fine. You're right. It looks fun. She knew her family would think it strange that she thought it looked exciting — she was supposed to be quiet, calm, and dependable. She'd never been the daredevil type, and she still wasn't. But . . . *Maybe there's a part of me that* does *belong here.*

«*Of course there is.*»

He sounded so confident, but how could he know?

«*Um . . . Mina?*»

Oh, right. You can read my mind. She grinned at him. Maybe he did know.

As soon as the sparks on the rods died, all four players dove down fast and disappeared into the blackness, presumably inside Mytris, and then electric lights began to snap on. She should have realized that the lightning school, of all places, would have the miracle of electric lights. Mina heard a buzzing around her, and then a bulb above them blinked to life. Soft amber light spilled across the station. A string of bulbs lit the stairs down from the dock and a river-like path toward a trio of black towers, which were now visible.

As they descended from the dock, Jyx was chattering. "All the best players will compete at the Ten-Year Festival. Bad luck for us with the timing — the festival's too soon for us to be good enough for it, and by the time it happens again, we won't be stormy anymore."

The Ten-Year Festival was, as its name said, held every ten years, to celebrate the founding (and saving) of Alorria. The next festival was in less than two months, and the new prime minister was said to be determined to make it the best ever. Everyone Mina knew had been talking about it for what seemed like forever. Sometimes Mina felt like she was the only one in the country who wasn't sure how she felt about the festival. There would be crowds, and she didn't like crowds. *Maybe I'll feel different now that I'm a storm guardian. Maybe I'll be different.* She wasn't sure how she felt about that, either. She didn't want to become someone she wasn't.

«*You're already who you're supposed to be, exactly as you are.*»

She realized Pixit was reading all her doubt and fear. She was broadcasting every bit of it. *Maybe. I don't know.* As much as she liked Jyx, now that she'd met another lightning guardian, it seemed as if all her doubts had doubled. Yes, part of her was excited, but a *lot* of her was nervous.

Jyx skipped alongside Mina as they started down the path. "Ooh, maybe we can help harvest lightning for it, and maybe they'll let us go and watch close-up! Imagine seeing the Ten-Year Festival from the sky!"

She wished she could be as sure of herself as Jyx.

«*I'll be your confidence, until you find your own.*»

That was sweet. *I'm not sure it works that way, but thanks.*

Jyx was still skipping and still talking. "My parents won't stop going on about when they were in the Ten-Year Festival, back when they were storm guardians — they said it was incredible, and it's such a shame I'm too young and inexperienced to really participate, even though I have Chauda."

Except for Jyx, it was silent in the barren lands. Away from the river, Mina couldn't hear the wind, nor did she hear any of the usual night birds or crickets that she heard in the farmlands. *We might as well be walking on the moon.*

The weak light from the bulbs was enough to light the path, but it only spilled a little ways beyond — the earth was blackened and dry. She saw no plants or trees, though maybe they grew farther away. She couldn't imagine a place with no green whatsoever.

«You did say it was called the barren lands.»

I thought it was just a nickname for the Northwest Barrens.

«Ooh, can I have a nickname?»

I like your name. Pixit's nice.

«You could call me Pixit, Master of the Skies. Or Pixit, Harnesser of Lightning. Or Pixit, King of Storms.»

Maybe we should train first?

«And then you'll call me King of Storms?»

Sure.

«Yay!» He pranced next to her.

She knew he was trying to distract her from worrying, but it still worked. Further proof that Pixit was a match for her. Mina couldn't help smiling at him. Whatever was going to happen, whether she succeeded or failed, at least she wouldn't be doing it alone.

«Never alone again.»

Laying her hand on his back scales, she sent as much warm love at him as she could.

They followed the path to an iron archway — the gate was

open, and through it stood the three towers of the school. Light bulbs blazed, strung on wires from window to window, winding up the towers. She'd never seen so many. Mother would have said it was frivolous — the farm had everything they needed, and they didn't need electric baubles — but Mina thought it was wonderful. Each tower ended in a metal pole that looked like an empty flagpole. *Lightning rods,* she thought. All the stones were black; the courtyard was black; the windows were dirty gray. Mina slowed, but Jyx marched past her, with Chauda trotting behind.

As they reached the massive door, decorated with a single silver lightning bolt, Mina looked for a door knocker or even just a handle. "How do we get inside?"

"Um." Jyx examined the door. "Maybe it's a test?"

Chauda flapped hard and rose into the air next to them.

"Chauda thinks we're all supposed to fly in," Jyx said.

Sounding panicked, Pixit said, «*Oh no, I can't lift you! I'm not strong enough! What if they don't let us in? What if they send us back, and it's my fault?*»

Okay, maybe he did absorb some of my worrying, Mina thought. In that moment, she could read all his fears: he was worried he'd disappoint her, that *he* wouldn't be good enough for *her,* which she thought was absurd. He was perfect as he was. She projected to Pixit: *Calm down. It's a door. It's meant to open.* She raised a fist and knocked. The sound was swallowed as if buried in a pillow.

Jyx pushed past her. "Let me try." She pounded on the door

76

with both fists. Landing with a plop, Chauda head-butted the door. "Hello! We're here! Let us in!"

Stepping back, Mina looked up at the silver lightning-bolt decoration. She tracked it down to the point, where she saw a divot in the door. She waited until Jyx paused, resting her hands on her knees and panting, and then Mina pushed on the divot.

A bell chimed.

"Seriously?" Jyx wheezed.

Mina shrugged.

The door swung open, and a squat man peered out at them. The light behind him was so bright that Mina could barely see his face. She got the impression of raisin-size eyes and a bulbous nose. "Ah, you must be the new ones," he said.

Jyx pointed at the door. "Was this a test?"

He blinked at her. "No. This is a door."

Grumbling, Jyx stomped inside. Pushing past Mina and Pixit, Chauda stomped in as well. Sparks shed from her tail, and the man in the doorway brushed the embers off his sleeves. Whatever his clothes were made of, it didn't burn. Pixit romped in after them. Mina was last. She wanted to ask if they were in the right place, if they'd done the right thing, if they were supposed to do something now that they were here, but she decided he would tell them what to do next.

He didn't.

Humming to himself, he trotted through the entryway and disappeared through another smaller door. Jyx, Chauda, Pixit, and Mina were left alone.

"Oookay," Jyx said. "Are we supposed to follow him?"

Mina craned her neck, trying to see everything all at once. The vaulted ceiling, high above them, was made of all black stone streaked with gold veins, as if lightning had been caught inside it. There were no windows, but a crystal chandelier filled with electric bulbs hung from the center of the ceiling. All around them were glass sculptures in strange shapes, like sprays of water frozen in midair. Each was displayed on a pedestal. She went closer to one, reading the plaque beneath it.

FROM THE CLASS OF SPRING 882

A woman's voice said, "Sand, when hit by lightning exactly right, can create magnificent glass sculptures. You see before you the proof of mastery of each graduating class since the founding of Mytris Lightning School. Mastery of the power of storms is what makes Alorria magnificent and sets her apart from all others."

"Wow," Jyx said.

"'Wow' indeed," the woman said. She was as tall as a cornstalk, with a thin face, sharp nose, and arched eyebrows. Her hair was black except for one white streak that had been pinned back behind her ear. She wore black robes that sparkled with yellow bolts, and she carried a metal cane with a black orb at its end. She looked, Mina thought, very dramatic. "Someday you may create such a masterpiece, perhaps. Not all succeed here.

The path of a lightning guardian is not an easy one, and there are those who fail to rise to the challenge."

Mina felt her mouth grow suddenly dry. Before she'd arrived, she'd never considered that failing to become a storm guardian was a real possibility, but now that she was standing here, it felt like more than just a vague fear.

I was so focused on everything that came before *this moment — the egg hatching, convincing my parents to let me go, traveling up the river — that I didn't stop to really think about what would come after.*

"We won't fail," Jyx said. "We were born for this! Right, Mina?"

I wasn't, Mina thought, but she buried that thought quickly, before Pixit could see it. She sensed Pixit sliding closer to her. He laid his head under her hand, as if to reassure her. *At least* he *was born for this. Maybe that will be enough.* Weakly, Mina whispered, "Right." She didn't think anyone heard her.

"If you succeed, you will graduate in six months, as the Class of Fall 894," the woman said. "Since storm beasts hatch throughout the year, our graduating classes are grouped loosely by season."

"Go, Fall 894!" Jyx whooped, then said in a more polite, talking-to-a-teacher voice, "I'm Jyx and this is Chauda. We're here to join the Class of Fall 894."

"Welcome, Jyx and Chauda." The woman paused. And Mina realized she was waiting for Mina to introduce herself, but Mina's throat felt so clogged and her heart was thumping so fast that she had to swallow twice before she could make a sound. By then, the woman had already continued. "You must be Mina and Pixit. I am Professor Werrin, headmistress of Mytris. If you will follow me, I will lead you to your dorm room. Counting you, there are eighteen students in your season, all housed near one another, but we train you in smaller groups to better tailor your lessons to your skill level. As our two newest students, you two will be both roommates and training partners —"

"Yes!" Jyx pumped the air with her fist. "Mina, hope you're ready to fly high and fast. Both my parents were lightning guardians, and they graduated top of their class. We're gonna do the same. At least as soon as Pixit and Chauda's wings can hold us."

But . . . but I've never even heard of lightning relay before tonight! And I don't know anything about lightning! Mina felt like sinking into the floor. Every bit of doubt and fear came rushing back again. Now that she was here, her daydreams felt silly at best — and at worst impossible.

«*We can do this!*»

I don't know that I can! I'm supposed to be a farm girl!

«*You're supposed to be you. And I know you can do that!*»

SEVEN

$\mathcal{P}$ROFESSOR Werrin led the way, with Jyx, Chauda, and Pixit trooping after her. Mina slunk along behind them, certain that at any moment the headmistress would notice she didn't belong. After all, the stationmaster and the river-ship sailors had seen it instantly, and her own family was certain of it. She stared down at her feet, not making eye contact with anyone, wishing she were better at hiding her thoughts from Pixit.

Pixit's thoughts were broadcasting clearly, and there wasn't a shred of doubt in them. «*This is going to be awesome. Stop worrying. We're going to fit in great!*»

As they walked through a corridor, she was hit by sound: shouting and laughing.

Mina felt like running in the opposite direction. She made herself keep walking forward.

"Lights out is in forty-five minutes," Professor Werrin explained. "Until then, all are encouraged to expend their excess energy. Quite literally, in fact." Stepping through an arch-way, she gestured with both arms. "Welcome to the heart of Mytris!"

It was a cavernous room that Mina would have called a din-ing hall, if you ignored everything except the rows of tables and chairs. You couldn't ignore everything else, though. Obstacles filled the walls and ceiling: a maze of metal rods, a climbing wall, chains that stretched from one corner to another, and metal ladders that dangled from the ceiling. Guardians and beasts zipped through the room, chasing one another, clinging to the ladders, and racing through the maze. Sparks flew in white-and-blue arcs between all the metal. And towering over everything was a black basalt statue of a lightning beast with golden eyes, which seemed to survey the chaos.

"Whoa!" Jyx breathed.

"Hands on your beasts," Professor Werrin said briskly. "They'll ground you."

"What about you, Professor?" Jyx asked.

The professor brandished her cane, and the orb opened into an umbrella-like metal net. She held it over her head. "Sensible shoes and an electricity cage will protect me nicely. Come now." She forded into the room.

«Oh, Mina, doesn't it look fun?»

It looked the opposite of fun.

The sound was nearly deafening — every student seemed to be shouting at the same time. Mina didn't know how anyone could hear themselves think. She hurried through. Out of the corner of her eye, she saw Jyx smiling and waving at everyone, loudly introducing herself and Chauda. Clearly, Jyx was going to fit right in.

If this was what she had to do to be a lightning guardian . . .

I'm doomed.

Only when they reached the other side did Mina feel like she could breathe again. She ventured a question. "Is it always like this?" She immediately wished she hadn't asked — she hadn't meant to draw attention to the fact that she wasn't like the others.

Professor Werrin looked at her curiously. "Of course not. There's order and discipline here as well. You will see in the morning. Breakfast is typically much more sedate."

Good, Mina thought. She'd considered her farmhouse loud, especially with the twins, but this was extreme. She glanced at Jyx. The other girl didn't seem at all intimidated. In fact, she was grinning broadly.

Pixit pranced beside Mina. «*Come on, be excited! Maybe they'll all be new friends!*»

Or maybe they'll see I don't belong.

He made a puffing sound. «*Or maybe they'll all be really great new friends! I don't remember you being this negative before I was born.*»

Yeah, well, it's easy to be brave when you're talking to an egg.

"Balloons will be sent to both your families, informing them of your safe arrival," Professor Werrin said, waving at a room stuffed with red message balloons.

At least she hadn't said a message would be sent saying Mina was unsuitable. Mina allowed herself a kernel of hope. She followed Professor Werrin and the others.

"And this is the library," Professor Werrin said, gesturing toward another room as they passed.

Inside, through the window in the door, Mina could see a tunnel-like room full of long rows of bookshelves, all wrapped in chains. So many books! Mina lingered by the window.

At one table, she saw the squat man with the bulbous nose who had opened the door for them. He was poring over a thick book with yellowed pages. Rising up onto her tiptoes, she tried to see what kind of book it was — she'd never seen such a fat one. It had to hold hundreds of stories!

As if he felt her gaze, he looked up and met her eyes. He shut his book, hiding the title.

"Mina!" Jyx called. "Keep up!"

Mina scurried on, with one more glance back at the beautifully quiet library.

«See, told you you'd find something you liked here.»

You never said that.

«I could have said it, if I'd thought to. It's totally the kind of thing I'd say.»

She grinned despite herself.

As soon as she and Pixit caught up with the others, Professor Werrin nodded briskly at her and then, hitching her robe up to her knees, climbed a set of stairs. "Dorm rooms are this way. Storm-guardian bathrooms on the left, beasts' on the right."

At the end of the corridor, the headmistress halted in front of a human-size door, too narrow for a full-grown storm beast, though plenty wide enough for Pixit and Chauda now.

Chauda snorted, a sound full of disapproval.

"There are external entrances to all the dorm rooms, for your beasts to use after they grow," Professor Werrin said — Mina thought she sounded a touch defensive. "Mytris School is a historic building with a rich history. These dorms are a legacy of a time before storm beasts, when doorways were narrow, and thick walls were needed to protect us from the weather. They remind all students and beasts of their purpose in Alorria."

Another snort from Chauda, but this one somehow managed to sound more polite.

Mina wondered what it would be like to need walls for the weather. Did the people beyond the mountains — "outsiders," as Mother and others called them — hide behind walls all the time?

She toyed with the idea of asking, but it seemed their brief tour was at an end. Besides, she wasn't sure she could form the words. Or that she should.

"This will be your room until you graduate and receive your assignments," Professor Werrin said, swinging a door open. "Morning bell will be your signal to wash, dress, and join your classmates for breakfast. After breakfast, you will meet your teacher outside on the practice field. Follow the other students."

Jyx began peppering the headmistress with questions: what was breakfast, when would training begin, when would their first flying lesson be, how soon until they went into their first thundercloud, what kind of lessons would they have.

Full of wonder, Mina moved past her into the dorm room.

She'd never lived anywhere but her family's farmhouse. And this looked exactly like she'd imagined a student room would look. Practical and perfect. She loved it.

It was all black, like the rest of the school. She touched the stone walls — they seemed to be painted with the same fire-resistant stuff she'd discovered on the ship. On each side of the room was a bed with a shiny silver blanket. *Fire-resistant too?* Pixit trotted over to one of the beds, and a spark leaped from his tail onto the silver blanket. «*Yep.*»

She liked that. It meant Pixit would be able to stay with her at night. In fact, it looked as if he was expected to. He had a bed as well, at the foot of hers, a large divot four times his current size, padded with rubber. There was a matching spot on the opposite side of the room for Chauda. One side of the room was all window, as wide as a full-grown storm beast, latched shut. *This must be how they're supposed to enter once they're bigger*, she thought. Mina crossed to it and opened it wide, expecting to glimpse the hills and maybe even the mountains beyond.

There wasn't anything to see.

All the bulbs had been turned off outside, and the barren lands were sunk in darkness.

"Lights out means lights out — interior lights will shut off shortly as well," the headmistress said. "I suggest you prepare yourselves for sleep. You have a long day ahead of you." She then backed out and shut the door.

Wait — that was it? The headmistress hadn't said a word about Mina not belonging here. In fact, she'd treated both of them with an air of almost boredom, as if this were routine, as if Mina weren't any different from any other student. And she hadn't answered a single one of Jyx's many questions.

Jyx didn't seem to mind.

"Ahh!" Jyx said as she flopped on her bed. "I'm so happy to be here! Away from home! Away from 'Jyx, you're in the way!' and 'Jyx, you're being too loud!' and 'Jyx, why won't you grow up?' Ugh! So nice to be on our own! Know what I mean?"

"Sort of." Mina sat on the bed. The silvery blanket wasn't as soft as cotton, and it crackled when she sat. She was still in shock that their welcome had been so ordinary. *Maybe I can find a place here, even with being different.*

«*Look around,*» Pixit said. «*You already have one.*»

A dorm room wasn't precisely what she meant, but she didn't argue.

Lying on her bed, Jyx fell silent, caught up in her own thoughts and leaving Mina to hers. On her side of the room, Mina pulled out her sketchbook and began to draw — pictures of the ship, Mytris, Pixit, and Chauda — until her hands stopped shaking and her heart quit thumping so hard.

Eventually, long after Jyx had stopped talking and long after lights out, Mina slept.

⚡

Mina didn't linger over breakfast — after one look at the hall stuffed with students, professors, and beasts, she scooped up a cinnamon roll and fled to eat in the peace and quiet of her room. Just because they were all seated at tables did not mean it was "sedate."

You should stay, she told Pixit.

«*But you'll be lonely!*»

You know I won't be. She'd be much happier this way. *Besides, I have you in my head. You eat your potatoes and play with the other beasts. Have fun.*

Only when the bell rang again did she scoot back out, trailing after the other students to the practice field, as Professor Werrin had instructed.

In daylight, Mytris Lightning School looked just as imposing and unfriendly and majestic as it had at night, with its three black towers and darkened windows. And the land around it — the barren lands — was as stark and intimidating as the name. The hills were blackened, the earth dark and dry, with no hint of grass or flowers or trees, just a few dead shrubs. Everything looked charred.

Rising above the black hills were the mountains, closer than they'd ever been in the farmlands. Mina thought the mountains looked wild, with jagged peaks, razor-sharp rocks, and sheer cliffs of exposed gray. From the safe distance of her family's farm, they had seemed picturesque — the gentle haze of distance had smoothed the slopes and softened the peaks, making them into a faraway backdrop of her world. Here they were in your face, as if proclaiming, *We are mountains, and you will tremble before us.*

Oddly, it was the sight of the mountains that calmed her. They looked so amazing, so unapologetically and defiantly what they were, that she forgot, briefly, to be nervous.

She remembered again the second she noticed the crowd.

Spread across the circular practice field were all the students at Mytris, about two hundred total, with their beasts, loosely clumped by class. So many people! And creatures! *They don't expect us to train all together, do they?* The idea of practicing in front of so many, when she knew nothing and most had been training for months —

"Hey, Mina!" Jyx trotted over toward her with Chauda close behind her. "Isn't this the awesomest?"

«*Yeah, Mina, isn't it?*» Pixit looked at her pointedly.

His exasperation tasted peppery in the back of her throat, and she couldn't help smiling. She laid her hand on his neck. *I promise I'll try my best. You know I want us to fit here.*

She felt Pixit's mood shift to a kind of sunny orange.

Side by side, Mina and Jyx and their beasts watched a procession of mostly older girls and boys, plus a few grown-ups, march onto the field to join the students. The storm-beast school had two kinds of teachers: older professors, who were former storm guardians whose beasts had lost their power, and

89

young teachers, who were still paired with active beasts. Both professors and teachers wore robes like Professor Werrin's, but only the professors carried the special electricity-cage canes. As they filed in, Mina saw the guardians and beasts flock to them — a few headed back into the towers with textbooks tucked under their arms, but most ditched their textbooks in shelves by the practice field and then flew out in groups of four into the barren lands. She eyed the textbooks, wondering when she'd get one.

It was organized chaos: everyone seemed to know whom to go with, and they went, crisscrossing one another, converging, then dispersing, until the only ones left on the field were Mina, Pixit, Jyx, Chauda, Professor Werrin, and the small man who had opened the school door for them the night before. Professor Werrin introduced him as Professor Dano.

"Seriously?" Jyx huffed. "He's Professor Dino?"

"Professor *Dano* is an esteemed educator at our institution," Professor Werrin said, leveling a glare at Jyx. "You are honored to have him as your teacher. In fact, he requested you two. Or, specifically, her." She switched her gaze to Mina, softening it slightly.

"Me?" Mina squeaked.

"He observed your interest in the library when you arrived," Professor Werrin explained. "Professor Dano is one of our premier historians."

"But . . . but I want to learn how to spark!" Jyx sputtered. "And fly! I'm ready for more than just books!"

"Your beasts are not," Professor Werrin snapped. "Neither

of them. Yours may be larger, Jyx, but Chauda's wings are still developing. Until your beasts have grown strong enough, you will learn what Professor Dano chooses to teach you. When *they* are ready, and not before, you will begin your practical training. All students here at Mytris follow the same curriculum: lectures first from a qualified professor, then 'sparking and flying,' as you put it, supplemented with textbook assignments from your flying instructor." She fixed her gaze on each of them. "I expect you to work hard and obey Professor Dano's commands. You will be judged both on effort and achievement. Succeed, and you will earn yourself a worthy future, as well as the pride and gratitude of your family and all Alorria." She then swept off the field, back inside the school, leaving them with Professor Dano.

Jyx was muttering under her breath. "Can't believe this. Professor Dino. My parents said he's the worst, droning on and on. We aren't going to learn anything useful from him."

Mina wanted to apologize — Jyx sounded so dismayed — but she couldn't help smiling instead. Their professor loved books! And, so far at least, he seemed nearly as quiet as Mina. *Maybe there's a way for me to fit in here after all.*

Pixit glowed beside her, happy that she was happy.

⚡

Until their beasts' wings grew stronger, Professor Dano informed them, they'd be learning storm-beast history. Jyx groaned at that, but Mina was thrilled.

Pixit was excited too. «*Story time!*»

He'd spent two years listening to Mina read to him. *I love that you loved that as much as I did*, she thought at him. He licked her cheek.

Waddling through the school, the professor led them to a windowless classroom and handed each of them a textbook. Mina flipped through hers eagerly. This was great! When it was time to spark and fly, they'd know exactly what to do.

"This is ridiculous," Jyx grumbled, ignoring her book. "We should be out there learning to spark right now."

Poring over a chart that detailed different storm-beast powers, Mina didn't reply.

Professor Dano took his position at the front of the classroom. "Your job is to listen and learn, not criticize." And so he began:

"The history of Alorria."

But instead of a dry recitation of dates, Professor Dano wove a tale worthy of Pixit's wish for story time. He told about the founding of Alorria, how it began as a small storm-ravaged country, hemmed in by mountains and the ocean. Crops barely grew in the weak soil, and its people were barely surviving. Many starved to death, until one day, a man found an egg, larger than any he'd seen.

"He would have eaten it right then, fed his young daughter and himself, but the man had foresight: if he waited for the egg to hatch, if he let the creature grow, then they would have a feast!" Professor Dano said. "And so he placed the egg inside his one-room hut beneath his daughter's bed. Days passed, then months, and the egg did not hatch. The man forgot it was there. But the daughter slept above it, dreaming and thinking and feeling and living, until at last, two years later, it hatched. And from that egg came the first storm beast: a rain beast, bonded to the girl. Together they drove away the storms that pounded their hillside, and instead they brought gentle rain. Crops grew, and word began to spread."

The funny thing was that the story was different from what Mina had learned from her parents and her teachers in the farmlands. In the story she knew, the farmer didn't forget about the egg — he hatched it with the intent to harness its storm powers, a deliberate choice for the good of his country.

"Are you saying it was luck?" Jyx asked, disbelief in her voice. She must have heard the same stories Mina had of the brilliance of the early Alorrians, of their insight and vision.

"Yes, it was chance alone that shaped our future," Professor Dano said. "Chance and absent-mindedness. And a certain disregard for cleanliness."

Mina turned that idea over in her mind. If that unknown man hadn't forgotten he'd stashed an egg under his daughter's bed, then all of Alorria would have remained like the rest of the world: at the mercy of storms. The way Professor Dano told it, it was pure luck that the power of the storm beasts had been discovered.

Other lectures were the same: a mix of familiar and different.

Each day, as Professor Dano expounded on Alorrian history and storm-beast theory, Mina drank it all in, every word of it, with Pixit beside her. As much as she wanted to learn to fly, she loved this.

On the fifth day, Professor Dano described the period when their country withdrew from the rest of the world. Before the discovery of storm-beast powers, Alorria had been part of a much larger world. "Isolationism — defined as caring only about your own country — had the benefit of limiting the area that the early storm beasts and guardians had to protect. Here's the important bit to understand: all the world's weather is connected, and more complex than you can comprehend. By solely focusing on the land within the mountains, the first storm guardians and their beasts were able to focus on controlling only a localized weather pattern. That's what made it possible for the early Alorrians to achieve perfection — by limiting the range of their control."

That sounded selfish, especially compared to the (literally) sunny tales Mina knew. She wanted to know more. *What about those who fail to control the weather? And what about those who can't? And what about those who live beyond the mountains?*

«*Ask,*» Pixit urged.

Mina glanced at Jyx, wondering if she was considering the same questions.

"Sooooo," Jyx drawled, "when do we get to play with lightning?"

━CHAPTER━
EIGHT

IT took only three weeks (and a *lot* of potatoes) for Pixit to grow to his full size. Mina noticed it the day that he failed to fit through the door, a week after Chauda had switched to using the window.

«*Oof!*»

Looking up from the book she'd been reading — *A History of Alorrian Agriculture*, written by a sun guardian who had coaxed twenty-six sun beasts into creating a tropical rainforest in southeastern Alorria — Mina saw Pixit crammed into the doorway. His head and front legs were wiggling ineffectively in the air, while his body, puffed with scales and feathers, filled every available space. He looked as if he'd become rectangular.

Mina giggled.

«*Not helpful.*»

Sorry. Closing her book, she jumped to her feet and hurried to him. She gripped his front paws and pulled.

He didn't budge.

Mina heard a *whomp* sound behind her as Chauda flew in through the window. The other lightning beast gave a snort that Mina had learned to interpret as *I told you so.* Chauda had a dozen different snorts, all of which meant approximately the same thing. And then, from the hallway, on the other side of Pixit, she heard Jyx's voice. "He grew! This is great!"

It would be great if Jyx would help.

"Tell her she could push," Mina said to Chauda.

She heard feet shuffle, and then Jyx shouted, "Okay, on three! One . . . two . . . three!"

Leaning back, Mina pulled with all her strength. She heard Jyx grunting on the other side, and then . . .

Pop — Pixit flew out of the doorjamb.

Thump — Pixit landed sprawled on the floor.

Jyx, who had belly-flopped forward on top of him, pushed herself up. She had a huge grin on her face. "Mina, do you think this means what I think this means?"

Mina grinned back at her. Of course she did.

«*It means no more doors,*» Pixit thought with a groan.

Punching the air, Jyx ran in a circle, jumping and hollering. "Tomorrow, we fly!"

Pixit shook himself like a wet dog. «*Really?*»

Yes, really! Mina threw her arms around his neck. She could feel his excitement bubbling inside her — he'd been looking forward to this ever since Chauda had been approved for flight with her guardian. The school doctors had told them that as soon as Pixit exceeded door width, he'd be ready too.

"No more boring story time with Professor Dino!" Jyx cheered.

Mina had never thought it was boring, but she knew Jyx didn't agree. As much as she wanted to fly like the other guardians, Mina liked listening to Professor Dano's version of Alorrian history and his explanation of how storm control worked: no beast created weather; it merely manipulated what was already there. She found that fascinating. There was no point in saying that to Jyx, though. Instead Mina said, "Thanks."

Mid-twirl, Jyx stopped. "For what?"

"For waiting."

Jyx could have started her practical lessons as soon as Chauda was approved, but she'd said she'd wait for her partner. "Sure. Best friends do things together."

"Yes, we do," Mina said. For someone who liked to be alone, it was a big thing to say. And she surprised herself by meaning it.

«*Can I say I told you you'd find a great new friend here?*»

You can say it.

«*Told you!*» Pixit chirped happily.

Laughing, Jyx grabbed Mina's hands and swung her around in a circle. They spun, both laughing, until they collapsed in Chauda's nest.

⚡

Outside, on the charred practice field, Mina climbed onto Pixit's back. She fit snugly into the curve of his neck, between his shoulder blades. His feathery scales were wonderfully soft. Beside her, Jyx was already mounted on Chauda.

The school doctors had given their okay after breakfast. Now it was up to Professor Dano to officially pronounce them ready for the next stage of lessons.

«*We're ready,*» Pixit said confidently.

Remember, he said just walk first. Get used to having me on your back, and then we'll try to lift off. Her heart thumped hard. This was it! Today they'd fly! She'd dreamed about this for so many years — the next step toward becoming a real guardian!

As Pixit walked forward, Mina began to slide to the left. «*Hold on!*» Grabbing on to one of his scales, she pulled herself upright. He took another step. Soon they were trotting in a circle.

"Excellent!" Professor Dano called. "That's enough for today!"

But they'd just started! And they hadn't even gotten off the ground!

«*I can do it!*» Pixit said. «*I'm ready!*»

Mina could *feel* his readiness — through Pixit's thoughts, she could sense the strength in his muscles and wings. His instincts were telling him *It's time!* so loudly that she was itching to fly too.

Jyx was protesting. "Hey, we're ready to fly! How are we going to collect lightning if we can't reach the clouds? And what about electricity lessons? Someone needs to teach us how to spark!"

Her words had zero impact. "Come inside," Professor Dano said, "and we will discuss why the phrase 'collect lightning' is incorrect. Lightning is the result of electromagnetic discharge, when positive charge is drawn to negative charge between the cloud and —"

"Yeah, I get that. Remember my parents were lightning guardians? Heard all that before. The time for lectures is over!"

"It's over when I say it's over," Professor Dano snapped.

Tilting her head back, Mina looked at the sky. Other storm beasts were circling the towers, silhouetted against the sun. She held her hand up to shield her eyes. Professor Dano wasn't going to be swayed by Jyx's pleading.

But there are other ways to argue. She remembered the letter she'd left propped on the kitchen table for her parents to read.

Nice weather, she commented to Pixit.

«*Yes, it is.*» She tasted his curiosity, sweet and fluffy like lemon pie. She knew he could sense that an idea was taking shape.

It would be sad to spend the day inside.

«*Yes, it would be. Very sad.*»

Both of them looked back at Professor Dano. He'd picked up their textbooks from the shelves by the field and was herding Chauda and Jyx toward the open doors. Inside looked damp and shadowy.

«*My wings are not too immature.*»

She trusted Pixit — and the opinion of the school doctors — but the problem was Professor Dano. He didn't seem to want to admit they were ready. She knew she couldn't convince him with words, even if she could find the right ones to say, but there were other ways to be heard. *If he sees with his own eyes . . .*

Pixit radiated excitement, with sparks jumping off the tips of his wings, as he read the idea in her mind. *«Let's fly!»*

He bounded across the practice field, stretching his wings out to either side and pumping them up and down. She heard Professor Dano calling after them, and Jyx cheering. She felt wind in her face and had to squint to see — ahead of them was the wall of one of the three towers.

Pixit ran faster. His claws scraped the dirt. His wings pumped harder. And then — she felt him lunge up into the air. And then thump down. Professor Dano called out to them to stop, but both Mina and Pixit ignored him.

Faster. And faster.

Wings up, down, up, down, up, down.

Another leap!

And this time they lifted into the air. Pixit pushed his wings down, and dirt plumed up in a cloud beneath them. Mina clung to his neck, flattening herself against him. She saw the tower zooming toward them.

«Squeeze tight!»

Mina held on as tightly as she could, and Pixit veered up, his belly parallel to the tower, flying straight into the air. She bit back a shriek. The wind shook her cheeks and wicked away any moisture in her eyes. The ribbon in her hair unraveled and sailed away on the breeze, and then Pixit leveled off, gliding westward.

She lay against his neck, panting.

It was both silent and loud in the air: Pixit's wing beats were loud and steady, a *thrum-thrum-thrum*, and the wind was a whoosh in her ears, but all other sound had been stripped away.

«*Open your eyes.*»

Mina realized she'd squeezed them shut. She pried them open. Over Pixit's shoulder, she saw the school: three black towers and the practice ring. Hills surrounded it, but from above they looked like ripples in a blanket. Beyond the hills were the mountains.

Facing them, Mina felt as if they were calling to her. There was something so wonderfully wild about them. Every road and river in Alorria had been planned with precision to cut through the land in the most direct and pleasing way. Every inch of the farmlands was tamed. Even the sea itself had been curbed within the harbor.

But no one had tamed the mountains.

She liked that — no one told them who to be. They determined that for themselves.

«*I don't know if I can fly all the way there,*» Pixit said apologetically.

And suddenly Mina realized that that was where they had been headed. Her wishing had steered them away from the fields of the school, toward the mountains. *Of course. We should head back. I didn't mean . . .* But there was no use pretending to Pixit that she hadn't been thinking about flying to the mountains, seeing them up close. And seeing what lay beyond.

Sorry, Pixit.

«*I wonder what's out there too.*»

They were supposed to be learning to become lightning guardians, not daydreaming about adventuring beyond the border. She thought of her family and how they always said she was so dependable. *We'd better turn around.*

They flew back to the school, and Mina held tight as Pixit spiraled down toward the practice field. He then folded his wings and smacked onto the ground. «*Oof!*»

She was jolted forward into the back of his head. "Ow!"

«*Sorry.*»

Mina patted his neck. *It's all right. We'll work on the landing.* It was their first flight, after all. They'd get better with practice. And soon they'd be able to fly farther and for longer, too. She was already itching to fly again and hear the wind in her ears and feel the air on her face. She looked up to see Jyx jogging toward her.

Mina felt oddly calm. She'd said what she'd wanted to say, without having to say anything. It felt good.

"That was incredible! You're amazing!" Jyx shouted. "Also, you're in trouble!"

Pixit gave a little whimper, and Mina stroked his ear as she dismounted. She walked beside him to Professor Dano, who had been joined by Professor Werrin. Professor Dano was glaring at her with his arms crossed. His nostrils were flaring like those of an upset horse. Beside him, Professor Werrin was expressionless, regarding Mina and Pixit as if they were stones, or as if she were stone.

Now Mina felt less calm. Her palms started to sweat, and she wiped them on her shirt. She hadn't thought about getting in trouble — she'd just been trying to show Professor Dano what she wasn't able to say.

"I never knew you were so brave," Jyx said.

I wasn't being brave. I was just . . . being practical. He wasn't hearing us.

«*You are brave. I know it, even if you don't.*»

When Mina and Pixit reached him, Professor Dano wagged his finger at them. "I did not give you permission to fly. Flying lessons will commence when and only when *I* say so. It is my responsibility to teach. It is your responsibility to obey."

Softly Mina said, "It's my responsibility to learn."

Professor Dano sucked in a breath to continue; then he blinked and stared at her. "What did you say?"

Mina felt as if the air had gotten stuck in her throat. She wished she hadn't said a word. *I flew! Isn't that enough?* Dropping her head, she stared at her scuffed work shoes. She hadn't owned any other footwear to pack. She noticed that Professor Werrin's shoes were golden. Their points stuck out under the hem of her robe.

She risked a glance up and saw that Professor Dano was struggling not to smile.

"That may be," Professor Werrin said sternly, "but disobedience is not tolerated in storm guardians. You didn't even wait for instructions! You could have flown beyond the barren lands! Lightning students are not permitted to fly their beasts beyond the hills! Did you even know that before you went flapping off?"

She hadn't known. Mina hung her head again.

"As punishment, you will complete an essay on the importance of obedience to the laws of Alorria and to the commands of your teachers and supervisors. Professor Dano will point you to the relevant texts. I expect to see historical references with examples that show how the loyalty of storm guardians and their devotion to their duty contributed to the greatness of Alorria." With that, Professor Werrin swept from the practice field back into the tower.

Everything was silent for a moment.

Mina snuck another peek at Professor Dano.

"Such a shame," he muttered. "First student in years who *listened*. But perhaps good can still come of this — if you can learn to *question* as well as listen." Louder, he said, "Follow me. Just you, Mina."

Mina hesitated. She didn't want to leave Pixit while he was upset. But she wasn't about to argue with Professor Dano. "I'll be back soon," she told Pixit. "Will you be okay?"

"I'll take care of him," Jyx promised. "We'll go to the dining hall."

He perked up. «*Potatoes?*»

As Mina followed Professor Dano into the north tower, she glanced back over her shoulder. Pixit was already trotting off happily with Jyx and Chauda. She felt him thinking of filling his stomach — he'd worked up an appetite with all the flying.

At least Pixit didn't stay unhappy for long. It wasn't in his nature. *He sparkles inside and out,* she thought.

Professor Dano didn't speak as he led her inside, which was fine with her. They walked through the quiet stone corridors — a few students were in classrooms studying, but at this time of day, most were out flying above the hills.

It was nice to be in the castle when it was nearly empty.

She began to hope this would be a pleasant punishment. Reading relevant texts? That sounded marvelous! If she had to spend extra time alone in the library . . . But he didn't lead her there. Instead he led her up a spiral stone staircase, too narrow for a storm beast, and halted outside a heavy iron door. After searching through his pockets, he found a key, opened the door, and shooed her inside before she could ask where they were or why.

It was a small, windowless room with books on every wall. She'd seen the school's library — vast shelves of books all chained in place. Books were too precious to be allowed near lightning beasts, and so access was strictly controlled. But the books here, in Professor Dano's special library, seemed even older, and they were all unchained. Their spines were cracked leather, and the pages looked crisp and yellow. She couldn't help but let out a little Pixit-like chirp of joy. *So many books!* Her fingers itched to seize one from the shelves, but she hesitated, unsure if she was allowed to touch them.

Professor Dano toddled over to one case and pulled out a book, then another, and another. He stacked them on his desk. "Read these. Don't remove them from this room. Shut the door when you leave — it will lock behind you."

She dared one question. "Flying lessons?"

He halted on his way to the door but did not turn around.

She waited.

He sighed. "Yes."

Mina smiled.

—CHAPTER—
NINE

CURLED up in Professor Dano's chair, Mina read for the entire day. She didn't mean to — she knew Pixit was waiting for her, she knew she was missing dinner, and she knew she'd have flying lessons tomorrow — but once she began, she couldn't stop. These weren't sunny, incomplete textbooks; these were journals, written by the very first storm guardians.

I am afraid, one long-ago guardian wrote.

The storms, she read, *they come faster now. It seems the more we try to fix the world, the more we break it.*

Although the early Alorrians had their storm beasts, they didn't know how to use them — they were just kids trying to make their world better, with no teachers yet to guide them. They'd create rain over a field — and cause a tornado in a nearby town. They'd use a sun beast to heat a field, and a pond elsewhere would freeze in the middle of summer, killing all the fish.

It took several decades before they were able to stabilize the weather in Alorria. Mina found one book, bound in red leather, that detailed with charts, tables, and maps exactly how the weather in each region changed day by day, with a list of how many storm beasts of which kinds were active by the hour.

There were setbacks. Devastating ones, in which entire harvests were destroyed. She found herself crying as she read lists of names of people who had starved in those winters, before winter itself was banished. She had to wipe her tears quickly so they wouldn't fall on the brittle pages and destroy them.

She wondered how many students had ever seen these books and felt like she'd been given a gift, not a punishment. Here was the terrible, painful past they'd moved beyond. Scientists had figured out that if the beasts worked together, under the guidance of the guardians, they could tame the weather across all of Alorria, which allowed for all the wonderful things that Alorrians now took for granted: food for everyone, a safe sea, no killer winters. Their combined efforts ushered in a grand era of art and architecture, where wants were met and needs were eliminated. She skipped through those pages and went back to the first journal.

She flipped to the last page and reread the final line: *It seems the more we try to fix the world, the more we break it.* She'd start her essay with that and then talk about how the guardians, working together, had succeeded in finding a way to fix the world.

Or at least, she thought, *a way to fix Alorria.*

She looked at the shelves around her and all the precious books. *Are any of them about the rest of the world?* she wondered.

But before she could continue that thought, the lights-out warning bell rang.

Mina hurried out of Professor Dano's special library, careful to close the door behind her, and down the spiral stairs, through the halls, and into the tower with their dorm room. She was panting by the time she reached the bathroom, brushed her teeth faster than she ever had, and ran to her door. She burst in, thinking she had at least a minute to spare to get to bed —

And the lights flicked out.

"Good night, Mina," Jyx said from her own bed, somewhere in the darkness. Chauda huffed at her, a snort that either meant *You're late* or *Don't bother me.*

Over the weeks at school, as they'd continued to grow, both beasts had learned to control their sparking, which was good for preventing random fire accidents but made their dorm room very, very dark. *Pixit? A little light?*

A spark arced in the corner, and Mina picked her way over Jyx's unwashed clothes and strewn-about schoolwork to her bed. She couldn't see to find her nightclothes, so she simply crawled under the covers.

«*Missed you.*»

Missed you too, Pixit.

«*Did you learn lots?*»

Yes. She hesitated, thinking of the mountains. They'd been so very tempting and so very wild, unlike the rest of Alorria. What lay beyond them?

«*Probably a lot of fast-asleep people. It's nighttime there, too.*» His thoughts felt sleepy in her head, and full — she wondered if he'd been eating the entire time she'd been in Professor Dano's library. She felt his thoughts become fluttery and heard a soft, whistling snore from beyond the foot of her bed.

She lay awake, thinking of storms and mountains.

$$\lightning$$

The next morning, after snagging her usual breakfast roll from the dining hall, Mina raced outside with the morning bell. *We're going to learn to fly today! And how to collect sparks! Or whatever Professor Dano wants us to call it . . . Oh, Pixit, we're going to be lightning guardians!*

He chirped in answer, and she felt his joy like bubbles in her throat.

Ahead, she saw Jyx and Chauda with two friends and their beasts, as well as an older girl in a teacher's robe, near the outdoor shelves of textbooks. Catching Mina's eye, Jyx waved her over.

Usually Mina picked an empty spot and waited for Professor Dano, but today was supposed to be different. Making herself smile in what she hoped was a friendly expression rather than a nervous grimace — it felt more like a grimace — Mina joined the others.

"No more Professor Dino!" Jyx crowed. "Vira is going to teach us from now on! This is her beast, Loon." She introduced the students, too: Zek and Ferro, with their storm beasts, Ragit and Brindle. "Everyone, meet Mina and Pixit."

No more Professor Dano? At all? She'd hoped they'd have both lectures and practical lessons. She thought of how annoyed he'd seemed when she'd flown — he hadn't wanted the lectures to end either. *Maybe that's why he tried to deny that we were ready,* she thought. After the lectures, Professor Werrin had said, came "sparking and flying" lessons with textbook assignments from their flying instructor, who was, it appeared, Vira. *Maybe I shouldn't have been so eager.*

Vira was not much older than they were. Her hair was shaved into zigzag patterns on her scalp, and her teacher's robe had been carefully ripped to just above her knees. She was leaning against a lightning beast with a scar across his right eye. *She looks like she'd rather be anywhere but here.* Mina wondered what her story was, why she was a teacher at Mytris, and where she'd rather be. But of course, she didn't ask any of that.

Zek and Ferro were both boys, one tall with his hair in a ponytail on the top of his head, which made him extra tall, and the other one short with eyebrows like woolly caterpillars. The tall one, Zek, grinned at her. His teeth looked like a rabbit's. "Hey."

The other one, Ferro, leaned toward her and shouted, "Nice to meet you!"

Mina blinked at him, not sure why his nose was so close to hers.

"Um, she can hear you." Jyx whacked him on the arm.

"Oh. I thought — since we heard she doesn't talk . . . Never mind." His face turned bright red, even to the tips of his ears. It made his caterpillar eyebrows stand out even more.

"Hi," Mina said.

They both stared at her as if she were a horse that had suddenly spoken.

"She *can* talk," Jyx said. "She just doesn't do it much, which is something you guys should totally try. Mina actually listens to me. First person I've ever met who's done that." She beamed at Mina as if she'd invented her, which was nice. Still, it was unsettling to have this many people staring at her, as if they expected her to say something clever or do something smart.

Zek elbowed Ferro. "If she were deaf, why would you think shoving your ugly face in hers would help? She can't read your lips if you're two inches from her nose."

"Probably shouldn't answer that," Ferro said, "on the grounds that it will make me look like an idiot." He was still blushing. "Sorry, Mina, didn't think it through."

"You're lucky she didn't punch you in the face," Zek said.

Mina thought about telling them she'd never punched anyone, but they seemed to be carrying on their conversation just fine without her having to say anything. She kind of liked that

— she was talking with them without having to talk, like with her family.

"Yeah? You're lucky *I* don't punch *you* in the face," Ferro said.

"Ignore him," Zek said to Mina. He was smiling at Mina sympathetically, as if he understood that she wanted to run and hide.

"Ignore both of them," Jyx told her.

"All right, enough chitchat," Vira said. She turned to Mina and Jyx. "Lesson time. You've seen other students playing with sparks, right? That's the key to literally everything we do. Lightning beasts can pull electric charge from the sky and store it within their bodies, but it's the guardian who channels it in useful ways. Just like wind beasts pull the wind, but the wind guardians direct it. You must learn to direct electricity, both into and out of your bodies. Tonight your assignment is to read chapter thirteen in your textbook — it will explain all the technical mumbo-jumbo behind what we're doing." She waved at the shelves of textbooks.

Mina had read that chapter already. It said that beasts and guardians had to work together to harness the weather. A storm beast had power, but it couldn't use it without a guardian.

"But it's hands-on lesson time now," Vira continued, "and before you can do anything else useful in the sky, your beast has to learn to transfer that stored electric charge to you. We start with that, here on the ground. As soon as you prove to me you can do it, we go up."

That was . . . direct. And also cryptic. Exactly how were they supposed to transfer electric charge? Their textbook had been equally vague about the details. She waited, hoping Vira would say more.

Vira lounged against her beast, Loon, and waited expectantly, as if they were supposed to suddenly start sparking. "Come on, this is the easy part. All lightning guardians do this. Show me there's a point to taking you in the air. I'm here to train storm guardians, not kids who want to fly with the birdies because it looks fun."

Mina glanced at Jyx and the two boys. Zek and Ferro raised their arms up and spread their fingers. Mina and Jyx mimicked them.

After that, though, Mina had no idea what to do. *Um, Pixit?* «*What am I supposed to do?*»

I was hoping you'd know.

Both Zek and Ferro had little sparks hopping between their fingers already. Clearly, they'd done this before. Mina looked at Jyx. She had sparks in her hair, causing strands of it to defy gravity, as well as sparks between her thumbs and her index fingers. *I think you're supposed to give me electricity? Channel it through me?*

«*I don't know how to do that.*»

Try?

He tried. She felt him concentrating — his thoughts felt like a weight, pressing against her mind. «*Spark, spark, spark!*» White and blue sparks danced all over him, across his scales.

She felt them tickle against her skin where they touched her. But no sparks appeared between her fingers.

"Good. Excellent," Vira was saying to the others. "Mina? Pixit? What are you doing?"

Mina winced. "Concentrating?"

"You look like you have gas," Vira said. "Look, this is easy. If you so much as scuff your feet on the ground, you build up electric charge. Happens all the time naturally. And your beast naturally absorbs it. All he has to do is transfer that charge to you. You just need to think like a lightning guardian."

But what does that mean? She thought of the books she'd read, both aloud to Pixit and in Professor Dano's library. Storm guardians made a difference. They made the world better. She didn't know, though, what it meant to *be* one, at least not the way Vira meant.

"Come on," Vira urged. "You're a lightning guardian! You are fearless! You are fast! You will not be stopped! You will not be silenced!" Her voice rose louder and louder. "You are a thunderstorm come to life! Loud and ferocious!"

Silently Mina wailed, *I'm not any of those things!*

«*You're my Mina. And we can do this!*»

"It should be instinctual, through your bond," Vira said. "You should feel drawn to the fire in the air. Use the fire in your soul!"

They tried again.

Mina thought back to her lessons with Professor Dano. He'd explained the science behind it, how everything was made up of atoms, how a charge was created when electrons were stripped away from their atoms, how positive and negative charges were drawn to each other, how electricity was the flow of that charge, how the beasts arrested that flow by storing the charge until it was ready to be discharged and used. He'd drawn lots of equations on the board, and she'd dutifully memorized them. Understood them too. But she didn't understand how to get electricity from Pixit's belly onto her fingers.

I don't have "fire in my soul"!

«You sparkle inside, your papa said.»

That's not the same!

"Are you sure he's not a rain beast you painted yellow? Keep trying. The rest of you, let's fly." Vira jumped onto Loon's back, and with a single massive flap of his wings, he rose into the air. Wind whooshed out beneath him. "You can join us when you're ready to be one of us, Mina."

"Awesome!" Jyx said as the wind knocked her back. Hurrying, she clambered onto Chauda. "Ready?" she said to her beast. Chauda snorted back at her. "Oh. Right. Mina?"

Mina smiled, albeit weakly. "It's okay."

"You sure? We're supposed to be doing this together. Best friends —"

She didn't want to keep Jyx from the air. Already they'd been waiting for Pixit to grow strong enough. It wasn't fair to delay her any longer. Mina shook her head. "Best friends don't hold each other back. Besides, we'll concentrate better alone."

"If you're sure?"

"I'm sure." Mina faked a smile.

"Join us as soon as you can."

"Lean forward as your beast runs," Vira instructed from the air, where Loon hovered. "Your weight position is important if you want a smooth takeoff." Huffing, Chauda thundered forward, and Mina watched as Chauda and Jyx lifted off, shakily but steadily rising.

Jyx whooped and punched the air.

"Once you're airborne, stay in formation," Vira ordered. "You'll be tempted to soar all over the place, but trust me — you don't want to see how mad Professor Werrin will get if you go flying off beyond the borders of the barren lands. That's one school rule you do *not* want to break. Understood?"

"Clear as day!" Jyx said, and then she grabbed for Chauda's neck scales as Chauda wobbled in the air. "Whoa!"

"Keep a tight grip," Vira called to her. "You fall, you die."

They should use safety harnesses, Mina thought. Tie themselves to the beasts the way she and her family harnessed themselves to the fence during wind days. She wasn't sure why the lightning guardians didn't, especially the students. She thought back to the stationmaster who'd called other lightning guardians reckless. Maybe it was because of pride? Or maybe it was trust, in themselves and in their beasts. Still, it wasn't very responsible.

«*Is Jyx going to fall?*» Pixit asked.

Mina realized her musing had leaked into Pixit. *She'll hold on,* she reassured him, *and Chauda won't let her get hurt. Don't worry. Just try to make my fingers spark so we can join them, okay?* She worked to keep her mental voice as light as possible.

This was a thing that all lightning beasts and guardians should be able to do. Easily, Vira had said. So they should be able to do it, with a little practice, right? *That is, if I really am meant to be a lightning guardian.* Mina squelched that line of thought as quickly as it arose. Luckily, Pixit didn't seem to hear her. He was still fixated on the lack of harnesses.

«*I'd never let you fall.*»

I know. Spark, please?

They kept trying. But the best that Mina felt was a tingle in the air. She didn't see a single tiny spark light her fingers. Not even once.

Vira had said, *You can join us when you're ready to be one of us.*

As she failed again and again, Mina couldn't stop the terrible fear rising up inside her, as every doubt and worry she'd ever had clamored to be heard: What if she never was ready? What if she couldn't be, no matter how much she wanted to? She wasn't loud or ferocious or fearless. She was just . . . Mina.

What if that wasn't enough?

━CHAPTER━
TEN

LYING in bed after lights out, Mina couldn't sleep. She heard Pixit flopping around in his bed as well. *Can't sleep either?* she asked.

«*Am I being too loud?*»

Actually, you're quieter than when you're snoring.

She slipped out of her blankets and felt her way to Pixit's bed. Her hands bumped into his feathery scales. She sat, leaning against his side.

«*Mina, I can feel you worrying, and I don't know how to fix it. I know you're a lightning guardian. I know it like I know air is for breathing and water is wet. But I don't know how to make you see it too.*»

She put her arms around his neck and burrowed her face into his scales. She didn't know how to reassure him, when she wasn't sure he was right.

«*Can we try again to spark? Maybe if we succeed, then you'll see what I see.*»

Of course we can try. Resting against Pixit, she spread her fingers apart. *Let's try now, when no one's watching.* Maybe it was the pressure of knowing that others were waiting for them, or that people could be watching them fail. She told herself she had to keep thinking positively, for Pixit's sake as well as her own.

They tried again, and again. Mina felt the air tingle. A few sparks skittered over Pixit's tail like a mouse scurrying across a floor. Stray bits of electricity danced between his ears and crackled on his nose. But none of it transferred to Mina.

At last, she fell asleep, next to Pixit. He snored with her.

In the morning, they joined Jyx and the boys outside, and the others flew while Mina and Pixit stayed earthbound, trying to make Mina spark. After a while, they sprawled on the dirt, Mina's head on Pixit's stomach and her hands with fingers still spread.

They failed. Again and again.

At last, Mina whispered in her head, *Maybe we should admit it: I'm not meant to be a lightning guardian. And it's not fair to you. You deserve a better guardian. One who can be a part of all of this. One who sparks. I don't spark.*

Pixit knocked her sideways as he suddenly stood up. «*Oops, sorry!*»

She got up and dusted the black dirt off her shirt. *I'm fine.*

«*I stood because I had something important to say. I was being dramatic. I didn't mean to knock you over.*»

Despite herself, despite all her worries and doubts and everything, Mina laughed. "It's fine, Pixit. What did you want to say?"

Sparks were dancing all over Pixit's body. Mina watched the bits of electricity sizzle in the air. «*You don't spark. And that's good. Sparks die. See?*»

She watched as each spark fizzled.

«*Ooh, ooh, maybe you're the rubber!*»

I'm the stuff that makes the lightning stop?

«*You're the stuff that makes the lightning safe!*»

That didn't seem quite right. *That kind of says I'm not a lightning guardian. I'm supposed to be able to handle electricity.*

He drooped. «*Okay, then, not rubber. It sounded good, though, didn't it?*»

Mina scratched behind his ears. He leaned against her, and she had to brace herself to keep from falling over — he'd grown a lot. She tried to think positively. *I'm different from the other guardians. So maybe I just have to find another way to be a guardian.* She remembered what the official letter had said, the one that had come with the river-ship tickets. *A true heart is never a mistake.*

«*Different isn't wrong,*» Pixit said with such utter certainty that Mina couldn't help but believe him. «*You might not spark. But I am still a lightning beast, and you are still my lightning guardian.*»

I just need to find a different way, a way that works for me.

«*Us.*»

Us. She climbed onto Pixit's back. *Let's go find our way.*

⚡

Flying over the blackened hills, they found Jyx and the boys with their teacher a mile away. Mina was going to tell them she hadn't succeeded in holding a spark yet. She truly was. But Jyx didn't give her a chance. "You did it! You finally did it! Oh, thank goodness! They wouldn't let me play until you came — lightning relay needs equal teams — and it's been so *boring!*"

After that, Mina didn't know how to tell her they hadn't done it, at least not yet. Jyx was so happy to see her. *I can't disappoint her.* She didn't say anything.

Vira clapped her hands. "All right, listen up. Ferro, Zek, and your beasts, to my left." She pointed to the boys. "Mina, Jyx, and your beasts, to my right. The game is lightning relay. It's designed to hone both your flying skills and your electricity-handling skills. Drawing sparks out of your beast was just the first step — to be an effective lightning guardian, you need to be able to pull electricity out of a thunderstorm, store it within your beast, and then deliver it to a lightning rod. The catching and throwing techniques used in lightning relay will help prepare you for that task."

Mina began to wish they'd stayed on the ground.

"The goal of the game is to get your electricity to the lightning rods at the top of the school towers. Jyx and Mina, your team scores if the lightning touches the north rod; Zek and Ferro, the south rod. Don't fall off your beasts."

«Whoa, wait, what?»

Steeling herself to pretend to be loud, Mina opened her mouth to ask Pixit's questions. But Ferro grinned, spread his fingers, and pulled bits of electricity from the air. *He's already mastered drawing it from the air,* Mina thought, *and I can't even draw sparks from Pixit.* Concentrating, he mashed the sparks into a ball, like Mother kneading bread.

On Chauda, Jyx zipped past her. "Come on, Mina, Pixit! You guard Ferro. I'll take Zek. Don't let them pass the bolt!"

Pixit wobbled in the air, and Mina clung to his neck. «*Oh. Um. I guess we're doing this. Mina, is this a thing we're doing?*»

Yes. She urged him toward Ferro.

«*But you can't catch a bolt! You can't even hold sparks. Oh dear, oh no, this was a bad idea. I'm sorry, Mina.*»

Maybe no one will throw it at me?

«*What if they do?*»

I duck? We're finding our own way, remember? Different from how others do it. On the plus side, at least this was a test of her theory — could she be different from the others and be a good lightning guardian? She'd already made friends with Jyx and Chauda. And she'd found a way to convince Professor Werrin and Professor Dano to let them out of the classroom, all without becoming someone she wasn't.

«*How do we play lightning relay if we can't catch or toss lightning? You heard Vira! That's half the point!*»

But only half. She didn't know, but she wasn't about to just give up. They'd have to be alert, look for things that the others hadn't seen, and try things that hadn't been done.

Ferro was bouncing up and down on his beast's back, waving his arms. "Over here! Zek, I'm open! I'm" — guided by

Mina, Pixit jutted in front of him — "not open. Go left! Down, no, wait —"

Jyx chased Zek. The tall boy held the ball of sparks over his head as his beast zigzagged away. But Jyx and Chauda were gaining on him, flying straight as he dodged and weaved.

Suddenly Ferro dropped down, his beast's wings folded. "Now!"

Zek hurled the ball through the air.

Pixit dove toward it, even though Mina had no idea what to do if they reached it first, but Ferro was faster — he snatched the lightning out of the air. "Ha-ha! Catch me if you can."

Then Ferro threw it back to Zek, who aimed it at the goal. The ball zoomed forward and hit the rod, disappearing in a crackle of sparks that traveled down the metal and into a black box at the base.

"One point for the boys!" Ferro crowed. He flew toward Zek and they high-fived.

The game continued.

Ferro and Zek, on Brindle and Ragit, scored three more times.

"Maybe we need a plan?" Mina suggested to Jyx.

Jyx brightened. "Yeah! Excellent. Do you have an idea?"

Mina studied the two boys, as well as the rods. So far, they'd been chasing after the boys, always a step behind them, reacting every time they passed the lightning back and forth. Suddenly she had it. "No more guarding Ferro and Zek. It doesn't matter what they do — what matters is the lightning and the goal. I'll guard the rod, and you be ready to catch the bolt when they fail to hit it."

"Great!" Jyx paused. "You mean you're just going to stay there, by the goal? No flying after them? Just wait for them to come to you?"

Mina nodded. "Exactly." It was a reasonable plan. Straightforward. And something that she and Pixit could do, even without being able to transfer electricity.

"But no one does it that way."

She wondered why not. It made sense: Ferro and Zek had to reach the rod to score. With Mina as goalkeeper, the odds of them hitting it dropped dramatically. And then, once the boys tried and failed, Jyx could easily steal the lightning and could score. True, it was less exciting than chasing them all over the sky and required more patience. But: "Is there a rule against it?" Mina asked.

"No rule. It's just much too boring. We're doing it my way!" Jyx declared. "You come in from the east, I'll come from the west, and we'll squeeze them between us. Knock the ball out of his hand. Okay? Great. Go!" Chauda, with Jyx, flew eastward.

Sighing, Mina guided Pixit to the west. *This isn't going to work. There are two of them — one will just catch the ball when the other drops it.*

This time, when Zek made the lightning ball, Jyx zoomed toward him from the east and Mina from the west. Leaning forward, Mina pressed against Pixit's neck — he flew faster and faster.

«Um, do I crash into him?»

I think that's Jyx's plan.

«It's a dumb plan.»

She also failed to see how crashing into other students was a useful skill to develop, but it was too late to argue, even if she wanted to.

Mina squeezed her eyes shut and held on, and then they crashed into Zek. She heard Jyx whoop and Zek yelp, and she opened her eyes to see the lightning ball spurt out of Zek's hands. "Get it, Chauda!" Jyx cried, switching direction.

But Ferro was already there, grabbing the ball and then zooming to throw it at the rod.

«Ow. I think I bent a scale. This is not fun.»

From the sidelines, their teacher called, "Nice try! Do it again! Come on, look lively! A storm won't wait for you to have a nice rest break."

Jyx and Chauda flew back to Mina and Pixit. "Hear that? We almost had them! Next time, try to crash a little harder, okay?" Before Mina could reply, she flew back into position.

Mina considered her, the boys, and the rods. *Guard the rod.*

«But Jyx said . . .»

I know. But Jyx is wrong. She doesn't have to listen, but we can show her. Like we showed Professor Dano that it was time to fly. Tugging on one of Pixit's scales, she urged him toward the school. He shot looks back over his shoulder, but he trusted her. *Land on the rod.*

«I won't fit. I'm bigger than it.»

That's why this will work. Wrap yourself around it with your tail and wings. They can't hit the goal if you're covering it. Jyx had said there wasn't a rule against goaltending. It just wasn't the style of most lightning guardians. They all liked being on the offensive.

From across the sky, Jyx called, "Mina, Pixit, what are you doing?"

Pixit landed with one paw on the top of the rod, then scooted down it, hugging it with his four legs and winding his tail around it. Mina wrapped her arms and legs around his neck so she couldn't fall off.

And then the game began again.

She watched as Zek called to the electricity, watched as Jyx and Chauda rammed into him, watched as this time Ferro was ready and caught the ball several seconds before Chauda could pivot in the air. He raced toward the rod.

Be ready.

«*For what?*»

For him to throw it.

«*And then what?*»

You catch it.

«*But I'm holding on to the rod.*»

Didn't you listen to Professor Dano's lectures? He'd spent multiple days on storm-beast theory. *You can absorb charge with any part of your body. You don't have to catch it with your paws.* A lightning beast's entire body functioned as a kind of battery, capable of storing electric charge. She was supposed to catch the bolt, and he was supposed to store it — but he could skip to just absorbing it, if the bolt came straight at them.

Ferro was flying closer. He looked confused, but still he rose up on Brindle and pulled his arm back to throw. Jyx was just a few feet behind him, with Chauda straining to catch up.

"Mina, he's going to score!" Jyx called.

He threw the lightning.

Pixit, eat it, Mina ordered.

Pixit opened his mouth — and swallowed the lightning.

Not a spark touched the rod. His body absorbed the electric charge and stored it all.

Jyx and Chauda pulled up short, staring. Also staring, Ferro and Brindle dipped down. Zek and Vira flew closer. All of them were babbling at the same time. "Did he just —" "Did that count?" "But it touched —" "No, it didn't." "But they didn't score, either!" "Is that allowed?" "That was a brilliant idea." "Is he okay?"

Are you okay? Mina asked Pixit.

Pixit burped.

"Game over!" Vira declared.

Jyx cheered as she steered Chauda over to Mina and Pixit. "Sorry for doubting you. Next time, I'll listen."

Mina smiled back at her, and Pixit purred happily.

ELEVEN

FIVE days later, they had their first thunderstorm. Mina saw the posting while the other students were crowded into the dining hall. She'd been lingering by the door, waiting for the room to clear out before she darted in for a breakfast roll, when Professor Dano waddled over with a hammer and a flyer.

She hadn't seen him since flying lessons began, but he nodded at her as if no time had passed. He had a bandage around his right arm. She wondered where he'd been and how he'd hurt his arm — no one had mentioned him in days — but she couldn't figure out how to politely ask. You didn't ask teachers personal questions, or at least she didn't. She wondered what he'd say if —

"Finished that essay yet, Mina?"

"Not yet, sir. I'm sorry." She wanted to explain that she'd been in the air every single day and every other night — Vira had started scheduling some of their lightning-relay matches after dinner, before lights out. When she wasn't flying, she was working with Pixit to coax electricity out of the atmosphere, or else completing the latest textbook assignment from Vira. She would have been satisfied with even a little static on her sleeve. *Maybe I should ask Professor Dano for help.* But after the exchange of pleasantries, he seemed to lose interest in her.

He nailed a piece of paper to the wall, made a humph sound, and then waddled off while she read it.

Thunderstorm
Three miles northeast of Mytris Lightning School
Tonight at eight o'clock
All students required

Our first thunderstorm!

She didn't know how she felt: excited, scared, or her usual jumbled mix.

Pixit! she called.

She didn't hear an answer — chowing down with the other lightning beasts, he was too distracted to hear her. She debated what to do. She didn't like going into the dining room, even during breakfast, when things were comparatively calm. Students weren't using the climbing wall or maze of metal rods this early. She usually maneuvered her way through the line to pick up her food, then fled back to her room, where she could eat in lovely peace and quiet. *I can do this,* she thought. *I'm a lightning guardian. Just like them.*

It was just . . . there were a lot of them, all in one place.

Across the dining hall, Mina spotted Jyx with Zek and Ferro, as well as a circle of other students whom Mina vaguely knew. They said hi to her sometimes, but she'd never eaten with them. *But Jyx will want to know about the storm.*

Taking a deep breath, she stepped into the dining hall. Immediately the sound washed over her. She felt as if she'd plunged underwater. She threaded her way between the tables, ducked beneath a potato that was tossed by a guardian into the open mouth of his beast. Another student bumped into her with a tray, and she and Mina both muttered an apology at the same time. At last she reached Jyx's table.

Jyx was talking, gesturing widely as she told a story. She broke off when she saw Mina. Jyx climbed up onto the table, between breakfast trays and textbooks, and strode across it to grab Mina by the arms. "You joined us! See, told you she'd come around eventually. Sit! Eat!"

Mina felt her face growing hot. She let Jyx herd her onto one of the benches, and she wished Jyx would lower her voice. People were staring at them. *I should have waited.* "I'm not — I only wanted to tell you that —"

"Mina's the one who came up with the new relay strategy," Jyx said. "Guard the rod. Eat the energy. Mina, all the teams are trying it now, or some variation." And several of the other students chimed in, each of them describing how they'd used their beasts to guard the rod. One on offense, one on defense, but sometimes it would be a trap, to trick the other pair closer . . .

So many were talking at once that Mina wanted to clap her hands over her ears. But she sat there, frozen, with a smile plastered on her face.

Slowly she began to relax. It felt surprisingly like being at home, with the conversation flowing around her — it was more like an embrace than an attack. They were excited she was here. She was introduced to more kids and their beasts. She greeted them with a hello that was far too quiet for anyone to hear, but no one seemed to mind.

And after a few minutes, she realized she didn't have to fake the smile anymore. They seemed to like that she was at their table, especially Ferro and Zek, who were proclaiming they wanted her and Jyx on their relay team from now on. "We want more of your ideas!" Zek said.

"Yeah, you have new ideas," Ferro said.

Zek jabbed a thumb toward Ferro. "Ferro here hasn't had a new idea since he was two."

Ferro nodded with fake solemnity. "I was a brilliant toddler. Sadly, it's been all downhill since then."

They continued teasing each other.

Eventually there was a tiny break in the babble. Just a breath. But Mina had been listening for it, and when it came, she spoke. "I saw on the board outside: There's a thunderstorm scheduled."

Jyx shrieked and leaped up. "Thunderstorm!"

Ferro and Zek high-fived.

Hearing Jyx, everyone erupted into shouting, running, and

climbing over tables. The teachers began shouting too, ordering everyone to calm down, stop running, and for goodness' sake don't walk over tables — and watch out for the food! Pitchers were knocked onto the floor, spilling water and juice everywhere. Several textbooks were trampled. Plates fell — the crash of breaking pottery was barely audible over the chatter and shrieks of the excited students.

And then Pixit was there, bounding across the tables, calling her name. «*Mina!*» She wrapped her arms around his neck and buried her face in his feathery scales. Throwing one leg over his back, she slid onto him. She felt his wings pump beneath her, and they were rising up toward the chandeliers of the dining hall — and then out through one of the broad open windows.

Blissful silence. Just the wind, Pixit's wing beats, and her heart thudding like a drum.

That was . . . loud.

«*They are excited. Our first thunderstorm! Aren't you excited, Mina?*»

Yes, of course, but . . . *I still can't hold bolts, and you still can't transfer electricity to me.* He was able to store it — they'd proved that when he'd absorbed the bolt during that first relay match — but a real lightning guardian needed to be able to draw the electricity out of her beast and then send it wherever it needed to go, usually to a lightning rod that led to a power line.

«*It will be easier inside a storm. You'll spark then, and you'll prove to everyone — and especially yourself — that you belong here.*» He sounded certain, so she decided to believe him, even though he had as much experience with storms as she did — which was none at all. Storms weren't allowed to reach the farmlands. She'd only read about them.

By sundown, all the students and beasts were outside, milling around the practice fields. A few pairs were playing lightning relay up by the rods at the top of the school, but Mina kept her feet on the ground and watched the mountains.

The storm was coming from the north.

A few hours earlier, she'd watched the rain beasts and wind beasts with their guardians race across the blackened hills. Since then, the clouds had been gathering above the mountains. She watched them churn, darkening into purple and blue.

She wondered where the storm had come from. Professor Dano had said that all the world's weather was connected, she remembered from one of his first lectures. So what had this storm been like on the other side of the border, before the beasts had drawn it to Alorria?

Jyx was beside her, hopping from foot to foot. "Mom and Dad took me to see a storm once. Thunder was so loud that I peed my pants."

Mina shot her a look and wondered why she was saying this. A warning?

"I was three years old."

Mina went back to looking at the clouds.

Pixit nosed Mina in the elbow. «*Ask her if Chauda is telling the truth.*»

What's Chauda saying? she asked him.

«*She says that inside storms, the rain falls sideways, the wind is so hard it can rupture your eyeballs, and the thunder will leave you deaf for seven days.*» Pixit shuddered so hard that his scales clinked. Sparks flew off him like dandruff.

Out loud, Mina asked Jyx, "Could you please ask Chauda to stop teasing Pixit?"

"Oh! Is she — sorry!" Jyx frowned, concentrating; then her expression relaxed. "Chauda said she'll stop. It's just that Pixit is such an easy target."

"All the more reason she shouldn't tease him," Mina said softly but firmly. She laid her hand protectively on the back of Pixit's neck.

"She didn't mean any harm," Jyx said. "She was just enjoying herself."

"That doesn't make it okay." You don't pick on the weaker, the smaller, the easier targets. Ever. She knew that from being a sister, from taking care of Pixit's egg, and from every story about every heroic storm guardian she'd ever read.

Jyx stared at her, silent for a moment, then said, "You're right." She turned to Chauda, whose wings began to droop. Chauda swung her head toward Pixit, and Mina heard Pixit graciously accept Chauda's apology.

It occurred to Mina that even though she hadn't spoken loudly, she'd been heard.

That was nice.

The professors, including the headmistress, were walking among the students, answering questions and offering advice.

"Stay with your partners," the professors were saying. "Students, stick together. Keep to the outskirts of the storm. Let the more experienced guardians take the brunt of it — they'll be coming from the city for the storm. Your job is to watch them and see how it's done. Collect stray electricity and store it in your beasts to deliver when you're done, but don't try to take on any of the major bolts."

The flight instructors were handing out what looked like crumpled-up bags. "For protection against the rain. If you haven't been inside a storm before, know that it will be intense and disorienting. You must recognize your limits and look out for one another. If it's too much, leave the storm. If you see another student who's overwhelmed, help them leave the storm. No heroics."

Mina looked for Professor Dano but didn't see him.

Crack.

Was that thunder? She didn't know what thunder sounded like, but that noise was like the time her father had felled a tree that had grown overlarge for its field.

Her mouth felt dry. She licked her lips, but it didn't help. Her hands were sweaty. She wiped them on her shirt before she took one of the rain bags. Checking first to see how others were doing it, she pulled the bag on — there was a slit for her head as well as two slits for her arms. The fabric crinkled as she moved. It was shiny and slick and reminded her a bit of the blankets on their beds.

Professor Werrin tapped her cane against a stone. "Attention, everyone! The city needs electricity, and we are going to provide it. Any you collect, deposit it in the outpost rods — they're located at the base of the mountains. This is not a game."

Mina exchanged glances with Jyx. She wasn't sure if it was good or not that it wasn't a game. They still hadn't won a match of lightning relay, even though they regularly kept their opponents from scoring.

"Mount up, students," Professor Werrin ordered. "Remember: Do not leave the barren lands. No bringing your lightning over any farms or orchards, and certainly no crossing the mountains. Stay where you won't do any harm. Anyone who disobeys will be prohibited from attending the Ten-Year Festival. Good luck, and happy storms!"

Mina climbed on Pixit's back. The rain gear was bulky, but she mashed it down and leaned forward, gripping his feathery scales. *Ready?*

«*No. You?*»

No. Let's do it anyway.

«*Okay.*» His voice felt as tiny as a mouse squeak, but he ran forward, his paws scraping up the dirt on the practice field. His wings beat hard. Out of the corner of her eye, she saw Chauda running with Jyx. And then all of them were airborne.

They flew near the center of the pack of students and their beasts as they aimed for the storm that spilled over the mountains. The purple-and-black clouds had swallowed the peaks and were obscuring the slopes. Occasionally, a cloud lit up bright white and then darkened again.

Another *crack*.

It had to be thunder.

Jyx shouted, "They say if you count the seconds between the lightning and thunder, it tells you how many miles away the storm is!"

Mina knew exactly how far away the storm was: not far enough!

I'm not ready! she thought.

It was swarming onto the hills now, as if it were invading. All the rain and wind guardians had backed off to a safe distance, watching the monster they'd summoned swell larger and larger into a bloated, ever-hungry piece of sky. Every instinct Mina had was screaming at her to turn around and fly the other direction. But the swarm of students was too thick. She couldn't flee even if she decided to.

«*It will be okay, Mina.*»

She wondered again how Professor Dano had hurt his arm. She thought of the lists in those old books of those who'd died in storms and of the people beyond the mountains without the protection of storm beasts. And she thought of her family, safe at home in the farmlands. She imagined the sun on the fields, the birds chirping as they swooped over the cornstalks, Gaton's sun beast lazing on the lawn, the twins screeching for their lunch. And then she and all the other students on their beasts flew into the storm.

TWELVE

THE storm ate them.

Mina felt as if she'd passed through the teeth of a hungry monster and was now within its stomach. The wind — it wasn't like anything she'd ever felt, even on a wind day. It hit at her and Pixit, tossing them sideways and upward. She clung to his neck.

«*Hang on, Mina!*»

Rain smacked her from all directions, immediately finding the gaps in the raincoat and sliding down her skin, so cold that it made her shake.

Around her, she heard excited shouts. "I feel it!" someone cried.

"It's coming!" Another voice.

"Ready, everyone!"

She couldn't see through the thick clouds.

Suddenly, bright white lit up all around her. A second later, a *crack*! She felt herself prickle all over, and not from the rain. *Did you feel that?*

«*Lightning! Yes!*»

Pixit flew forward — at least she thought it was forward — toward the darker clouds. Mina wondered which way was north and whether they were flying toward the school or away from it. *Remember, we're supposed to stay on the outskirts. Let the older guardians harvest the lightning.*

«*I can feel it, Mina!*»

She felt his excitement — it coursed into her until she was eagerly watching the clouds, trying to see where the next strike would be. The trick to harvesting from thunderclouds, she'd been told, was to intercept the strikes — you had to gather the energy *before* it finished discharging.

In other words, you had to catch the lightning.

There!

She saw the bolt this time: a white line that snaked through the cloud and then branched into a dozen different fingers. In the light she saw a storm beast swoop beneath it, and the bolt vanished as the guardian caught its energy and his beast absorbed it — and then all was dark again.

Crack.

She could feel the tingle — it was stronger to the left. *Left!*

Pixit flew left, beating his wings against the rain. She wiped the water from her face with one hand, then clutched his scales again, blinking fast to try to see. She heard shouts around her:

"Next one!" "Ready!" "I feel it!" "It's coming! Catch it before it strikes!"

Lightning.

Beautiful, white, branching into a hundred different lines right in front of them.

CRACK.

And then beasts were flying fast around her, past her. One bashed against Pixit's wings. He dipped sideways, then struggled to stay aloft. Mina slipped to the side. «*Mina!*» She squeezed tight and yanked herself back up between his shoulder blades.

A blast of rain and wind slammed into Pixit, catching his wing and flipping him over. Mina screamed, clinging hard to him as he tumbled through the air.

Somersaulting wing over wing, he fought against the wind and rain. «*Hang on, Mina!*»

She held on.

She knew others were in the storm, lots of others. Jyx was somewhere. And Zek and Ferro, and all the other students and their storm beasts, as well as the guardians who'd come to harvest the lightning. But with the storm around her, Mina felt as if she and Pixit were alone.

«*We can do this! Just hang on!*»

Another strike, directly in front of them, and immediately *crack!* Pixit reared back, and Mina's fingers slipped on the wet feathered scales. She scrambled to grab on, but with all the rain, his hide was slick.

I can't hold on!

His feathers slid through her fingers. She grabbed at empty air.

A scream burst out of her: "Pixit!"

He dove for her. «*Mina!*»

His claws seized her shoulder, and she felt a sharp pain shoot through her arm. He loosened immediately, and she grabbed on to his leg.

A voice called through the cloud. "Mina?"

Jyx! She wanted to cry. She tried to shout: "Jyx, we're here!" But then the clouds lit white, as lightning struck farther away from them, followed by the clap of thunder that swallowed her words.

She tried again: "Jyx! Chauda! Here!" She dangled from Pixit's leg as he flapped, desperately trying to stay aloft. Rain smashed into her. Pain throbbed in her shoulder.

Through the purple-and-black clouds, she saw a shape — and then Jyx and Chauda burst into view. "Mina! What are you doing? Can't you follow a simple order?" Flying beneath her, Jyx reached up to grab her, and Mina let go of Pixit's leg. She flopped down onto Jyx.

Chauda instantly sank.

"Stay with your partner," Jyx said. "That's what they told us! But I couldn't find you! I looked. I called for you. Couldn't you hear me? Why didn't you call back? Mina, you're bleeding! Your shoulder! Chauda, we have to land. Mina's hurt." Another flash, closer. "What do you mean you can't hold us both? This is not optional, Chauda."

Mina began to sit up. She had to get back on Pixit —

"Whoa! Stay still!"

But Chauda was off balance. She tipped, and Mina slid. Jyx grabbed for her, and the shift in weight knocked Chauda all the way sideways. Her wings slapped together and she began falling. With a cry, Pixit shot after her, and then all four of them were tangled — a knot of arms, legs, and wings — falling through the storm.

They plummeted.

Thunder cracked around them, and in the next flash of lightning Mina saw the ground, the jagged rocks of the mountain racing toward them. She flung herself at Pixit, her arms around his neck, and the four of them broke apart: Jyx with Chauda, and Mina with Pixit.

Pixit stretched his wings out, slowing their fall, and they crashed down and tumbled, knocking rocks free, falling with the rocks, until at last they stopped.

The rain slackened.

She heard the thunder, more distant.

Lying on the side of the mountain, Mina felt as if every inch of her skin were bruised. Her shoulder throbbed. *Pixit?*

«*I'm here.*»

"Jyx?" she croaked.

"Over here!"

In the darkness, Mina could only tell that Jyx was some-where above her. "Are you all right?"

"Keep talking — we'll find you by your voice."

Mina felt a laugh bubble into her throat, and she swallowed it back. She knew this wasn't the time for laughing, but she still felt like she was about to burst into unstoppable giggles. Or cry. Or both. *They need me to talk. Me.* "That wasn't how the first storm was supposed to go," Mina said. She wasn't sure what else she should say, but Jyx needed more words to follow. "I'm sorry you were paired with me. It's not fair to you. You deserve someone who's better at this."

"You didn't mean to fall," Jyx said. "Don't be so hard on yourself. You're always so worried about being fair to other peo-ple, but you're not being fair to yourself!"

"I lied about being able to summon a spark," Mina con-fessed. "We still can't do it."

"Okay, *that* I'm a little mad about. Why didn't you tell me? We could have helped you!"

Mina heard pebbles tumbling, above and to the left. She wished the lightning would flash again so they could see. But when it did flash, it only lit up the sky high above them, silhou-etting the peak of a mountain. "I thought we were supposed to figure it out on our own."

"We're supposed to be partners. And your problem is obvious: you still don't believe you're meant to be a lightning guardian."

How is that obvious? She'd tried to hide her doubts. Appar-ently Jyx was more observant than she'd thought. *Or maybe I'm just that bad.* "I'm the worst lightning guardian Mytris School has ever seen. After this . . . they'll probably send me home." Her throat closed up. Professor Werrin wouldn't want a guardian who could neither summon electricity nor fly in a storm.

The thought made her feel ill. She'd dreamed about being a guardian for so long . . .

Another cascade of pebbles. "Mina, talk more. Tell me about your home."

"I love our farm. It's perfect." She fell silent again, imagining it, the way the wheat looked when it first burst through the earth, the way the air smelled on a summer morning, the way the apples tasted sun-warmed and fresh from the tree.

"So tell me about it. Come on, Mina. *Talk.*"

Haltingly, Mina described it. She told Jyx about her family — her older brother, the twins, and Mother and Papa. She talked about how excited they'd been when she'd received her egg, and how proud she'd been. She'd wanted this so badly, and they'd wanted it for her. They'd been so sure she'd hatch a sun beast or rain or wind and that she'd stay on the farm with them.

"And you ended up with a lightning beast?" Jyx said. "Why?"

«*Because it's who you are, Mina,*» Pixit said stoutly. «*Because you have things to do beyond the farm.*»

What do I have to do? I'm a disaster.

«*I don't know. Things.*»

"Mina? Keep going. How come Pixit's Pixit?"

"Because . . . because . . . because . . ." She had no answer at all. He was *not* a mistake. But maybe *she* was, a farm girl who wanted more but couldn't handle more when she got it. She heard Pixit in her mind, telling her she was perfect as she was, but she didn't believe him. She couldn't help but think that she didn't deserve to be a guardian at all. That was why she'd fallen in the storm, and that was why she still couldn't hold a spark. "I keep thinking of that old guardian saying — you know, the one they put on the welcome letter: 'A true heart is never a mistake' — and I wonder if maybe I'm the first."

"Ah, there you are." Jyx's voice was right next to her. Mina squinted up and saw her shape, a darker shadow against all the other shadows. Chauda was a squat shadow beside her. Jyx plopped down next to her.

"How badly hurt are you?" Jyx asked.

Mina pushed herself up to sitting. Her head spun, but it wasn't too bad. She touched her shoulder and winced. She drew her hand away. "I don't know."

"As soon as the storm fades, we'll fly back to the school. Straight to the sick room."

The rain was lessening. Mina squinted as she looked out, trying to see the lights of the school. Even with the storm, she should be able to see them.

She heard another crash of thunder behind them, beyond the mountain peak.

And a terrible thought occurred to her.

The storm was *behind* them. *Beyond* the mountain.

Which meant that they were on the other side.

"Jyx, why can't we see the school?"

"Because of the storm. Remember the storm? Hard to see? Lots of clouds? Lightning? Very exciting? Did you hit your head?"

«*Oh no.*» Pixit understood.

"Jyx, we crossed the mountains." Mina tried to keep her voice level and calm, but she failed. *This is bad. Very, very bad.* Not only had she failed to spark and fallen when she'd flown in her first storm, but she'd also broken one of the school rules: don't leave the barren lands. "I think . . . we crossed the border. We're not in Alorria."

‑CHAPTER‑
THIRTEEN

RAIN fell steadily, softly, *pat-tat-pat-tat*, on the rocks around them as Pixit panicked in her head and Jyx panicked next to her. «*Oh no, oh no, what did I do? Oh no, oh no, I'm so sorry!*» And Jyx: "We're doomed! We are so, so, so doomed! What are my parents going to say? I know what they're going to say. They're going to freak out. They're just waiting for me to mess up. They already think I'm never going to be as great as they were. What are we going to do? This is terrible. This is disastrous. This is catastrophically bad! Mina, what do we do? What do we say?"

Her head throbbed. Her shoulder ached. But Mina took a breath and then exhaled. *Don't panic,* she told Pixit. It wasn't a catastrophe; it was a simple mistake. And the answer was simple: stay quiet. "We don't say anything. We fell in the storm; that much will be obvious. We don't say where."

"We lie?"

Is it lying if you were silent? *Yes, it is.* But it wouldn't be fair for Jyx to be punished just because Mina wasn't a real lightning guardian.

"Okay, fine," Jyx said. "I mean, it's not like we meant to do this. And we could easily have fallen on the right side of the peak. Just bad luck."

Mina heard a shuffling and grunting, and she saw the shadow that was Jyx climb onto Chauda. She felt a puff of wind and rain spatter her face as Chauda stretched her wings. Taking a deep breath, Mina pushed herself over to Pixit and crawled onto his back.

Pixit spread his wings, and then hissed. «*Ow, ow, ow!*»

Mina slid off his back and landed on the muddy rocks. *Are you okay?*

«*Hurts!*»

She stroked his neck soothingly. *Where?* It was too dark to see any injuries, and he was too wet for her to tell if she was feeling water or blood. *Are you cut? Anything broken?* She ruthlessly quashed any feelings of panic that bubbled up — she couldn't let Pixit feel her fear. He was scared enough.

Pixit let out a strangled little sob. «*Left. My wing. It hurts when I move it. Think I landed on it.*»

Out of the corner of her eye, she saw a shadow in the rain above them. "Mina, Pixit, come on!" Jyx said. "The longer we stay here, the more likely someone will notice we're missing."

"He hurt his wing," Mina said, trying hard to stay calm. Pixit was hurt! *It's my fault.* If she'd been a better guardian, or if she'd urged him to be more careful in the storm . . . If they'd flown

149

sooner or practiced more, or if she'd listened to her instincts and worn a safety harness, even just a rope, instead of doing what everyone else did and trying to pretend she was like everyone else when she knew she wasn't . . . Again she clamped down on her feelings. "I don't know if he can fly."

"He has to! We can't be caught on this side of the mountain. You heard Professor Werrin. We broke a major rule!" Jyx and Chauda circled them, spattering rain. "It's one thing to break a rule on purpose, for a reason. But this — if we get in trouble because of a mistake, that will be *bad*. You don't know my parents, Mina. They were star guardians. I can't make a mistake! Not one this size!"

Pixit, can you try? Even if you could just make it over to the other side of the peak . . .

He moaned.

The rain was only a drizzle now. Struggling to shine through the clouds, the moon cast layers of shadows over the mountainside. Mina could see farther, nearly to the peak. *We still have some time. But not a lot of it.* Per orders from the city, the rain and wind guardians were driving the storm south, following the mountain line, so the lightning guardians could harvest as much lightning as possible, before they sent the storm back across the border. The thunder and lightning wouldn't be allowed to reach the pastures and orchards, much less the city and the farmlands beyond. Once the storm was gone, all the students would be herded back to the school — and someone would notice that Jyx and Mina and their beasts were missing.

If we can just reach the other side of the border before then, everything will still be fine.

«*I'll try. Climb on again.*»

Mina climbed back on. She wrapped her arms around his neck, trying to stay away from his wings. She felt him tense as he opened one wing, then the other. He flapped — and the pain shot through her, too. *Stop! You'll make it worse.*

«*I'm sorry! Mina, go with Chauda. I'll fly when I'm better. I'll find you.*» He sounded both heroic and pathetic at the same time.

I'm not leaving you. Besides, Chauda can't carry me and Jyx — you know that. She looked up the peak, trying to guess how far it was. *Not impossibly far,* she thought. "Jyx, you and Chauda need to go for help."

«*No!*»

"Are you crazy? I'm not leaving you!"

"He's hurt." She eyed the peak again. From the shadows, she could tell it was steep, and the rocks were slick with rain. *You can't fly. But can you walk?*

«*All the way to school? I don't know.*»

All we have to do is cross the peak. If we're on the right side of the border we'll be fine.

«*Yes! Or at least I can try.*»

"By the time you get help, Pixit and I will be across the border." She tried to sound much more confident than she felt.

Jyx and Chauda circled them again. "It's dark, it's steep, and it's wet. You'll never make it!"

Mina hated arguing. It made her feel like her insides were

squishing together. But she didn't have a better idea. "Please, Jyx! You don't have to tell them you fell too. Just say you saw us fall. Be vague about where."

"I don't know, Mina."

"Remember with lightning relay? You said you'd listen to me."

Jyx opened her mouth, shut it, then glared at Mina before she said, "Fine. But you'd better be alive when I get back, not buried at the bottom of an avalanche. Spark extra so I can find you again, okay?" With a final snort from Chauda, they flapped away.

Mina watched as the smudge of their shadow flew up toward the clouds and then over the peak. She tried not to feel abandoned, especially since this was her idea.

Pixit's voice quivered in her mind. «*Avalanche?*»

She wrapped her arm — the one that didn't ache — around his neck. *Come on. Let's climb a mountain.* Together, slowly, they started up the slope.

The rocks were slippery, and she had to be careful with every footstep. She kept a tight grip on Pixit. Beside her, he was concentrating too. She felt his thoughts: «*One, two — easy, there. Steady, steady. Don't step there. Careful. Three, four. Right, left, back right, back left.*»

It continued to drizzle, as if the clouds were crying.

Higher, it became steeper, with sheer vertical rocks they had to go around. Mina wondered what they'd do if it became too steep to climb. But she couldn't think about that. She had to focus on one step at a time.

Behind her, she heard a voice: "Up there!"

A man's voice. A stranger's.

Mina had managed to stay calm when they fell, when Pixit was hurt, when Jyx was panicking, and when Jyx and Chauda left them alone to climb in the dark and rain. But hearing the sound of a stranger . . .

Mina panicked.

Pixit, climb faster!

«*It's Jyx! She found help!*»

It was too soon. And the voice was below them — help would come from *above*, from storm beasts. *That's not help!* Mina reached for the next handhold, but her fingers felt only slick, flat rock. *Pixit!*

He held still so she could boost herself up on his leg. She stretched, reaching for a crack or bulge or anything — but there was no place to grab, nothing to hold. She heard multiple voices now, calling to one another frantically. Two women had joined the man.

"Stay where you are, child!" a woman called. "It isn't safe!"

Terror shot through her like a lightning strike, and she scratched at the rock, trying to find some way up, away, *now!* Her fear poured out of her into Pixit, and he screeched, spreading his wings. His thoughts were frantic, tumbling over one another, amplifying her fear, which then fed right back into him.

«*We must escape!*»

You can't fly!

«*Grab hold!*»

Mina wrapped her arms around his neck, and he lifted up. She felt him strain, and his wing folded when they were only a few feet up. They fell down, hitting the rocks, and tumbled together, his wings wrapped around her.

She blacked out.

When she blinked her eyes open again, she saw brightness — a blob of searing orange. Her eyes watered, and she threw her arm in front of her face. Voices were talking, soothingly, with an accent she'd never heard before. "Shh, you'll be okay. Lie still. You fell. But you're all right. No broken bones."

"Pixit?" she croaked.

"Is that your beast's name? He'll be all right too. We're patching him up now. Rest. That's a good girl. Here, drink this. It will make you feel better." She felt a cool mug pressed to her lips and liquid sloshed against her mouth. She swallowed. Bitter warmth flowed down her throat and spread through her lungs.

She didn't want to drink anything. She wanted to make sure Pixit was all right! She tried to struggle. *Pixit! Are you okay?*

She felt only fuzziness where his thoughts should be. "Pixit!"

"Poor dear, let her see him. She'll upset herself." She heard shuffling. Someone's hands were behind her back, helping her sit up, and the amber light — a lantern, she realized, though with a steady glow, not a flame — was shifted. She saw Pixit, lying on a blanket. A man and a girl about Mina's age were wrapping bandages around his wing, while an older woman was beside Mina.

Outsiders, she thought. She'd never seen clothes like theirs, bulky coats with zippers and buttons all over. And the woman's accent! She didn't sound like anyone in Alorria.

"You're helping? But . . ."

The woman chuckled. She was holding a clay mug and dressed in layers of brown. Frizzy hair poked out from under her hood. "You were told all non-Alorrians were pathetic creatures who can't even help themselves, or some such nonsense? We're the search-and-rescue team from Dern — that's the nearest outpost." She gestured toward the base of the mountain. "My name's Neela, and this is Varli and Eione. We're out every storm, looking for strays. Usually it's a sheep. Or a foolhardy trader who thought she could make it home before the weather worsened. We don't see many of your kind."

Mina swallowed. Her mouth felt chalky, and her head was swimming. It was hard to think. Instead she focused on the lantern with its odd light. "I don't . . ." She wanted to tell them she didn't know anything about outsiders. She'd always been curious, but she'd never really expected to meet them. *Especially not like this.*

She felt her shoulder, poking it gingerly. It had been dressed in clean white bandages, and it felt better. It barely hurt.

"We put bone-ache medicine on it. You tell that to your doctors — you'll need to put fresh medicine on in a day if it's to keep healing. And use your arm as little as possible. Same goes for your storm beast. He's to fly as little as possible until he heals."

"But we have to —"

Neela stopped her, not unkindly. "Cross the mountain. I know. You're not the first guardian to be blown off course. These storms you play with are dangerous, whether you know it or not."

The mushiness inside Mina's head was beginning to fade, and she noticed that the rain had stopped. She wondered how much time had passed. *Jyx will be coming back soon. We need to cross the mountain!* "How soon —"

"As soon as he's patched up, we'll help you cross. Your own people will find you on the other side." Smiling warmly, she patted Mina's unhurt shoulder. She reminded Mina of their neighbor, a woman who mothered every child who came within five miles of her farm. Mina had eaten plenty of sunflower muffins on her porch.

One of the other rescuers, Varli, a man with a bushy brown beard, spoke. His voice was gentle, as if she were a deer he didn't want to startle. "Just the next time you want to play with the weather, we'd appreciate it if you'd steer your storm *away* from our outpost? It's only a few buildings. Shouldn't be hard to go around."

Neela clucked at him. "She's just a child. She's not steering storms on her own." To Mina she said, "Still, once you're trained, perhaps you could think more about who you hurt with your fun and games."

Mina felt herself flush with embarrassment. *But I didn't hurt anyone!*

Did I?

Guiltily, she remembered how excited she'd been: their first thunderstorm. Everyone had cheered, and none of them had thought for more than a second of the people in the storm's path. The guardians had made sure no Alorrians suffered, but clearly no one had been careful of where the storm hit *before* it crossed the border. When the rain and wind guardians had summoned the thunderstorm, the one she'd flown through, had they guided it over the outpost?

But that's not my fault!

Maybe it was no one's fault. Maybe it was an accident. Maybe they hadn't known the outpost was there. She couldn't believe anyone would steer a storm through a place with people intentionally.

The third rescuer — a teenage girl with black straggly hair and a scar on the corner of her lips — snorted, reminding her of Chauda. "She's not going to do anything. None of them care what happens to us."

"Don't talk like that, Eione," Neela scolded. "They don't know any better, that's all."

Eione snorted again but didn't say anything else. She bent back over Pixit, affixing his bandage with a dot of resin that she warmed between her fingers — Mina had seen Mother do the same when Gaton had sprained his arm falling out of the old apple tree.

"We can weather the storms," Neela said, as she dug another bandage for Pixit out of her pack. "It's these poor dears who are always surprised when they can't, thinking they can control the uncontrollable."

We can control it, Mina wanted to say. *I'm just not good at it.*

"We can weather *most* storms, yes," Varli said. "Eione here has been through some terrible ones. But stars and moon help us all when the ten-year storms come." He pressed his fingertips to his forehead, like Mother did sometimes to ward off bad luck. It was so strange to think of these people as having any of the same mannerisms as her family. She'd expected outsiders to — well, she hadn't known what to expect. None of her books had been about non-Alorrians. *Maybe they're not so different from us.*

"I suppose you're not going to ask her to do something about the ten-year storms?" Eione said.

"She's only a child," Neela repeated. "Younger than you."

"Dangerous child," Eione muttered.

Mina wanted to ask what the "ten-year storms" were, what they thought she could do about them, and why Eione thought she was dangerous. Her questions must have shown on her face, because Varli answered her.

"The last ten-year storm flattened the outpost," Varli said sadly. "We didn't have the early warning we have now, and not everyone made it out in time. Lives were lost."

"Like I said, her kind don't care," Eione said. "I don't know why you're bothering pretending she does."

Of course I care!

But Eione's face was flushed and she was still talking, louder and louder. "They think they're so superior, when they're so dependent on their dragons for every —"

"Enough, both of you," Neela said. "She's hurt, she's wet, and she's scared. We need to help her back home before her people panic. You know they'll assume the worst. Get the stretcher beneath that storm beast."

All three of them worked together to unroll a hammock-like sling that was wrapped around two poles, and then to shift Pixit onto it. "On three. Careful now. Easy with the wing. One, two, three!" Pixit grunted as they pushed him into the sling. His eyes fluttered open.

Pixit? Are you all right?

His sparks flared.

The rescuers jumped back. "Whoa!" Eione cried.

Mina crawled to him. *It's okay.* She stroked his neck. *They're helping us. Look — they bandaged your wing. And they're going to help us over the mountain.* She felt him calm as she talked to him. His sparks settled down, sizzling in the rain. *It's going to be fine.*

Neela and Varli hefted Pixit into the air, resting the poles on their shoulders. Carrying the strange lantern, Eione led the way up. There was a narrow path that zigzagged around the rock. It was nearly invisible in the dark and the rain, which was why Mina and Pixit had missed seeing it earlier. Mina had to concentrate on stepping carefully — the pebbles shifted under her feet, and the mud was slick — but at least it was walkable. Twice she had to catch her balance on the rocks. Her rescuers didn't pause, proceeding up as sure-footed as mountain goats, as if they'd done this a dozen times.

Maybe they have. They'd said she wasn't the first to cross. But she'd never heard of any storm guardians crossing the border before. All beasts stayed in Alorria. It was just the way it was. Their duty was to their people.

But these are people too, she thought. The guardians who'd summoned the storm should have checked to make sure the way was clear.

At last, the rescuers halted.

"We aren't allowed to cross into Alorria," Neela said. "Otherwise we'd never dream of leaving an injured child and her beast alone up here."

"*Your* country's laws," Eione added.

Wait — there was a law about this? She hadn't heard that. She'd thought it was just a school rule that she and Pixit weren't allowed to leave the barren lands. She hadn't known there was a law forbidding others from entering Alorria.

"There's a nice ledge. You'll be safe until your people come. Just rest." Neela pulled out a satchel and handed it to Mina. "Food and water, enough to keep you for another day. And if for some reason your people don't come for you, follow this path down to the Dern outpost. We'll house you for as long as you need." She pointed down the mountain to a cluster of amber lights — lamplights, Mina guessed, or lanterns. It couldn't be electricity, could it? How could they have electricity without lightning beasts? And outside a city?

"I — I don't know how to thank you," Mina said.

Eione rolled her eyes. "Maybe quit it with the killer weather? That would be a start."

Neela shushed her. "It's our job to help, and the right thing to do. We're just glad we were able to. Safe storms, child."

"My name's Mina. And this is Pixit." She wished she could give them more than their names. Maybe she could come back and . . . *I can't return. Stop being ridiculous.* It was unfair that the storm had hit their outpost, but there wasn't anything she could do about that. She was still just a student — and not a very good one. She couldn't even manage to hold a spark. "Thank you."

She and Pixit crawled over the ridge of the mountain onto a ledge that was exactly where they'd said it would be. It was wide, flat, even comfortable. In the distance, she could see the three towers of Mytris, blazing with electricity. There was no trace of the storm left in the sky on this side of the mountains. The stars and moon shone brightly down on Alorria.

Behind her, the outsiders began their climb down their side of the mountain, back to their storm-ravaged home.

⟅CHAPTER⟆

FOURTEEN

O N the ledge, Mina curled up against Pixit. He folded his unhurt wing around her, and they slept — until a shriek startled them both awake: "Mina! Pixit! Where are yoooou?"

Mina pried her eyes open and shook Pixit. "Spark, Pixit! Spark so Jyx can find us!"

Groggily, he began spraying sparks.

More!

He concentrated, spewing sparks in all directions like he was a fountain of fire.

She heard Jyx call, "There! I see them! Chauda, down!" And then a moment later: "Mina, I'm so glad you two aren't dead!" Jyx and Chauda swooped toward them, with two other lightning guardians behind her: Zek and Ferro on their beasts. It was still night — a clear, beautiful night now — and the elec-tric lights still blazed at Mytris, far in the distance, so Mina knew she hadn't slept for long. Zek waved at them. Ferro was carrying what looked like a bundle of ropes and couldn't wave, but he beamed at them with a huge smile, visible in the bright moonlight.

"And how lucky you fell on *this* side of the border! Yes, that was extremely lucky!" Jyx was shouting extra loud. Circling around them, she waved in Zek and Ferro. "We brought a net, which we did *not* steal."

Both Zek and Ferro nodded vigorously. "We left a note," Zek said.

"Students are supposed to help each other," Ferro said solemnly.

Mina couldn't help smiling at all of them. She'd never been more happy to see people. Babying her own injury, she helped them secure the net under Pixit, and she climbed in with him. It was coated in a layer of fire-resistant rubber.

Each holding a piece of the net, the three other beasts flew away from the cliff. Mina and Pixit were dragged off the ledge and then into the open air. For an instant they all sank, and Mina almost screamed. Pixit did yelp.

"Up, up, up!" Jyx cried. "Flap like you mean it!"

They flew steadily on to the school.

Ferro began talking. "I broke my arm once. Three years old, and I was running toward the house, really excited because I'd seen this butterfly —"

"You were excited over a butterfly?" Zek asked.

"It was a cool one. Fuzzy antennae."

"You're joking."

"Never seen one before. Three years old, remember? And there are butterflies worth running for. Imagine if you saw a butterfly that spat fire —"

Jyx jumped in. "That would be awesome."

"And impossible," Zek said.

"It was a hypothetical example!"

"You're a hypothetical example," Jyx told him.

"Nice timing on the insult," Zek said, "but that doesn't actually make sense."

They continued talking and teasing one another, and the words flowed around Mina. But instead of making her feel anxious or like she wanted to hide from all the talking, they made her feel safe. Their babble felt like a cradle, keeping her from falling.

It felt like family.

All the bulbs were still blazing when they reached the school. Mina peered through the holes in the net, trying to see which teacher would catch them and how much trouble they were in. «*Are we going to be expelled?*»

Of course not! Why would you think that? Besides, as far as anyone knows, we didn't do anything wrong. She tried to put as much confidence into the thought as she could. After all, both Zek and Ferro and their beasts had only seen them on this side of the mountain, and not even Jyx knew that Mina had talked to outsiders. *We'll just have to keep that a secret.*

She thought of how Eione had said she wasn't going to help, and Mina felt a stab of guilt. Lying wasn't the way to pay them back for what they'd done. If the outsiders hadn't helped her and Pixit . . . *Or we'll keep it a secret for now,* she amended.

«*I'm good with secrets.*»

I know you are. He'd kept secret the fact that she couldn't spark.

«*It's easy to be excellent at it,*» he said modestly. «*I can't even talk to humans other than you, and Chauda mostly just grunts.*»

Mina smiled.

The storm beasts flapped across the practice field, then dipped down. "Gently now, people! Okay, lower . . . lower . . . on three. One, two . . ."

Thump. Pixit and Mina crashed to the ground. «*Oof!*»

"I didn't say 'three' yet!" Jyx said. "Seriously, it's not difficult. One, two, three. Land on three." Much more gracefully, Jyx and Chauda landed beside Pixit and Mina. Jyx jumped down and pulled the net off them. Zek and Ferro helped.

"Are you two okay?" Ferro asked. "I mean, aside from the crash landing. Sorry about that. Blame Zek." He dodged as Zek aimed a punch at his arm.

Then Zek glanced up, beyond Mina. "Brace yourself. Incoming."

Mina pushed the rest of the net off and stood up. Professor Werrin, Professor Dano, and three of the flight teachers were hurrying toward them. She felt the eyes of everyone else on the field. Her face was hot. This would be all anyone talked about — not the storm, not the lightning, but the fact that Mina and Pixit had had to be carried back in a net.

The professors and teachers swarmed around them, fussing over her and Pixit's freshly bandaged injuries, as Jyx very loudly told them how Mina and Pixit had fallen in the storm, and how she, Zek, and Ferro and their beasts had discovered them on a ledge on *this* side of the mountain and carried them back to the school. She continued, wailing about how she'd been afraid they'd broken their necks when they fell, how she'd been worried she'd find them dead, how she'd been so relieved to find them alive, albeit hurt. Zek and Ferro jumped in, stoutly confirming everything she said.

Other students pressed closer, eager to hear the story, and Mina wished with all her heart that Pixit's wing were healed so she could fly far, far away. She even wished she were still on the cliff, so she wouldn't have to be the center of so many people gawking at her at once.

As if they sensed her discomfort, Jyx, Ferro, and Zek clustered around her.

Just that made her feel ten times better.

Professor Werrin and Professor Dano shooed the other students and teachers away and escorted Mina and Pixit into the school, through the halls to the sick room. Jyx and Chauda came with them, along with Zek and Ferro. Inside the sick room, two school nurses scurried around them, examining Mina's shoulder and Pixit's wing.

"Nicely bound," one of the nurses said. "You've had training?"

Mina didn't know what to say. She opened her mouth but no words came out.

Jyx jumped in. "She grew up on a farm. Lots of broken arms there. Dangerous places, farms are."

Ferro nodded. "Yeah. All those cows."

It's a wheat-and-corn farm, Mina thought, but she still didn't say anything out loud. The nurses seemed to buy that explanation. She felt as if a band around her chest had loosened and she could breathe a little more easily.

She wondered if Zek and Ferro had guessed the truth. If they had, she was doubly grateful to them. She wanted to put this whole mess behind her as quickly as possible.

"Luckily, it's not broken," one of the nurses said to Professor Dano. "Just a sprained wing for the lightning beast and a bone bruise for the girl." Addressing Mina, she said, "It'll ache for a while, but you'll be able to use it. You, though, my friend" — the nurse turned to Pixit and wagged his finger — "are grounded until you're fully healed. You'll injure it worse if you try to fly too soon."

Mina swallowed. She knew they'd gotten off lightly. No one seemed to suspect where they'd landed. But the thought of being grounded at all . . . She was already so behind the others. She still couldn't draw electricity from Pixit, much less catch a lightning bolt in midair, and they'd clearly failed dismally within the storm itself. They needed *more* practice, not less. But if Pixit was hurt, there was nothing to be done. So she merely nodded.

"Think of the bright side," Professor Dano said. His voice was as dour as always. "Now you'll have time to finish that essay."

Ferro wrinkled his nose. "I don't think that's a bright side."

"*You* don't have to write it," Mina said, softly but clearly enough to be heard.

Jyx, Ferro, and Zek burst out laughing. Mina grinned at them.

"Well, that is a bright side for me," Ferro said.

⚡

At her desk, Mina worked on her essay while everyone else practiced flying and summoning electricity. She wanted to do a brilliant job at it, to prove in at least some small way that she was worthy of being here with the other lightning guardians, but every few minutes, she sighed. She missed flying with Pixit, and she missed him being near her. He was stuck in the sick room, because he couldn't fly up to their window. He was still able to hear her sighs, though, mind-to-mind.

«*I'm sorry I got hurt.*»

It's not your fault.

She stared out the window at the mountains. She wished she could stop thinking about what had happened over there, and the things the outsiders had said. Had the guardians dragged the storm through their outpost? And what were the "ten-year storms"? She'd never heard of regularly scheduled storms outside Alorria, especially deadly ones.

How did they know a storm was going to come every decade? Without beasts, nature should have been unpredictable. It didn't make sense.

Mina frowned at her paper. She was supposed to be writing about the importance of obedience to Alorrian law, using historical references, but as near as she could tell, history had been one disaster after another. *I guess that's the point. It was only when guardians and beasts began working together that the disasters ended. For us, at least.*

The outsiders still faced plenty of disasters.

She chewed on her lower lip.

"'It seems the more we try to fix the world, the more we break it.'"

«*You know, I'm supposed to be resting,*» Pixit complained. «*It's difficult to sleep when you're thinking so hard that you sound like you are in the same room, shouting.*»

Sorry.

But Mina couldn't stop her brain from whirling. In the journals of the first guardians, when the guardians and beasts were learning how to control the storms, they made things worse by creating terrible storms elsewhere, resulting in those horrifying lists of names. *What if that's still happening?*

It was a ridiculous thought.

Storm guardians and beasts had learned from the past. They worked together, obeying the law, to make life safer for everyone.

But what if by controlling the weather in Alorria, we're making it worse somewhere else? Like in Dern?

Jyx burst into their dorm room. "Mina, Mina, Mina! Guess what?" She didn't even pause for Mina to try to guess, which

169

was good because Mina had no idea why Jyx was bouncing up and down. "We get to go to the city! All of us! All the students at Mytris are invited to meet with the prime minister, and she's going to present to us the plans for the festival!"

"All of us?" Mina thought of Pixit. He was still too injured to fly. *And maybe I don't even deserve to say "us" yet.*

«*Of course you do, Mina.*»

Jyx couldn't hear them, naturally. "Yes, Pixit too! We'll go by river ship. Because it's easier to keep us together that way. They don't trust us not to get distracted and fly off. I think they've hired, like, five ships to take us all. Oh, Mina, this is amazing! We'll be able to watch some of the rehearsal! It won't be at full power, of course, but we'll see a taste of it. And then soon: the festival itself! Guardians and beasts from across Alorria — they'll all come to the capital to perform. And oh, the water shows! And the lights! It's going to be incredible! I don't remember the last festival. I was two. You were two. You can't remember it either. But I heard it's amazing! And this year, the prime minister is promising it will be the hugest ever!"

Jyx's excitement was contagious. Mina found herself grinning back at her. The Ten-Year Festival was celebrated with magnificent displays by the storm guardians and beasts, showcasing the best of the best commanding the weather —

Every ten years? That was how often the bad storms came, the outsiders had said.

«*You don't think there's a connection between . . .*»

Of course not.

The Alorrian government would never let the celebrations proceed if they were dangerous to anyone, even people outside the borders. It was a harmless display. And it was rumored to be just as amazing as Jyx said. Galon remembered the last one and talked about it all the time. The sky would light up with colors, and snow and rain would dance — dance! — across the land as if to music. Day would become night, and night would become day, and the clouds would be formed in the shapes of animals that chased one another. So many miracles! It was supposed to remind Alorrians of how lucky they were and to encourage the next crop of children to volunteer for eggs.

Of course it had nothing to do with the outsiders' storms. Storms were a natural occurrence. It was only that the outsiders didn't have their own storm beasts to prevent them. "When do we leave?" Mina asked.

"That's the best part! We go tomorrow! Forget that stupid essay and pack!"

Promising herself she'd finish her work later, Mina packed alongside Jyx.

Jyx chattered about the things she knew they'd see and the things she hoped they'd see. To listen to her, you'd think the city was the most marvelous place ever invented, where anything and everything was possible. *And maybe that's true,* Mina thought. She remembered the glimpses of it she'd seen from the river ship, and she couldn't wait to see more.

When she finished packing, she pulled out her sketchbook. She was too excited to sleep yet. She drew pictures of the city as she remembered it until it was lights out.

Caught up in her own thoughts, Jyx was quiet too. It was nice lying there in the darkness, knowing Jyx was feeling the same way, sharing a wordless excitement.

Neither of them slept much, though Chauda snored enough for all of them. But at morning bell, both Mina and Jyx sprang out of bed. They washed and dressed quickly and were down in the school entrance hall before the last bell rang, joined by Pixit. He flapped his bandaged wing at Mina. «*One more week, they said — then I can fly again!*»

Good news. But stop flapping it. Today we'll sail.

Zek and Ferro were in their group, as well as three other pairs of beasts and guardians: Trina, Saril, and Kita, with their beasts, Hava, Quil, and Uma. All of them jostled together, talking and laughing, giddy, and for the first time, Mina felt like she was one of them. She was as excited as everyone else. They all greeted her by name just as cheerfully as they greeted Jyx, Ferro, and Zek.

"Stick together," Jyx said to Mina.

"Yeah, that way if anyone sees a butterfly that spits fire —" Zek began.

Ferro punched him lightly in the arm.

"Ow, I'm wounded!"

"Guess you'll have to go to the sick room instead of the city," Mina teased softly.

"I'm healed!" Zek said.

They all laughed.

They were herded by teachers onto a river ship that had been coated in the lightning-resistant rubber. Beasts were crowded together as far from the flammable masts and sails as possible, while the guardians were free to roam around the ship. Jyx and Mina ran from side to side as a wind guardian filled the ship's sails. They waved goodbye to the school.

Mina hadn't seen the barren lands when they'd arrived, since it had been nighttime, though of course she'd seen them many times from the windows of the school and from the air. Somehow, seeing the blackened hills from the raised river ship felt different. Leaning against the side of the ship, she felt the wind in her face and breathed in the briny smell — in this direction, the river would be fresh water, but the ship still smelled of seaweed and fish and salty air. They'd make the return trip tomorrow, when the current reversed direction. On either side of the raised river, the hills looked beautiful, even though they were charred like burned bread — there were variations in the blackness: silhouettes of leafless trees, rocks that huddled in circles like travelers around a fire. Beyond the black hills, the mountains watched the river ship wend its way toward the city.

Out of the corner of her eye, she noticed that Ferro had come to stand beside her. "Missed you at lightning relay," he said.

She was so startled that she gawked at him.

"You think of new stuff." He shrugged. "It's funner."

Zek joined them. "'Funner' is not a word."

"I said it. Must be a word."

"Not the only criterion. Definitely not a word."

"She understood what I meant," Ferro said. "That makes it a word. Right, Mina? You knew what I meant; therefore we had communication. Therefore, it's a word."

Zek snorted. "Saying 'therefore' doesn't make you sound smarter. Being right does. Mina, tell him he's an idiot. He doesn't believe me when I say it."

Mina looked at Ferro, then at Zek. She was saved from answering by Jyx, who jumped in, saying, "You're both idiots. But luckily, you're with us, so that raises the average intelligence on this side of the ship." She winked at Mina, who grinned back.

I think I really do have friends.

«*You do,*» Pixit said warmly.

"Look!" Jyx cried, pointing. "The city!"

FIFTEEN

LAUGHING and jostling one another, the students and their beasts poured off the river ships onto the dock, and then they all crammed together into one of the trains. Mina was in the middle of it all — Zek's elbow rammed into her side, Chauda's fishy breath on her neck, and Pixit's shoulder pressed against her back. But for once, she didn't mind the crowd — she was with friends.

She belonged.

The doors slid closed, and the train zoomed away from the dock. All around her, the students and their beasts pointed and shouted at everything around them.

On the street below, a lightning guardian was creating a flower out of streaks of electricity. It sizzled and vanished before their eyes.

Farther on, two sun beasts were beaming light onto the

glass panes in a skyscraper, in a rhythm that made it seem like it was a kind of dance.

By a fountain, six rain guardians were practicing their routine. One tossed a water-ball into the air, and another caught it and then threw it at a third, who then shot the water up into a spray that rained down like sparkling confetti, landing back in the fountain pool without a drop missed. The lightning kids cheered, Mina included. *Did you see that?* she asked Pixit.

«*Do you see* that?» He was looking up above the train, where six wind guardians flew in a V formation like geese. A hundred pieces of paper were tumbling in the wind behind them, and as Mina watched, the wind whipped the sheets into a spiral and then twisted them, folding each one quickly, until they became a hundred paper birds flying behind the guardians.

"Step lively, children!" Professor Werrin called. "There's much more to see!" Thumping her cane and then holding it up so they could all follow, Professor Werrin led them off the train and across a bridge.

Looking down, Mina saw that the bridge itself was glass. She thought of the masterpieces in Mytris, made by graduates, and wondered if this was lightning-made glass. Or it could have been regular glass, heated by a sun beast and shaped by a sun guardian. Through it, distorted, she could see the streets of the capital, teeming with people and beasts and various carts and contraptions that ran on their own with so many gears that they looked like the innards of a clock.

Beside her, Jyx was bouncing as she walked. "Mina, I think we're going to see *her*!"

«*Who?*»

Mina asked out loud for Pixit. "Who?"

"The prime minister! Remember? I told you she's going to speak to us, but I didn't think it would be *now* or that we'd be allowed *inside*!"

«*Inside where? Mina, I can't see.*» On all fours, Pixit was shorter than the humans, and unlike the other beasts, he couldn't use his wings to fly up for a better view.

Craning her neck and walking on tiptoes, Mina tried to see over the heads of those around her. Up ahead was an archway painted with images: storm beasts, with blue sky behind them. At the apex was the Alorrian sun symbol, its rays inlaid with gold, along with the words "A true heart is never a mistake." Seeing those words — the same words as in the letter that came with the river-ship tickets — Mina smiled. She felt as if they were welcoming her personally, as if she was supposed to come here.

Nearly everything famous that had happened in history — every decision made, every law passed, every judgment rendered — had happened through this archway. Inside the capitol, the prime minister met with the advisors, and together they led Alorria.

It was the most famous place in the whole country.

And we get to go inside!

«Do you think they have a place for me to pee?»

Oh, Pixit.

«It was a long river ride.»

We'll look, she promised. She thought of Beon and Rinna and how they needed bathrooms at the most inconvenient times too. She imagined telling them about seeing the archway and the city with all the people and buildings and fountains and trains. With a twinge of guilt, Mina realized she hadn't thought of home in a while. She should be missing her family more.

She wondered if they'd be amazed to see her in the midst of all the other students, as if she were no different from any of them.

As they all filed through the archway, Mina gawked at the capitol. The domed ceiling was filled with more murals, each showing a scene from Alorria's history: the great storms of the past, the taming of the skies, the plowing of the fields, the building of the city, the closing of the borders. She wished she'd brought her sketchbook. She could have at least tried to capture it all to show her family later.

A woman's voice, unnaturally loud, boomed across the hall. "Welcome, lightning guardians and beasts, to the capitol." Her voice echoed, seeming to come from multiple locations at once.

Mina strained to see who spoke. At last she spotted the speaker: a woman dressed in reflective silver standing on a platform next to an odd tangle of metal tubes.

"Welcome to the birthplace of Alorria. It was here that the first laws that governed the use of storm beasts were passed, here that it was determined how to save and protect Alorria, here that the country changed from chaos and poverty to peace and prosperity!"

Jyx elbowed her. "That's her! That's — oh, no, wait. It's not. It's just an underminister." The prime minister appointed dozens of underministers to help with the day-to-day running of the government. "Do you think we won't get to see her? Ooh, Mina, the underminister is using a speaking tube! I've heard of them. Lightning-powered. Makes your voice twice as loud. Three times. A hundred times. The more lightning, the louder your voice. They'll use them at the festival. Ooh, look, it has a projector, too! That's a device that throws your image onto a wall." A somewhat watery image of the underminister, five times larger than life, rippled across one of the walls. Mina had never seen anything like it. It was amazing!

«Mina? I really need to go.»

"Be right back," Mina whispered to Jyx. She threaded through the press of students and beasts, bringing Pixit with her, until she reached the edge of the group. Professor Dano was on the outskirts — all the professors who had come were positioned around the group, keeping the students and their beasts herded in a clump. In a whisper, she explained what Pixit needed.

He rolled his eyes but pointed to a door half-hidden behind a gold curtain. She hurried through and was relieved to see that the doorway was wide enough for a storm beast. Pixit dashed after her.

It was easy to find the bathrooms — clearly labeled, one for beasts and one for humans. Mina waited in the hall while Pixit ducked inside.

Even the hall outside the bathrooms was gorgeous in the capitol, covered in murals made of bits of glass. Mostly blue and green, they showed a storm over the ocean, with waves as high as the skyscrapers and tiny boats capsizing on them. She wondered what she was missing and hoped Jyx would fill her in when they got back. *Hurry up, Pixit. This is a once-in-a-lifetime treat! We're in the heart of Alorria!*

«*You know they put jewels around the —* »

Pixit.

«*Sorry. Hurrying.*»

She heard footsteps, and she flattened against the wall. *Pixit?*

«*One minute. Can't rush this.*»

She reminded herself they were supposed to be here. All the lightning students had been invited today. Other students would visit the capitol on other days, but today they were supposed to be here, and it was okay that she was in the hallway waiting for her beast.

But as footsteps and the hum of voices approached, Mina wished she could turn invisible. A woman with a face she'd seen thousands of times before — on banners and signs — came around the corner, tailed by an entourage of women and men in dark blue uniforms.

The woman had graying hair, soft cheeks with smile wrinkles, and kind eyes. She wore a white sheath dress — not unlike what Mother would have worn to a dress-up occasion. The only hint at her rank was the amulet with the Alorrian sun symbol that hung from her neck.

Mina was sure she'd forgotten how to breathe.

She stared, and every single thought fled her head except for one: *It's the prime minister.*

«*Who? Where?*» Pixit asked from inside the bathroom. «*Wait for me!*»

Mina didn't know what she was supposed to do. Bow? Curtsy? Faint?

The prime minister smiled warmly at her, as if Mina were a beloved neighbor, not a strange girl lingering in the hallway. "Ah, you must be one of the lightning students. Let me guess: you're waiting for your beast to finish in the bathroom."

Mina could only stare. She didn't remember how her throat worked. She felt as if she'd never formed a word before in her life.

"They're wonderful dears, but they can be so inconvenient sometimes." She gave Mina a wink. "Don't tell my beast I said that. Did you know I used to be a wind guardian, back when I was your age?"

Mina nodded, then shook her head, then just stared more.

One of the men beside the prime minister darted forward and whispered in the prime minister's ear. She nodded but waved him back. "Don't be silly. I can spare a moment for one of our brave volunteers. Truly, it is because of the loyalty and devotion to duty shown by our young people that Alorria prospers today." She laughed at herself. "Oh, don't I sound pompous!"

She didn't. In fact, she sounded like any of Mina's neighbors, friendly and ordinary. Mina tried to think of a response. *I have to say something!* When she got home and Gaton asked her what she'd said when she was face-to-face with the prime minister, she couldn't say she'd said *nothing*.

He'd expect that, though, she thought.

There was no one who would be surprised if Mina said nothing at all.

"Would you like to ask me a question?" the prime minister asked. "I'm always happy to answer questions our young people have."

Mina opened her mouth.

Nothing came out.

The prime minister laughed again, but it wasn't unkind. Mina felt as if she was laughing with Mina, not at her. "You'll think of a thousand when I'm gone, I'm sure. But you can ask your teachers. I'm certain they're training you well. You must be excited for the Ten-Year Festival. I know I am." She shared another smile. "In a way, it's my first too, at least my first as prime minister, and I promise you it will demonstrate just how amazing Alorria is and how worthy it is of your service."

The man who had whispered to her before darted forward again with another whisper. This time, the prime minister didn't wave him away. She gave Mina yet another of her warm, motherly smiles and said, "Happy storms, child." And she started past Mina.

Her perfume smelled like oranges, and as the scent wafted

past, a question popped into Mina's head, and she blurted it out:

"Does the festival cause the ten-year storms beyond the mountains?"

The assistants gasped. A few of them whispered to one another.

The prime minister stopped. She didn't turn. "Oh, how very disappointing. That's not an appropriate question, lightning child. I think it best if you do not attend the rest of today's events." She then swept on, and her assistants scurried behind her, all except one.

The one who remained, a large man with bulging muscles beneath his tailored uniform, took Mina by the arm and began to haul her down the hallway, in the opposite direction. *Oh no, what did I do?* She tried to think of what to say and how to apologize, but the prime minister was already out of earshot.

«*Mina?*» Pixit bounded out of the bathroom.

It's my fault. I said something I shouldn't.

«*I heard you. I thought you asked a good question! Why did she get mad?*» He wanted to spark lightning at the assistant who was marching Mina down the hallway, away from all the other students. «*And where is he taking you?*»

I don't know. Get Professor Dano, she told him. Someone had to be told she was being taken . . . somewhere . . . and Professor Dano at least wasn't the headmistress. Mina didn't want to even imagine the look on Professor Werrin's face if she heard that Mina had insulted the prime minister.

The overly strong assistant deposited her in a room lined with gold chairs. Before she could figure out how to ask how much trouble she was in, the man had left without a single word, closing the door behind him. She tried the door — it wasn't locked — but she didn't dare leave and risk getting in more trouble. She hoped Pixit would return soon.

Mina waited. She tried sitting in one of the chairs, but then sprang up after a second and began pacing. She didn't think the question had been so terrible. It was one she'd been worrying about — a real question, not a how-are-you-today small-talk question. Wasn't that what the prime minister wanted? Wouldn't she want to be asked an important question?

I didn't do anything wrong.

I don't deserve to be punished.

The more she thought about it, the more convinced she was that this wasn't fair. She thought of the words over the archway to the capitol: "A true heart is never a mistake." Well, she'd been true to her heart. The prime minister had invited her to ask a question, and so she had. A good question. One that mattered. Just because the prime minister hadn't liked it . . .

Why hadn't she liked it?

Maybe it wasn't that she didn't like the question . . .

Maybe the prime minister didn't like the answer.

Mina stopped thinking about how unfair it was to be punished for asking a question and started thinking about what the prime minister's reaction meant. If the prime minister hadn't known what Mina was talking about, if the question had never been asked before, if the answer was that storm guardians were innocent and what a silly child she was for even worrying, then Mina wouldn't be here, sequestered in this room, away from the other students, safely prevented from asking that question where anyone else could hear.

"It means the answer is yes," Mina said out loud.

Worse, it meant the prime minister *knew* the answer was yes.

⟞CHAPTER⟝
SIXTEEN

*W*E'RE *here to rescue you!»* Pixit cried as he burst through the door — and promptly got stuck in the door frame. If she hadn't been so anxious, Mina would have laughed.

Behind him, she heard Professor Dano's voice. "Stop. You won't do any good shoving forward — your shoulders won't fit. You need to back up and wait here."

Chastened, Pixit wriggled backward, freeing himself, and plopped down in the hallway just outside the door. He looked in, forlornly, at Mina. *It'll be okay*, she reassured him. As Professor Dano came through the door, though, Mina wished she'd prepared what to say.

"Can you explain why your ridiculous storm beast dragged me, with his teeth, out of the hall?" he demanded. "Are you hurt?"

She shook her head.

He softened his tone. "Overwhelmed? I know the city can be over-the-top."

"I . . ." Mina swallowed. She had to speak. "I offended the prime minister." Her voice was barely more than a whisper, but he heard her anyway. "She said I can't attend the rest of today's events, and one of her assistants put me here."

Professor Dano frowned. "What precisely did you say?"

She found the words to answer that: "I asked the prime minister if the festival causes the ten-year storms."

She'd expected to see anger. Or exasperation. Or disappointment.

She hadn't expected to see fear.

Or, she thought, maybe even a little awe.

His face went pasty pale, and his eyes wide. For a second, he didn't speak. Then he sputtered, "'Ten-year storms'? You really said that? To the prime minister?"

"Yes. You said in one of your lectures that all the weather in the world is connected, and so when I heard about the storms, I started to think —"

"How did you know the ten-year storms exist —" He cut himself off. "You crossed the mountains that day, in the thunderstorm, didn't you?"

He didn't seem to need an answer, but Pixit tried to answer for her. «*It was an accident. I was hurt, and we crashed...*» Of course Professor Dano couldn't hear him. «*Mina, you need to tell him it's not your fault.*»

I don't think it matters whether it was or wasn't, she told Pixit.

"Why, by the grace of storms, would you question the prime minister herself? I know I wanted you to ask questions, but I meant ask *me*." He sounded torn between exasperation and pride.

She didn't have an answer for that, and Professor Dano didn't seem to need one. He placed his hands on her shoulders so she had to look directly into his eyes. "This is important. Did anyone ask your name?"

"Um . . ." Had they? She tried to remember. She didn't think so. Mina shook her head.

"So the prime minister doesn't know who you are? Just that you're a lightning student?" He exhaled as if he hadn't been breathing properly before. She wondered why it mattered, and then jumped as he took her arm, the same way the assistant had, to tug her forward. "We have to keep it that way. They stashed you here to keep you from causing a scene during the prime minister's talk. When it's over, they'll return for you and most likely ask questions you don't want to answer. Come with me. I'll get you back to the ship before that happens." He herded her out of the room. Pixit wagged his tail, excited to see her. Professor Dano kept talking in a low whisper. "You'll stay out of sight. Tell everyone you were sick. If you can manage to vomit a few times, that would be excellent. *Don't* tell them what happened, or what you said."

Grim-faced, he propelled her through the hallway and through a nondescript door. This next corridor was plain gray, with no murals or any other decoration, and lit with a few electric light bulbs. She guessed it was for the cleaning crew. She didn't think this was the time to ask for a tour.

Professor Dano seemed to know the way. He hurried her and Pixit through a storage room filled with brooms, mops, and buckets, and then out a door onto a narrow bridge. It was barely wide enough for Pixit. It ran directly below a far wider bridge, like it was tucked into its shadows. "Where are we?" she asked.

"Maintenance bridge," he replied. "Beneath the archway. You'll tell people you never left the ship this morning. You were too sick."

"But people saw me."

"Fine, then. You left the ship, but you came back sick. Were any of the other students close enough to tell you weren't ill? Did you talk with any of them?"

"Yes. I talked to Jyx, Ferro, and Zek. Are they going to be in trouble too?"

"They can get *you* in trouble, if they tell the wrong person you weren't sick." He grimaced. "You'll need to prove to your friends you've been sick so no one suspects you were the one who spoke with the prime minister. Vomit on one of them, if you can. With luck, by the time anyone thinks to question them, that's all they'll talk about."

«*You should throw up on Chauda,*» Pixit suggested. «*That would be funny.*»

Nothing about this is funny, Mina told him.

In a very small voice in her mind, he said, «*That would be a little bit funny.*»

"Once we're back to Mytris, you'll be given a leave of absence to visit your family. That way, if the prime minister sends any-one to the school to identify you, you won't be there to be iden-tified. You won't have to answer any uncomfortable questions, and you won't have to admit you crossed the border. A week should be sufficient. The prime minister should lose interest in you quickly enough — in the grand scheme of things, this was a minor infraction. Unfortunately, we'll need to label the absence an academic suspension in order for Professor Werrin to approve it. It will be on your record."

Mina stumbled over her feet, and Professor Dano hauled her upright. "It's that serious?" She hadn't thought a simple question could cause that much trouble. She didn't understand why Professor Dano was reacting this way.

"Just a precaution. You wouldn't know this, of course — how could you? — but you asked a sensitive question at a sensitive time. Rumors have been flying between storm guardians for a while about the connection between our weather control within Alorria and the devastating storms beyond our borders. The prime minister has been attempting to squelch those rumors — and she sees the festival as proof that all is well, the rumors are baseless, and change is unnecessary."

Did that mean . . . *Am I right? There is a connection?*

"Given the closeness of the festival and the sensitivity of the issue right now, I don't want the prime minister to decide to make an example of a promising student by expelling you for promoting so-called 'false propaganda.'" He stepped off the bridge and strode straight across the platform onto a train.

Pixit hopped behind them, barely making it on before the doors shut.

"I'm . . . promising?" That wasn't a word she'd thought any professor would apply to her. She still hadn't made a spark on her fingers, much less caught a bolt in lightning relay. She was so-so at flying, and with Pixit's wing hurt, she couldn't even do that.

"Oh yes. There's more to being a great guardian than spark and sizzle." And Professor Dano smiled at her — one of the only times she'd seen that expression on his face.

The train sped away, taking them back to the ship.

$$\lightning$$

She was tucked into a cot belowdecks, where it smelled bad enough that she thought she might really throw up. Professor Dano procured a bucket with the dregs of fish stew in it to serve as proof of her illness, and he warned the sailors that she might be contagious. He also splashed some of the stew on the hem of his teacher robes. Then he bustled off, back to the capitol, to spread word that "Oh, poor little Mina, she's so ill. I took her back to the ship. Look — she was sick on my robes. Such a shame. For her, of course, not the robes, though they'll need to be laundered. She was sad to miss all the excitement."

Mina wasn't sad at all.

She was mostly terrified.

Lying in her cot, she imagined all the ways this could go

horribly wrong. Every time the stairs creaked, she was sure it was someone here to take her away. Her parents would get a letter, drifting in on a beautiful red balloon, saying their daughter had been expelled for spreading "false propaganda," whatever that meant. She'd be sent home, and she'd lose everything she'd ever dreamed of becoming. *And it would all be my fault, because one time I didn't stay quiet.*

«*It's not your fault,*» Pixit said.

He was directly above her, on the rubber on the deck. *Yes, it is.* She'd finally started to feel like she belonged — she had friends! She fit in! — and then she'd had to go and put it all in jeopardy.

«*It's not wrong to ask questions. And if the prime minister is afraid of the answer, maybe that means you asked the right question. And maybe it means you need to ask more.*»

She chewed on that thought for a while, until she heard the clatter of the students and beasts returning to the river ship. Pixit broadcast his thoughts to her as he greeted Chauda, Brindle, and Ragit. He told them all, as planned, that she was ill belowdecks and that they should encourage the guardians to see her and tell her what she'd missed — but that they should keep their distance because she was really sick.

Flopping limply in the cot, Mina waited for the sound of footsteps on the ladder. It wasn't long before Jyx, Ferro, and Zek half climbed and half jumped down into the hold. "Gah!" Ferro said. "This smells worse than my grandmother's socks!"

"This smells worse than your grandmother," Zek said.

"Seriously? You're insulting Grammy?"

"Sorry," Zek said. "It was just so easy."

Jyx hurried into the tiny room with the cots. She skidded to a stop several feet away from Mina's cot. "Mina! You look awful."

Mina tried not to be offended by that, since she wasn't actually sick. She gave her a halfhearted wave, as if she didn't have the strength for anything more. She then screwed up her face and grabbed for the bucket as Zek and Ferro came into the room. She coughed hard into it, and then looked up to see that all three of them were clustered by the door.

"We can, uh, leave you alone to rest," Zek said.

Mina leaned back heavily, as if the exertion had taken all her strength. She knew how to play sick — Gaton had done it often enough to avoid being sent to sell on market day. "It might make me feel better if you tell me what I missed?" Mina made her voice sound pathetic.

Brightening, Jyx launched into a description of the inside of the capitol, as well as the various acts they'd seen practicing for the festival. And then Ferro chimed in with an impression of the prime minister, quoting bits of her speech about the glories of Alorria.

The glories of Alorria, Mina thought as he prattled on. *And what is the cost of those glories? Doesn't anyone else wonder about that?* Professor Dano said rumors had been flying for some time. *But is anyone doing anything about it?*

She watched her friends and their excitement over the

upcoming festival. She wondered how they'd feel if they knew that all the celebrating caused terrible storms.

«*Tell them,*» Pixit urged.

I can't. If they go and tell the wrong person . . .

But she also thought of the outsiders she'd met. She remembered Varli pressing his fingers to his forehead and saying, "Stars and moon help us all when the ten-year storms come." Knowing what she knew now, how could she stay quiet?

On the other hand, what good would speaking up do? She'd asked one innocent question, and it had very nearly caused a world of trouble — and still could. If she spoke again, she'd do more harm than good. After all, it wasn't like the prime minister was going to cancel the festival just because one kid thought maybe she should.

I'm sorry, Pixit, she thought. *I can't.*

I have to find another way.

⌐CHAPTER⌐

SEVENTEEN

As Mina rode a river ship away from Mytris, toward the farmlands, she kept coming back to the same thought:

They should cancel the festival.

Unless the prime minister was 100 percent certain that the rumors were false, why risk people's lives and homes for the sake of a celebration? The festival was two weeks away — it wasn't too late to cancel.

«*You should tell people the truth.*»

He made it sound so simple.

«*It is simple.*» Munching on a potato, Pixit didn't look at her. He'd been sulking for most of the trip, and she knew it was because of her. «*You know what you should do. We found something wrong in the world; we should fix it.*»

She knew she'd disappointed him by not shouting from the rooftops what she'd learned. But if she tried, she'd be expelled, and then how would she make a difference in the world? The festival would *still* go on, and the ten-year storms would *still* hit the Dern outpost, as well as anyone else who lived beyond the mountains.

«I know you, Mina. I know what you're capable of. You do sparkle. Or you could, if you let yourself.»

She hated the way disappointing him made her feel, as if she were squirming inside her skin. *I'm sorry, Pixit,* she thought miserably.

«I just wish you'd do what I know you want to do.»

At last, they reached their destination. Shouldering her pack, Mina walked off the ship. Pixit followed behind. She stopped at the top of the steps and glanced back at him. *You're going to have to walk down these. Do you think you can fit?*

The doctors had told him that by the time they returned to Mytris, he'd be able to fly again, but until then he wasn't supposed to do anything to strain his wing muscles. Mina had told Jyx and her other friends that this was the reason for her visit home: so Pixit could rest and recover. She wished Professor Dano had used that as the reason too, instead of marking the week as an academic suspension.

Pixit poked his nose over the edge and chirped, *«I see Papa!»*

She looked over with him. Down below, far below, was a tiny cart with a horse. Seated in the driver's seat was a man with a broad blue hat — Papa!

Excited, Pixit squeezed himself down the stairs. His much-wider-than-before body pushed the rope railing out, and he stretched his good wing for balance. On the plus side, now that he was older and more mature, he could control his sparks better, so he didn't fry the rope. «*Can I hug Papa today?*»

Yes! She'd make sure of it. This time, she'd be Pixit's voice. She smiled, feeling a fraction better at the thought of making him happy.

When they reached the ground, Pixit bounded to the cart. «*Tell him I'm safe!*»

Jumping down from the cart, Papa ran to Mina. He scooped her up, pack and all, and swung her in a half circle before putting her down again. "You've — well, you haven't grown. But Pixit has. Hello, Pixit." Papa smiled broadly at Pixit.

Pixit was hopping from foot to foot. A little drool had pooled at the corner of his mouth. He licked it away with a quick jab of his tongue and kept hopping.

"He'd like to hug you hello."

Papa drew back. "Now, as I recall . . ."

She tasted Pixit's disappointment, like limp vegetables, and she thought of how she'd let Mother keep him from her bedroom after he was born. She kept disappointing him. *Not this time.* "He missed you too," Mina said firmly. "After all that time with me talking to him in his egg, you're like his papa too." Her heart was beating faster as she spoke up. She couldn't remember ever having interrupted her father before. "He's learned control, and it would make him happy — and me — if you'd let him hug you."

"Oh, well, in that case." Papa opened his arms, and Pixit bounded up to him like a puppy, leaning hard against him.

Papa patted his back as he hugged him, and Mina felt Pixit's rush of joy.

Pixit hadn't been safe to touch before, it was true, but Mina still wished she'd said something about how he'd felt, back when he'd first hatched. Maybe her family would have been happier to see him, if they'd known he cared about them, but there had been all the craziness with the fire in the fields and then the letter . . .

At least she'd said something now. *Better late than never.*

«Which is why you should speak up about the festival and the ten-year storms!»

That's different.

She could feel him disagree with her — it was like a whiff of curdled milk. She wished she could shut the feeling off. She didn't want to argue with someone within her own head.

«I'm not arguing,» Pixit protested. *«I'm having an opinion.»*

Can you not have it inside my head?

«You're inside my *head.»*

Oh.

"Come on, let's get you two home," Papa said. He guided Mina to the cart and helped her up onto the seat. He then pointed to a blanket in the back. "You didn't shock me, so I'm going to assume you've learned enough at that training school to avoid burning that to a crisp?"

As an answer, Pixit jumped up into the back of the cart. Papa climbed into the driver's seat and snapped the reins, and the horse jolted forward into a trot.

In silence, Papa drove between farms, and Mina drank it all in: the deep green of the hip-high wheat, the pale green of the just-planted beans, the rich brown soil between the rows. It smelled right too. She inhaled the familiar mix of old manure and fresh greenery. It was near sunset, and the sun was a hand's spread away from touching the distant mountains. Already some of the clouds had started to pinken.

As the sun sank, she saw their farmhouse in the distance, framed by a glorious array of rose, orange, and golden clouds.

Gaton had said that when she came back, home would feel smaller than it used to. But this didn't feel that way at all. Home felt just right. As they drew closer, she saw the twins running around in the yard — from this distance they looked tiny, but she was sure it was them.

"Mina," Papa said hesitantly. "I want you to know no one blames you."

Blames me for what? She felt as if her heart were squeezing inside her. *Did Professor Dano tell them what I said to the prime minister?* He wouldn't have. Not after he'd insisted she lie to her friends. Not after he'd lied to everyone in the school.

"I know training can be difficult," Papa said. "Especially when you're, well, you . . ." He trailed off. "Anyway, we're happy to have you home. And if you don't want to go back, we'll support your choice. We know you tried."

"I . . ." Mina wanted to tell him she hadn't been sent home because she was failing, except that it was true that she hadn't succeeded in getting lightning to spark on her fingers yet, and

Professor Dano had used that — and the fact that she'd tried to hide it — as the excuse for the academic suspension. Apparently, he'd been keeping a close enough eye on her to notice she *was* failing to perform even that basic skill.

«*We aren't failing. We just haven't succeeded yet.*»

If only she'd managed to spark!

"I just need to figure a few things out," she told Papa.

Papa smiled as if he understood, and he steered the cart toward home. She heard Rinna and Beon joyfully shrieking as Orli swooped over them. The rain beast was dangling a ribbon from her talons, and every few seconds she'd fly lower so it dragged on the grass. The twins chased after it, trying to catch it, and an instant before they could seize it in their pudgy hands, Orli would swoop back up.

"It's their new game," Papa said. "Gets them nice and tired for naptime."

It was brilliant. She wished she'd thought of it.

He whistled to the horse, and they stopped in front of the porch. Mina climbed down and went to help remove the horse's bridle, but Papa stopped her. "You go on in. Get settled. Rest. You've had a long journey."

"Papa . . ." She tried to think of the right words to say what she meant without *exactly* saying what she meant. "If you found out that the game Orli was playing with Rinna and Beon made them happy but somehow also, I don't know, made another set of kids somewhere . . . sick, or something, what would you do?"

"Tell them to find another game to play," Papa said promptly. "But don't you worry: this game isn't hurting anyone. Orli is careful not to lead the twins anywhere they could get hurt, and she's smart enough to know when they need a rest."

That was sort of an answer, she supposed. Papa unhooked the horse from the cart and led him toward the stable.

Pixit jumped off the back of the cart and brushed by her on his way up to the porch. «*That was a start.*»

He didn't understand what I meant.

«A *start for you, not for him.*» She felt blanketed in warm encouragement. He had faith in her, even though she'd let him down. Maybe, somehow, she could find a way to talk about what she knew about the storms beyond the border in a way that would help the people she wanted to help.

Pixit nosed the front door open and then hesitated. *You can go inside*, Mina told him. They'd widened the doorways years ago to fit Orli. Even as much as Pixit had grown, which was a lot, he'd fit through. *You aren't going to burn the house down, not now that you're older.*

He put a paw across the threshold.

"You can't come inside!" Mother shrieked from the kitchen. Pixit froze.

Mother poked her head out the window. "Sorry, Mina, Pixit. It's not you. I just washed the floor. Can you come to the back?"

They trotted around the house. As they went past, Rinna and Beon broke off their game and attached themselves like barnacles to Mina's legs, one on each side. "Mina, Mina, Mina, you're home! And you brought the sparkly pony! Can we ride him? Please, please, please?" It was all said in a jumble so fast that she didn't know which of them said what.

Laughing, she knelt and hugged them both.

«*Tell them they can ride me if they want.*»

"He said yes."

Cheering, the twins flung themselves at Pixit and then scrambled onto his back. Rinna poked at a spark of electricity. "Hee-hee, it tickles!"

"Ooh, ooh, me too!" Beon grabbed for a spark as if it were a bubble he wanted to pop.

Taking care to control his electricity, Pixit walked in a circle around the yard while Rinna and Beon shouted and clapped and cheered. Mina was happy to see that Papa didn't try to separate the twins from Pixit.

This is good, Mina thought. *They're treating him like he belongs.* She guessed it had just taken a while for them to accept that Pixit was who he was.

«*Just like your family and friends will accept you, when you act like the person I know you are.*»

She didn't reply to that.

Going inside, she went toward the kitchen to greet Mother, stopping just shy of the kitchen floor. It still glistened from its recent scrubbing, and Mother was under the sink with a wrench in her hand. "Hi, Mother."

Mother scooted out from under the sink and smiled at Mina.

"Welcome home, sweetie." Her face crinkled as she smiled, and Mina suddenly realized how much she'd missed all of them.

Fingers tickled her from behind, and Mina jumped forward, her toes landing on the kitchen floor. "No walking on the floor," Mother said, at the same time as Gaton, behind her, said, "Ha! Surprised you! Glad you're back. On a totally unrelated note, I'm not doing your chores anymore, and the chickens need to be fed."

"*Gaton*," Mother said. "Mina, he's kidding."

"Actually, I'm not," Gaton said. "Okay, yes, I am. Sort of."

"Go rest," Mother said to Mina. "I'll call you when dinner's ready, though we won't have it in the kitchen, because the floor is perfectly and beautifully —"

The twins burst through the kitchen door and tumbled inside, wrapped in a muddy ribbon. Clumps of dirt flew across the room and smacked into the cabinets, then dribbled down onto the floor.

Mina smothered a giggle as Mother sighed theatrically.

Beon and Rinna took one look at her face, yelped, and bolted back outside.

"I'll help you wash it again," Mina offered.

Mother waved away her words. "No, thank you. I think I will strap sponges to the twins and just roll them around the kitchen."

«*I want to watch that,*» Pixit said, his head poking in through the open window.

I don't think she's serious. Or not very serious. Backing into the living room, Mina watched Gaton pull on his boots, preparing to head to the chicken coop. "Gaton . . ." She tried to figure out what exactly she wanted to ask her brother, about what he knew about weather being connected and about storms across the border, but before she could, Gaton was out the door. He'd been a guardian longer than she had, and Professor Dano had said the rumors had been circulating for a while. Had Gaton heard them?

But he was gone before she could think of the words she wanted to say.

Or if she wanted to say anything at all.

⚡

A week passed quickly at home. Mina took back all her old chores, and she tried to tell herself that there was nothing that she could do to stop the Ten-Year Festival and help the people beyond the mountains. She was just one lightning-guardian-in-training, and not a very good one at that. She couldn't even spark. Who would listen to her, even if she did speak?

«*I'd listen.*» Pixit was watching her from the other side of the chicken-wire fence as Mina fed the chickens scraps from breakfast.

You're the only one.

«*That's not true,*» he thought quietly.

Squawking, the chickens pecked at her feet. She scooted

back and tossed the food across the coop, far away from her toes. *I can't.*

She looked up at the mountains, softened by distance into a nice background landscape, like a painting on a wall. Miles and miles away, Neela, Eione, Varli, and everyone they cared about were preparing for the ten-year storm. *I don't know how to stop the festival. And if I tell anyone what I know, I'll be expelled, and what good would that do? I can't help anyone if I'm expelled.*

«*Your family won't expel you,*» Pixit pointed out. «*They love you.*»

She finished with the chickens. That was true. *They're going to yell.*

He considered that. «*Probably.*»

It was tempting. If she could get them to listen . . . *They aren't going to even let me say it all before they start to yell.*

Pixit considered that, too. «*Talk really fast.*»

She wanted to tell them, especially if there was a chance they'd believe her and support her. She didn't like carrying this heavy secret. *But what's the point in telling them? How are they going to stop the festival? It's happening in just one week!*

Pixit trotted to the house. He was so excited that sparks hopped between his scales like minnows stranded on a beach. «*Let's find out! Come on, Mina, make a start!*» His excitement spilled into her, and she felt like she had the first time she'd seen lightning relay — surprised at her own excitement. She jogged toward the house, matching his pace.

Inside, Gaton was sewing ribbons onto Beon's festival

costume, or trying to. He was wrestling with a sleeve, while Beon wrestled on the floor with Rinna. Rinna had curled herself around what looked like one of Arde's chew toys, and Beon was trying to pry it out of her arms. Mother was reading in a chair next to the fireplace, and Papa was frowning at a ledger.

Beon and Rinna quit wrestling each other the moment they saw Pixit, and they pounced on him. "Sparkly puppy! Wing fixed? Fly now?"

Pixit looked at Mina with plaintive eyes. *«Tell them my wing still hurts, please?»*

He should have been healed by now. She eyed him with concern — they'd taken a few trial flights around the house just this morning. He hadn't complained of any pain then. *Does it still hurt?*

«Only when your brother chews on it.»

She looked down to see that Beon had stuffed the tip of Pixit's wing into his mouth.

"Spit it out, Beon," Mina told him firmly.

He looked startled — she rarely spoke like that. Pixit, though, couldn't speak for himself. She was getting better at speaking for him. "But I like how it tickles!" Beon objected.

Mother snapped her book shut. "Beon, you heard your sister. We don't eat our friends."

Sadly, Beon spat out the tip of Pixit's wing.

At least this had drawn everyone's attention. Mina felt them all looking at her and Pixit, and she wanted to dart outside and find another chore to do.

"Everyone . . ." Mina began. "I, um . . . You know how I was suspended? I want to tell you . . ." She swallowed, as all the words seemed to desert her.

Papa looked up from his ledger.

"It's all right, Mina," Mother said gently. "We aren't angry with you. If anything, we're angry with ourselves for letting you go, when we knew all along Mytris wasn't a good fit for you."

Papa nodded. "We worried about this — not that we didn't believe in you, but we worried that you wouldn't be happy at a lightning school. We worried that they wouldn't appreciate you. Sweetie, you don't have to return if you don't want."

The kindness in their voices, coupled with their complete misreading of who she was and what she wanted, kept her speechless. She stared at them both. Not return?

Gaton snorted. "Don't be ridiculous, Papa. She has to finish her training, become a storm guardian, and train until her 'sparkly puppy' fizzles out."

"Everyone has a choice," Papa told him sharply.

"Yeah, but Mina wants to be a guardian," Gaton said. "Right, Mina?"

This was not what she wanted to talk about. "I do, but . . ."

Papa pressed. "If she's unhappy there, then she doesn't have to stay. I'd never force one of my children to do anything that makes them unhappy."

Gaton muttered, "You make me clean the goat pen."

"This is serious, Gaton," Mother said. "Mina, are you unhappy? Do you want to stay at home?"

Mina cleared her throat. "Really, that's not —"

"I know it's serious!" Gaton stood up, the ribbons falling off his lap. "Do you know how many families enter the lottery for an egg? How many kids dream of their own beast? Only one in four ever has the chance, and the rest miss out. I know Mina wants this!"

Beside her, Pixit bristled. He leaned against her. «*They're not listening to you.*» Sparks crackled over his scales. Mina felt the hair on the back of her neck rise. Her skin began to tickle. But her family kept arguing, about her, about what they thought she wanted, without letting her say a word.

She wanted to be a guardian. Gaton was right about that. She wanted to make the world a better place. She wanted to do the right thing. She wanted so very much!

Mina raised her hands, fingers spread. "Stop, please. All of you, stop!"

And sparks jumped between her fingers.

She stared at them. Tiny white bolts of electricity hopped from her thumbs to her index fingers to her middle fingers to her ring fingers to her pinkies. Closing and opening her hands, Mina watched the little bits of lightning dance on her palms.

Everyone stared at her.

"We did it," she said to Pixit.

«*We did it!*» he howled in her mind.

"How did we do it?"

«*Do it again!*»

Mina concentrated, and a ball of fuzzy light coalesced on her palm. *I can do it! I really am a lightning guardian!*

«*Of course you are. You always were!*»

Is it because I finally acted like one? I was finally loud?

Pixit snorted. «*No. It's because you finally let yourself be you. The you I know you are. The you who has something to say and finds her own way to say it. Not loud, but determined to be heard.*»

She threw herself toward Pixit and wrapped her arms around him. He curled his neck around her and hugged her with his wings. Peeling back, she turned to her family, smiling so hard that her cheeks hurt.

With words tumbling over one another, she said, "I'm going back to Mytris to become a lightning guardian. But first, I need to tell you that I believe controlling the weather creates storms on the other side of the mountains. Most of the time, the outsiders manage, but during the festival, we manipulate the weather so much that it causes deadly storms that kill lots of people and destroy lots of towns beyond Alorria. Even worse, the prime minister knows but doesn't want anyone to talk about it and doesn't plan to do anything to change things. I asked her about it, which made her mad, but she doesn't know who I am, so my professor sent me home to keep me safe. Now that I'm going back, though, I want to do something about it, because it's not right. If you see something in the world that isn't right, you have to try to fix it."

EIGHTEEN

For the first time in her life, Mina struck her entire family speechless.

It felt kind of nice.

But then they all started yelling.

Gaton: "Wait — you heard the rumors too? And you asked the prime minister?"

Papa: "I'm sure you're mistaken. The storm beasts *prevent* storms, not cause them. What happens beyond the mountains has nothing to do with us."

Mother: "You insulted the prime minister? She's a national hero! She isn't keeping secrets from her people! That's ridiculous!"

Gaton: "You're seriously brave. I've heard stories about the prime minister — she hates to be wrong. So you're saying this why you were suspended? I thought it was because you couldn't spark. Which, by the way, you just did."

Papa: "The weather in Alorria doesn't cause deaths beyond the mountains. I think you're overreacting. Yes, there has been discussion – "

Mother: "Lies. The festival doesn't 'kill lots of people.' Storm beasts keep people safe! That's the entire point of the celebration! Haven't you read your history?"

Gaton: "History approved by the prime minister! All weather is connected – the sky is all one piece. You can't dismiss facts just because you don't like where they lead."

Papa: "Now, now, I'm sure our government wouldn't deliberately lie. And I'm sure there's another logical explanation for these 'deadly storms.'"

Mother: "If they even exist. Has anyone seen a shred of proof? All I've heard is talk from people who have never even been beyond the mountains."

Gaton: "Are you saying Mina's lying?"

Papa: "Of course no one is saying that."

Mother: "I'm saying she's mistaken."

Gaton: "She talked with the prime minister!"

Mother: "But she didn't see any proof –"

Gaton: "She doesn't need proof; she has logic!"

Papa: "Let's all calm down."

The twins jumped up and began clamoring for attention.

Beon: "I want sparkles on my hand! Give me sparkles too!"

Rinna: "I don't want sparkles on my hand! Get them away!"

Everyone was shouting all at the same time, overlapping, with each of them getting louder and louder, trying to be heard. Mina inched closer to Pixit, and he kept his wings folded around her, like a shield. She wished his wings could block out the noise.

In a gap when everyone took a breath, Mina quietly quoted the old journal: "'It seems the more we try to fix the world, the more we break it.' The first storm guardians knew it. And the prime minister fears it. If you'll just think about it, you'll see it makes sense. As Gaton said, the sky's all connected."

Papa crossed the room but stopped just short of her. He didn't reach out to her — Pixit was still spraying sparks. "Mina, sweetie, these ideas, these thoughts . . . Even if there's some truth to them, I'm sure it's exaggerated. If it were true that 'lots' of people were being killed, we'd know, and we'd do something about it."

Mother nodded, worry in her eyes. "Pursuing these accusations is only going to get you in trouble. You've already been suspended once."

Now Papa put his arm around Mina's shoulders, sparks and all. "Mina wouldn't ever cause trouble. She's a good girl. She's not going to do anything foolish. She made a mistake, and she's sorry, and whatever happened with the prime minister is done now."

Mina felt herself deflate. *What if they're right? What if I'm overreacting and the storms aren't so bad?* After all, she only had the word of three outsiders.

«*And the prime minister's reaction.*»

That was true.

«And what you read in Professor Dano's books. It couldn't have been an accident that he told you to read them.»

Also true.

When did you get so wise?

«*I grew.*»

But if she couldn't make her own family do anything to stop it . . .

«*I believe you, Mina. And I believe in you.*»

His words made her feel like a warm fire was inside her rib cage. *Still, though, we're back to the same problem we had when we got here. If I start telling the world that the rumors are true and the festival needs to stop, I'll be expelled, and then what do I do? One expelled student can't stop an entire festival full of storm guardians* —

An idea began to form in her mind, as beautiful as lightning.

One student couldn't stop the festival. One voice shouting was easy to dismiss. But if *all* the lightning students at Mytris were to speak up at once . . .

That many voices have to be heard!

Beside her, Pixit sparked brighter than he ever had.

⚡

Before Papa drove her to the river station, Mina promised her parents she wouldn't get in trouble, she wouldn't get expelled, and she wouldn't insult the prime minister to her face ever again. Given that she had no intention of getting caught, these were easy promises to make.

"Alorria needs its storm guardians," Mother said. "If you don't cause any more trouble, I'm sure they'll let this slide. Focus on your training."

"I will," Mina said.

She then kissed everyone, and everyone fussed over her and Pixit. Mother sent her with a sack of "your favorites, sweetie, to eat on the journey — don't eat that fish stew." On the cart ride to the station, Mina peeked inside: honey cake and jelly.

Even though she'd upset everyone, they still loved her.

Mina smiled and tucked the sack into her bag for later. She rode in pleasant silence with Papa through the farms, and when they said goodbye, she promised to try her best at Mytris. And then she and Pixit were on the river ship again, ready to ride northwest, toward the barren lands.

The ship left late in the day and sailed through the night. She slept in the hammock, with Pixit on the rubber beside her, and arrived at Mytris shortly after breakfast. They found the other students outside on the practice field, and for an instant Mina felt as if she'd never left. Dropping her bag by the text-book shelves, she and Pixit slipped quietly onto the field with the others, certain that no one had noticed —

"Mina!" Jyx squealed. "You're back!" She barreled across the practice field, grabbing Zek's arm with one hand and Ferro's arm with the other and propelling them toward Mina. Their beasts all bounded after them. "Mina!"

They crowded around her, talking so fast that they over-lapped.

"Lost three relays this week!" Zek complained. "Vira's scheduled a ton of extra practice to get us ready for the festival. We need you!"

"Yeah," Ferro agreed. "You've got the best ideas. Even if you never catch anything."

Jyx jabbed him in the stomach. "Be nice."

"I *am* being nice!"

They began talking simultaneously about how nice Ferro was (or wasn't), who had scored how in their last match, and how they'd begun to practice for their role in the festival.

Mina slowly began to smile at them.

«*They missed you,*» Pixit told her.

I guess they did.

"Mina, you're just in time!" Jyx announced, bouncing again. "Lightning-collecting test today!"

Mina felt as if her heart skipped a beat. She hadn't had a chance to see if the sparks at her family's farmhouse had been a fluke.

«*We can do this.*»

Yes, we can. She believed that. Didn't she?

"Mount up!" Vira ordered.

Mina climbed onto Pixit's back and settled between his wings, and the old doubts and worries began to creep back in. What if she failed, spectacularly, in front of her teacher and her friends? Pixit murmured words of encouragement and optimism in her mind, but they couldn't penetrate the swirl of panic.

It was blue sky again, of course, except for one carefully

curated thundercloud. It had been delivered by wind guardians and fed by more experienced lightning guardians, in order for students to practice. At Vira's command, the four pairs of guardians and beasts, plus their teacher and her beast, took to the sky.

Mina felt her stomach clench as she looked at the thundercloud. *Pixit.*

«*We've got this.*»

Do we?

«*Maybe?*»

He was nervous too. She could feel it in her mind, his emotions skittering past hers. With the others, they circled the cloud.

Vira shouted to them. "Here's the test: one by one, I want you to enter the cloud, gather up lightning — no wimpy sparks, people, I want a fireball — and then come out. Then I want you to throw your lightning back into the cloud so it's there for the next one of you losers. Ferro, you're up first."

Mina saw Ferro gulp hard. She wasn't the only one who was nervous. She wasn't sure if that made her feel better or worse. Hanging back with Jyx and Zek, she watched as Ferro guided his beast, Brindle, into the cloud.

At first, they looked blurred within — Brindle's sparks lit up the wisps of cloud on the edges — but then they disappeared entirely. The cloud itself brightened, then darkened, as if someone had switched an electric light on, then off.

Mina realized she was holding her breath. She made herself exhale and inhale again — and then Ferro and Brindle popped out of the cloud. Ferro pumped his fist into the air. His hand was encased by a white sparkle of energy.

"Great!" Vira called. "Don't lose focus!"

He twisted in the air, Brindle's wings flapping hard, and then, concentrating, stretched the sparkle into a skinny bolt. He hurled it like a javelin toward the cloud.

It hit the gray wisps and was devoured.

Ferro whooped and punched the air. Mina, Zek, and Jyx clapped and cheered. His face bright with victory, Ferro flew back to them.

"Jyx, next!" Vira called.

"Wish me luck," Jyx said to her friends.

Mina watched with just as much nervousness as if she were the one diving into the cloud. But she didn't need to worry. Jyx performed the test perfectly, emerging with a bolt and then hurling it back into the cloud. All of them congratulated her enthusiastically.

Zek was next. He too successfully completed the challenge, though Ferro noted that his bolt was not quite as impressive as Ferro's. Less sparky.

"Mina!" Vira shouted. "Show us what you got!"

Suddenly Mina wanted to flee. Run past the towers of Mytris. Sail away on the river. Or just keep flying all the way across Alorria until she reached her farm, where she could hide safely in the chicken coop.

«*But Mina, the chickens smell bad.*»

That surprised a laugh out of her. *Well, since you put it that way, we'd better try.* She thought of the moment she'd spoken up to her family and the way her fingers had sparked. It hadn't been a coincidence that she'd been able to handle electricity on the day she'd decided she had something she wanted to say.

Pixit flew toward the cloud, then he flattened his wings, and they dove inside. The day instantly dimmed — she couldn't see the sun anymore, or her friends, or the ground. For one brief disorienting second, she lost track of which was up and which was down.

«*Down is the way we fall,*» Pixit said helpfully.

Thanks, she replied dryly. She then reached out her arms and spread her fingers. *Okay, let's do this.* She felt tingling on her skin, as if a hundred feathers were tickling her.

But nothing happened.

«*Keep trying.*»

I am.

A few sparks jumped around them. She heard them crackling as they ran over Pixit's wings and down to the tip of his tail. She concentrated on bringing those sparks into herself.

«*How did you do it last time?*»

I don't know! she wailed. Last time she hadn't been thinking about it. She tried to remember what she *had* been thinking about. Her family had been arguing, loudly, assuming as they always did that they knew what she thought and felt better than she did, and she wanted them to stop and listen to her. She'd had something important she wanted to say.

She wasn't like other lightning guardians — that was true — but that didn't mean she didn't have things to say.

«*You are a lightning guardian. You create lightning. You are the spark that can ignite the world.*»

Maybe he was just saying that to make her feel better, the way he'd told her before that she was like rubber, the stuff that made lightning safe. She didn't know if this was any more true than what he'd said then. But maybe it was. Maybe she could spark change. Hearing it in her mind, from Pixit . . . for an instant, she believed him.

And that was all it took.

I am the spark.

The lightning came to her. It swarmed over her hands, and she felt it tingle all the way up her arms. Marveling, she brought her hands together, drawing the lightning into a single ball and then stretching it out into a bolt.

"It's beautiful," she whispered.

Beneath her, Pixit shifted and flew out of the cloud. She emerged into the sunlight with the bolt in her hands. A little ways away, Jyx, Ferro, and Zek erupted in cheers as Pixit pivoted in the air.

Rising up in her seat, Mina threw the lightning bolt back into the cloud. Just like a lightning guardian was supposed to.

If I do this, what else can I do? she wondered.

Pixit answered her as if it weren't a rhetorical question. «*You can do what you always dreamed. You can change the world.*»

━CHAPTER━

NINETEEN

STANDING on the threshold of the dining hall, Mina debated whether she should go in. *We can just talk to Jyx later.* In the nice, peaceful quiet of their dorm room, rather than here. In the hour before lights out, the dining hall was the opposite of peaceful. As Mina peeked inside, a student on her beast swooped through the maze of metal rods that dangled from the ceiling, while another pair scrambled up the climbing wall and yet another played on the metal ladders. Others cheered them on from below. But as Mina turned to go, Jyx spotted her and waved.

«*Remember: you're the spark.*»

Steeling herself, Mina crossed the hall and halted in front of the table with Jyx, Ferro, and Zek. This was unusual enough that all of them stopped chattering and stared at her, and she remembered suddenly how her family had stopped and listened to her when she'd had something to say. *When did they become like family?* she wondered.

Out loud, she said, "I need to talk to you all."

Ferro blinked at her. "That's new."

In her head, Mina heard Pixit talking to the other storm beasts — Chauda, Ragit, and Brindle — telling them this was important and to please come and listen to Mina. Chauda snorted, a *this better be good* kind of snort. She then herded her guardian and the boys out of the dining hall.

All of them trooped up to Mina and Jyx's dorm room. The beasts flew in through the window and filled the available floor space, while Mina, Jyx, Ferro, and Zek sat cross-legged on the beds.

"It's like we're having a secret meeting," Ferro said.

"We *are* having a secret meeting," Zek said. "Wait — why do we need to have a secret meeting? I was next up on the maze."

"Because," Mina said, studying each of them: Jyx with her heart-shaped scar on her chin and her eager bounce that said she was ready for any adventure; Ferro with his woolly caterpillar eyebrows above eyes that were constantly looking around as if searching out his next joke; and Zek, who liked to act as if he knew more than Ferro at all times, as if his height automatically made him more mature and knowledgeable. *My friends.* "Because I have a secret to tell you."

«*Make them promise not to turn you in.*»

"But you have to promise you won't tell anyone I told you."

"Ooh!" Jyx bounced on her bed, causing her pillow to tumble off and hit Chauda. Chauda snorted. "We can all tell secrets! Ferro, you go first."

Ferro scrambled away, his back against the headboard. "Wait, what?"

"Fine. Me first," Jyx said with an eye roll. "I used to be scared of skunks."

"Good to know," Ferro said. "Filing that away for future use."

Leaning over, Jyx plucked the pillow off Chauda and used it to whack Ferro. "No using secrets against anyone. That's the point. We're *trusting* each other." She looked at Mina, suddenly serious. "Right, Mina? You have something important to tell us, but you don't want to until you're sure you can trust us."

Mina nodded, surprised that Jyx understood so clearly. «*Well, it's not like you call them all together to talk very often. Or ever.*»

True, she thought. It was just that Jyx was usually so loud, Mina sometimes forgot Jyx could be quiet and listen too. She remembered when they'd first met, both of them side by side up the mast, looking silently out at the city. It was so easy to see someone as just one thing, like loud or quiet. But that wasn't fair to either of them.

Jyx took a breath. "Okay, real secret. My parents don't believe in me. Never said that to anyone before, but it's true. They think I'll never be as good a guardian as they each were, and they're jealous I have Chauda when their beasts lost their power years and years ago." Chauda laid her head against Jyx's leg — Mina had never seen the beast act comforting before. "The closer Chauda got to hatching, the meaner they got. So before we left, Chauda and I 'accidentally' burned a few of their papers, including tickets they were planning to use to come visit us here."

Ferro nodded, solemn. "I lost Brindle's and my river-ship tickets, before we came. Dropped them somewhere. Don't know where. But I didn't want to tell my parents — they're always yelling at me about how I have to be more responsible, and I knew if I told them . . ."

"So what did you do?" Zek asked. "You got here."

Studying his shoes, Ferro mumbled, "Stole two tickets."

"Okay, I'll go next," Zek said. "My secret is: I don't have any secrets."

Jyx bumped him with her shoulder. "Come on, Zek. You have to have done something wrong at some point. Thought something you're ashamed of."

"For example, you could have used the beast bathroom instead of the human one in the capitol," Ferro said, "because there was a really long line for the human one."

"You did that?" Zek asked.

"Totally. You know the beast bathroom in the capitol is decorated with jewels? What if the beasts miss?"

Mina grinned and glanced at Pixit.

«There were jewels. I didn't miss.»

She repeated that to the others, and Ferro high-fived Pixit, hand to paw.

223

Zek thought for a moment. "I was mean to Ferro once," he said finally.

"Just once? Not daily? Oh, wait, actually mean?" Ferro frowned. "I don't remember that."

"You didn't know it was me," Zek said. "I told people you wore burned underwear. Said you had Brindle spark on them and then you wore them, on purpose. I thought it would be funny. But you didn't think it was." He was staring at the wall as he talked.

"I didn't," Ferro said quietly.

"Sorry."

"I had no idea that was you."

"Yeah."

There was an awkward silence.

Mina said, "Our storms are killing people. And I think the prime minister knows and is refusing to do anything about it." It was easier to say this time, especially after what everyone else had just volunteered. "I know this because I crossed the mountains, talked to outsiders, and then confronted the prime minister, accidentally, and I would have been expelled, but Professor Dano saved me."

All three guardians and their beasts stared at her, every mouth open.

"We're going to need a *lot* more detail than that," Jyx said.

And so Mina told them everything: Professor Dano assigning the old storm-guardian books, the disaster in the thunderstorm and the crash on the other side of the border, the three search-and-rescue-team outsiders from the outpost, and word for word what she'd said to the prime minister and what had happened after.

It was the longest she'd ever spoken in her life, and it made her feel like she wanted to crawl out of her skin, hide under her bed, and let the shell she'd left behind continue talking. But she knew it needed to be said, so she didn't stop.

"Wow," Jyx said when she'd finished.

"You are way cooler than I thought you were," Ferro said admiringly.

"You really did that?" Zek asked. "I don't think you're lying," he added quickly. "I've heard rumors about guardians causing storms, I think we all have" — beside him, Ferro nodded solemnly — "but I didn't know you were brave."

"Just because she's quiet doesn't mean she isn't brave," Jyx said, throwing her arm around Mina's shoulders. "Really glad you didn't get expelled."

"Is it true?" Ferro said. "About the ten-year storms? And people dying?"

Mina nodded.

"So why did you tell us this?" Zek asked. "What do you expect us to do?"

"Um." Mina glanced at Pixit. He nudged her foot with his nose and filled her mind with encouragement. "Well, I'd like you to talk about what we're not supposed to talk about and do stuff that could get all of us expelled. And I think the first thing we need to do is cross the border and visit the outsiders."

All of them stared at her again.

She wished she could read their minds. She worried that they didn't believe her, that they were going to yell at her, that they were going to turn her in, that they were going to say no.

"Cool," Jyx said.

$$\text{\Lightning}$$

As the four of them trudged out to the practice field, they whispered to one another. "So we aren't going to actually tell anyone we're doing this, right?" Ferro said. "That part's secret?"

"Right," Jyx said as Mina nodded.

"And if we're caught?" Zek asked.

"We aren't going to be caught," Jyx said.

Mina loved her confidence — and the lightning-guardian recklessness of all three of her friends. They'd been quick to agree to this crazy plan. Jyx might have freaked out when they broke a rule by accident, but she didn't hesitate when it was time to break that same rule on purpose. All she needed was a good reason.

Up ahead, their four storm beasts were waiting for them. Mina felt Pixit's anxiousness ripple through her — he'd been so nervous he hadn't eaten a single potato for breakfast. She'd pocketed a few in case he got hungry later.

"But if we *are* caught?" Zek said.

"Then it was an accident, and we're really, really sorry," Jyx said. She grabbed Mina's arm. "Okay, Mina, you're up. There he is."

Following Jyx's gaze, Mina spotted Professor Dano across the field, deep in conversation with another teacher. "Maybe someone else should talk to him."

That was part of the plan: one of them was going to ask Professor Dano to distract Vira so they could fly to Dern. Except not in those words. Last night, flush with the excitement of sharing her thoughts with her friends, Mina had agreed to be the one to talk to him — Jyx had insisted that Professor Dano liked her best. But now that it was time . . .

Clapping her on the shoulder, Zek gave Mina an encouraging nod.

«*You can do it, Mina. We all believe in you.*»

It was her idea. *I can do this.* She wasn't addressing the entire school. All she had to do was talk to one teacher whom she'd talked to plenty of times before.

She jogged across the field toward him.

By the time she reached him, his conversation had ended and the other teacher had waded into the flock of students in search of his trainees. Professor Dano's eyes crinkled in worry as she approached, but he didn't let it enter his voice as he said, "Mina, is everything okay?"

She spat out the speech she'd prepared, the words running into one another and shaking much more than they had when she'd practiced. "Professor Dano, I need to do some follow-up research for my essay, based on what I learned from our trip to the city. My friends have agreed to help me. I was hoping that you could . . ." She faltered.

In her mind, Pixit prompted her. «*Meet with Vira.*»

"Meet with our teacher, Vira, who has been training us in flying, to discuss . . ."

«*The next step in our training.*»

". . . the next step in our training, while I do my research." There. She'd gotten it all out.

Professor Dano blinked owlishly at her. She wondered if she should have hinted more, or been clearer, or whether it was better (as they'd all decided last night) to be cryptic. At last, he spoke. "I don't know if it would be wise."

She swallowed. She wanted to retreat, but this was too important. "I have questions that really need answers."

His eyebrows shot up. She realized he'd never heard her sound so determined before. She hadn't raised her voice, but she hadn't wavered, either. "Last time you had questions, you weren't so careful who you asked," Professor Dano said. "Perhaps you should ask me."

It was a reasonable thing to suggest. Her mouth felt dry. She felt as if her face was flushed as red as a tomato. "It wouldn't be the same."

He studied her for a moment longer, and she wished she could flee. "I suppose it wouldn't be," he said. "It wasn't for me."

He understands!

«*I knew he would.*»

No, you didn't.

«*I hoped he would,*» Pixit amended.

"It won't do for you and your friends" — Professor Dano glanced at Jyx, Ferro, and Zek, who were all waiting for Mina by their beasts — "to be idle while I speak with Teacher Vira. You should practice your flying in her absence. Perhaps work on long-distance flight to improve your endurance."

Mina felt every muscle in her body unknot, and she wanted to slump into a relieved puddle on the grass. "Exactly what we had in mind."

She felt Pixit's pride beaming into her. «*You did it!*»

"Very good," Professor Dano said. "I will tell her not to expect you four back before dinnertime. After that, I expect you to be safe and sound within the walls of Mytris." He paused, then added, "Understand that an endurance flight involves certain risks. I would not approve this if I did not think you showed potential. Don't make me regret my trust in you."

"Yes, sir." She knew he wasn't just talking about the flight. Feeling giddy, Mina ran across the field to her friends. Other students and teachers were taking to the air, beginning their day's lessons. A few matches of lightning relay were already in progress. She shot a look back over her shoulder to see Professor Dano striding purposefully across the field to intercept Vira.

"Mount up!" Jyx said, glee in her voice.

All four of them climbed onto their storm beasts. Mina felt Pixit rumble beneath her as he ran forward, flapping his wings, and a moment later they were airborne. He flew up toward the blue sky and then out across the blackened hills.

Her friends flanked her, Jyx on one side and Ferro and Zek on the other. They caught the same airstream and soared away from the towers of Mytris. Behind them, the shouts and cries from the lightning relays faded into the distance. The only sound Mina heard was the steady roar of the wind.

Flying with friends, as far as they could fly, felt wonderful. She felt as if her heart were roaring to match the wind. The sky was clear, as always, and the morning sun was soft and sweet. Below, the hills were a beautiful mix of textures, like black silk and black velvet. A few birds flew on an airstream below them.

"Bet I can reach the mountains first!" Ferro called into the wind.

"Oh, I don't think so!" Jyx shouted back, and urged Chauda faster.

Pixit propelled himself and Mina forward, shooting past Ragit and Brindle. Laughing, Jyx and Chauda raced her, and then Ferro was in the lead, quickly matched by Zek. Mina and Pixit soared higher, catching a faster stream of wind, and soon they were ahead. The others steered upward, and they chased one another all the way to the mountains.

She knew once they crossed them, everything would change. None of them would see the world the same way ever again. If what she thought proved to be true, none of them would be able to continue to live blithely in the cocoon of ignorance. As they flew north, the mountains grew larger. She loved how wild and untamed they looked.

«*Kind of like Beon's hair,*» Pixit commented.

Mina was startled into a laugh, because it was a little bit true. *Hey, I was having a serious moment.*

«*Serious as "the cocoon of ignorance"?*» He giggled beneath her.

That was poetic! She then sobered. She'd always done things her own way, but this was the first time she'd deliberately broken a clear rule: Don't leave the barren lands. Don't cross the border. She'd never thought of herself as a rule breaker.

«*You said we'd find our own way.*»

You're right. I did say that.

A few more wing beats and they'd be across.

On either side of her, she heard her friends calling to one another, giving encouragement and checking to make sure they weren't being watched.

She and Pixit flew over the border.

Jyx, Ferro, and Zek, on Chauda, Brindle, and Ragit, followed.

They sailed above the other side of the mountain, beyond the border, and Mina was surprised to see that it was beautiful. The mountain itself was exposed rock with a few twisted pine trees wedged into the cracks, but the valley at its feet was overrun with green.

It was beautiful in the same way a tangle of colorful yarn was beautiful. Unlike in Alorria, the farms weren't laid out in squares in a perfect patchwork quilt. Instead they were trapezoids and thin triangles, wedged in between rivers and streams that meandered across the land. There were no neatly laid-out forests with carefully manicured paths and bushes. Here the forests were clumps of trees wrapped in vines and greenery so thick that it knotted them together. And the roads were shiny black ribbons that wandered up and down hills like the streams did — she couldn't tell what they were made out of.

Mina spotted the outpost, nestled against the base of a mountain. It was small, a tight cluster of a half-dozen buildings that looked like sturdy metal boxes. She guided the others toward it.

One after another, the students landed. Mina dismounted and patted Pixit's neck. *Nice flying. How's your wing feel?*

«Perfect. I want to say thank you to Neela and the others. Will you speak for me?»

Always. Let's find them.

Together, they walked toward the buildings.

A few people came outside — five men and three women, wearing clothes similar to what Neela, Varli, and Eione had worn: sturdy, practical, and made of materials that Mina didn't recognize. *Guess we didn't escape notice.*

«This is what we want,» Pixit reminded her.

Yes, but she hadn't thought about what she'd *say* to these people.

Luckily, she didn't have to. She had Jyx. Bounding forward with a big smile on her face, Jyx said, "Hi! We're looking for the search-and-rescue team who saved my friends! Can you help us find them?"

The men and women were eyeing them with a mixture of curiosity and suspicion. Mina guessed they didn't get many visitors. *Especially from our side of the mountains.*

"Their names are Neela, Varli, and Eione," Mina said.

Jyx echoed her, louder. "The people we're looking for are Neela, Varli, and Eione."

At that, one of the men scurried off, hopefully to fetch them, while the others continued to linger, staring at the four kids and their beasts and whispering to one another.

"I don't think they trust us," Ferro said under his breath.

«*Can you blame them?*» Pixit asked, and Mina relayed his words.

"What is this place?" Zek asked.

It had an official look, as if all the structures had been built for a purpose, not for beauty. A few, though, had homelike touches: flowers planted on either side of the door and curtains in the windows. "They said it was an outpost," Mina said.

"But what does that mean?" Ferro asked. "What do they do here?"

"You mean, besides stare at us?" Jyx asked, staring back at the outsiders.

Coming out of one of the buildings, the three rescuers jogged toward them. Neela was in the lead, followed by Varli and Eione. Eione was wearing a tough leather apron with various tools tucked into its broad pockets. Neela wore black boots that reached up to her knees. Mud and grass clung to them. She had a grass stain smeared up one arm. Varli was the only one dressed as she remembered: in climbing gear, with a heavy jacket.

"Mina, Pixit," Neela greeted them. "And friends. Welcome to Dern."

"Not to be rude," Eione said, "but why, by the storms, are you here?"

Mina glanced at her friends. They seemed to be waiting for her to speak. She felt a flutter of nerves in her stomach and reminded herself that this was her idea, she could do this, and Pixit believed in her. «*Always,*» he said in her mind. Out loud, she said, "Pixit and I wanted to say thank you. And . . . we were hoping you'd be willing to tell us more about the ten-year storms."

TWENTY

MINA curled up with Pixit in Neela's kitchen. It was cramped with all of them in it. Two of the storm beasts, Ragit and Brindle, had volunteered to wait outside and keep watch, in case any teachers had seen and followed them. Inside, Neela served tea.

Varli was perched on a stool, and Eione was squatting on the floor. She kept her distance from Chauda and Pixit, eyeing them warily, but Neela seemed unperturbed by the sparking beasts inside her home.

Mina, for her part, couldn't stop staring at the lantern on the table. It wasn't lit with a candle — it gave a steady amber light, as if it was powered by electricity. «But that's impossible,» Pixit thought. «They don't have storm beasts.»

She repeated his words out loud.

Eione snorted. "You don't need storm beasts for electricity. You need technology. But you Alorrians are so dependent on your storm beasts you can't imagine inventing anything, can you?"

"Eione," Neela scolded. She then smiled kindly at the storm guardians and their beasts. "Without storm beasts, we've found our own way of doing things over the years. Our cities rival yours for grandness."

Mina felt her eyes widen in surprise, and saw that her friends wore matching expressions. They'd always been taught to pity the outsiders, when they thought of them at all.

"No offense, but this doesn't seem so grand." Jyx waved her hand at the outpost outside the window with its squat, gray buildings.

"That's because it's so close to *you*," Eione snapped.

"This outpost exists to keep an eye on Alorria, to try to predict when your people will cause the next storms," Neela said. "We have advance warning now for the ten-year storms, thanks to a few conscientious Alorrians, but your everyday activities still cause a lot of damage to crops and homes. It's our responsibility to try to predict upcoming changes to the weather patterns. Especially any killer storms."

"When you say 'cause' —" Jyx began.

"Yes, *cause*." Eione cut her off. "Every time your beasts play with the weather, it messes with the world. You have any idea what it's like to face a killer storm? No, of course, you don't, because in Alorria you only have perfect summer days with mild wind and endless sunshine as you live your perfect, mild lives of endless selfishness."

"Eione," Neela warned. "They came as guests."

"Yeah, guests who want to *know*." Eione leaned forward. "Since you're so curious, let me tell you what it's like to face a beast-made storm. You hear the wind first, from a distance, and it sounds like the howl of a monster. Everything gets dark, even though it's the middle of the day, and you see this . . . this . . . gray wall. It advances toward you, and you know if you don't run, if you don't hide, if you don't take everything you know and love with you and bury it and yourself as deep down as you can get, it will all be flattened and then swept away."

Mina and her friends didn't move or speak. Motionless, they stared at Eione.

"And then — *bam!*" Eione slapped her hands together, and all of them jumped. "It hits. And you think the sky has fallen and all the stars have collapsed to the ground. Everything shakes. Everything screams. And you can't even tell if you're screaming because it's all so loud. And that's when you realize the earth is being pulled apart and the rivers are rising and the mountains are crumbling, and you can do nothing — absolutely nothing — to stop it, except hope that your storm bunker is sealed well enough that it doesn't flood and built strong enough that it doesn't collapse. Because if it's not, you'll die."

Neela had stopped pouring tea. She, too, was listening to Eione, but Mina saw there was no surprise on her face. There was only a resigned kind of sadness. *I don't think she's exaggerating,* Mina thought at Pixit.

«*I think I'm going to have nightmares.*»

"And when it's all over, you come out of the holes you've hidden yourself in, and it's like you are on the moon. Everything that made it your world, everything that made it *home*, has been wiped away. Cities are ravaged. Towns are destroyed. Fields are drowned in thick, murky lakes. The houses — the homes where you woke up every day, said hello to your parents, ate your breakfast, complained about your sisters, fixed your socks, did all the daily little things that you used to take for granted — are broken bits of wood. The table you ate every dinner at is firewood. That is, if you can find it, if it hasn't been flung miles away by the wind. Any animals you had that you couldn't take with you belowground are lost. And any people who failed to hide well enough, or the people in hiding places that flooded — " At this, Eione stopped abruptly. She stood and stalked out of the house, slamming the door behind her.

They stared after her.

"That was dramatic," Ferro said. "Is it true?"

"Sadly, yes," Neela said. "Come with us. There's something we should show you."

"All right," Jyx said in a small voice. She looked as haunted as Mina felt.

Neela washed the teacups, wiped her hands on a towel, and then, with Varli, led them all outside. Eione didn't rejoin them, but Mina saw others peeking out their windows and watching them from wherever they were — by the chickens, at a butter churn, near the well, by a stable.

It didn't take long to cross the outpost. They passed the houses, the sheds, and the dilapidated buildings. "Eione mentioned storm bunkers?" Jyx asked.

"Ours can withstand an ordinary storm, but to survive a catastrophic ten-year storm, you need the heavy-duty bunkers they have in the cities," Varli said.

Neela chimed in, "Thankfully, some of your storm guardians have shared the date of your next festival. We'll leave here in six days, before your celebration begins and the next ten-year storm arrives. In the past, before any of your people understood the connection between your displays of power and the storms, we had no warning that these storms would be worse than the usual. And there were consequences."

Varli pointed ahead of them. "See the consequences."

Neela and Varli led them to a meadow of wildflowers. An apple tree grew in the center, and a stream babbled across its pebbled banks. All around the meadow were flat, upright stones.

Gravestones.

These weren't the fancy engraved markers Mina had seen in Alorrian cemeteries. This graveyard had different kinds of headstones — some red, some black, some gray speckled with mica — and the shapes were irregular. They were loosely flat rectangles, but some were fatter and some taller. The guardians and the beasts walked between them, reading the names.

"Look at the dates," Zek said.

Mina read more closely. Not all of them were the same, but

many were. And the majority of the dates were every ten years. Exactly the dates of the prior festivals.

↯

None of them spoke much on the flight back.

Landing outside Mytris, they blended in with the other students who had completed their practice for the day, and they trooped inside to the dining hall. All four guardians, with their storm beasts clustered around them, ate together — mostly in silence. Every once in a while, Mina would look up from her plate, catch the eye of Jyx or Ferro or Zek, and then have to look down again.

We can't unsee it, Mina thought.

«*Um, I thought that was the point?*»

It was. The truth wasn't just rumor anymore. The truth had faces. And graves.

A little part of me wishes I didn't know. She'd been happy living in — what had Eione called it? — her "endless selfishness." After a few more mouthfuls that she barely tasted, she carried her tray to the trash. Behind her, she heard her friends doing the same. All of them left the dining room and climbed the stairs, by unspoken agreement, to Mina and Jyx's room.

Mina sat at her desk as her friends began talking in low voices about what they'd seen, what they thought, and what they felt. While she listened to them talk, she pulled out her unfinished essay for Professor Dano. She glanced at what she'd written and then set it aside and reached for her sketchbook.

She opened it and began to draw the graves.

She kept going until she thought she had it right: the shadows on the stones, the dates, and the silhouette of a lone figure — she realized she was drawing Eione, though with just the silhouette, you couldn't tell who it was. She kept Eione's face in shadow.

When she was satisfied, she drew it again on a fresh piece of paper, all the graves with their dates and Eione mourning the dead, and then she began to write underneath it. Not her essay. Or at least not the essay she'd meant to write, and certainly not the essay that Professor Weirin had intended her to write.

Instead she wrote the truth.

She altered her handwriting and used no names. Nothing that would identify her or any of her friends, or the people of the Dern outpost. Just the facts, including the history and the details of her interaction with the prime minister. And then a call to action:

> Tell everyone.
> We are killing people.
> It has to stop.
> End the festival.

Mina laid down her pencil and stared at what she'd written. The solution was simple: don't celebrate. Your celebration hurts people, so don't do it. As Papa had said when she'd asked him that question about Beon and Rinna, *Tell them to find another game to play.* All they had to do was convince the other guardians to refuse to participate.

No guardians, then no festival.

She hesitated for a moment longer. What if her friends didn't like it? What if they laughed? What if . . .

«Mina. We won't laugh. Show us.»

Taking a deep breath, Mina picked up the piece of paper and, turning in her chair, held it up for her friends to see. Jyx took it from her, studied it, and then passed it to Ferro and Zek. Keeping it away from any sparks, they showed it to the storm beasts.

«It's perfect,» Pixit said.

"How many copies can you make?" Jyx asked.

"If you find me more paper, I'll make as many as I can."

Ferro and Zek scurried off to their room, then came back with stacks of paper. Jyx rummaged through her desk and came up with another wad. "You know how everyone leaves their textbooks on the shelves by the practice field when they go out to fly? After breakfast tomorrow, we put the essays in the textbooks while everyone else is airborne," Jyx counseled. "And then we listen. Anyone who sounds like they might agree, we pull them aside and we talk to them. We don't say *we* are the kids in the essay. We don't say *we* saw the graves. Or even that we know who did. But we listen, and every time we hear outrage, we agree with it. We fan it. We tell *them* to talk to their friends. Meanwhile, Mina will keep drawing and writing more. And we spread this idea — this truth — throughout Mytris."

"And then?" Ferro asked.

"And then we spread it beyond Mytris, to every guardian in all of Alorria," Jyx said, and threw her arms open wide, as if she could touch the edges of Alorria with her fingertips. In that moment, Mina believed she could.

—CHAPTER—

TWENTY-ONE

THEY began, as planned, the next morning.

As guardians and beasts clattered into the dining hall, Mina supplied her friends with a stack of essays. And then she snagged a breakfast roll and went back to her room to sleep, something she hadn't done all night. She'd drawn and written by the light of Pixit's sparks until dawn. He was worn out too. His scales were a pale, flat yellow, and his entire body mushed into the sleeping divot as if his bones had melted. He snored very loudly. Mina slept anyway.

She woke around mid-afternoon, drew and wrote more, and had another stack of essays to give Jyx when she came back after training. Her hand was cramped from using a handwriting that didn't look like hers. "Told Vira you were sick," Jyx reported. "But Vira didn't care. She just wanted to talk about some illustrated essay she found in her copy of our textbook." Jyx snickered. "She had no idea how it got there."

"What did she say about it?"

Plopping down on her bed, Jyx said, "She thought it was lies from a sick mind. But not your kind of sick. I mean, not your kind of sick if you weren't fake sick."

She didn't believe it. Mina's shoulders sagged. She looked down at a half-drawn image of graves. Her fingers were aching, and the side of her hand was stained gray from the pencil.

"But that was just Vira," Jyx said. "You should have heard Kita and Saril. Kita was *crying.* She said she'd always suspected it was true, because how could the weather *not* be connected to the world? And Saril said she was going to write to her dad — he's a professor at a rain-guardian school, I think in the southern orchards. Or is it the lake district? Anyway, she said he'd been grumbling for years about how the government wouldn't consider new ideas. So that's good, right?"

Mina nodded, agreeing.

"You know what I think? I think people already know it's true, or at least guardians do. But no one ever stood up and put it in words — or pictures — and turned it from a whisper into a shout. I think people are ready to hear this. How many more did you finish?" She counted. "Twenty-three. Great. Keep going. I'll bring you food. Except you're going to have to come out tomorrow. Otherwise they'll send the nurse to check on you, and we don't want that. If you're stuck in the sick room, you can't draw more."

Jyx left for dinner without waiting for Mina to reply, which was fine because she didn't have enough energy to respond to any of that. She bent over the desk and kept drawing and writing.

«*Mina, is it morning?*» Pixit asked sleepily behind her.

No, it's almost nighttime.

«*Oh. That's good.*»

He fell back asleep, but only lightly, so he'd continue to spark. She kept going.

$$\lightning$$

At breakfast, Mina braved the dining hall. Instead of darting in for a roll, she picked up a tray and joined her friends at their table. Each of them nodded welcome as she sat. She'd expected them to be surprised to see her again, but they weren't. It felt right to be here.

"You look terrible," Jyx said. "Maybe take a break tonight."

Ferro leaned over to whisper, "Everything's going great. Don't even need to hand out more leaflets — everyone's sharing them. By now I think everyone in the school has seen one."

Mina smiled at him and ate her roll.

As her friends chattered around her, Mina listened to them and to a smattering of other conversations. She heard a lot of whispering and not as much laughter as usual from the tables around them. Glancing up, she thought she saw a flash of paper in another student's hand — Saril, the girl whose father was a rain-guardian professor, was passing it to another student, Trina, who read it with her mouth in an O shape. *I wonder if that's my essay.* Craning, she tried to get a peek at it.

But then Trina stuffed the paper under her seat as Professor Werrin strode through the dining hall. Mina watched the headmistress as she stepped onto a platform next to a fifteen-foot-tall sculpture of a lightning beast. She thumped her cane heavily for attention.

Announcements were rare during meals. Usually it was so loud in the hall that none of the professors bothered, but Professor Werrin caught everyone's attention precisely because her actions were so unusual.

"Students, I have an exciting announcement to make!" Professor Werrin said. Her voice projected across the hall, even though it didn't sound like she was shouting — it was only that the students and their beasts were, for a rare moment, quiet. "Our participation in the festival has been confirmed: five days from now, on the morning of the festival, we will be conducting a lightning-relay tournament in the southeastern farmlands!"

Home, Mina thought.

Before visiting the outpost, she would have thought that was an honor: to serve as a lightning guardian in front of her family and all their neighbors.

Murmurs spread around the hall.

"Graduates, of course, will be having their showcase tournament in the city, and don't worry, our tournament will be considered preliminary — you'll be finished in time to watch the finals. Indeed, the prime minister has promised to reserve seating for students participating in the festivities."

The murmurs grew into a rumble. Mina tried to hear what people were saying. It was odd — she'd expected cheers. Students always participated in the festival in some way, but this, an official lightning-relay match, should have been greeted with excitement.

Professor Werrin frowned. Clearly, she'd expected excitement as well. "This is an honor for all of us at Mytris Lightning School. In past years, students have been relegated to the background, but for this festival, the prime minister wants to highlight the promise of our youth."

Students began to shift in their seats.

Jyx whispered, "I'm going to say something."

"Don't," Ferro whispered back. "They'll know it was us. You'll get us caught."

"But we've spread all the leaflets. Now's the time to speak up!" Jyx was still whispering, but it was a louder, more insistent whisper that Mina was sure could be heard at the next table.

Mina glanced over her shoulder at the table behind them and saw Kita looking at Jyx. Kita was a tall, dark-haired girl who'd been at Mytris three months longer than Mina and Jyx. *Jyx said she cried when she read my essay,* Mina remembered.

Jyx gave Kita a nod.

In a loud voice Kita said, "Yes, now is the time to speak up." And Kita stepped onto her chair and then onto the table.

The students around her gasped.

Professor Werrin shifted her frown to Kita. "Sit down, please. Tables are for food, not feet."

"Professor Werrin, please tell the prime minister that we reject her invitation," Kita said in a ringing voice. "And we condemn the festival itself. It causes death and destruction!"

Students began to cheer.

Others shouted for her to sit down.

And then others shouted at them to shut up.

"The festival is an abomination, and it must be stopped!"

All around the dining room, students leaped to their feet, cheering and shouting. A few fights broke out, but they were quickly subdued. Still sitting, Mina marveled at what was happening around her.

We did this.

«*You did this.*»

Jyx grabbed her arm and hauled her onto her feet. Mina glanced around the room in wonder, and Professor Dano caught her eye. His expression didn't change, but he gave her a brief, barely noticeable nod.

«*I told you,*» Pixit thought smugly. «*This is what a spark can do.*»

$$\text{\Lightning}$$

Stealing away in the aftermath of the chaos, the four of them and their beasts crammed again into Mina and Jyx's room to plot more. Jyx perched on her pillow and tossed potatoes to

Chauda, who caught them one after another. "Chauda wants to know what our next move is," Jyx said.

All of them looked at Mina.

Mina flushed. *Why are they all looking at me?*

«*Because you're our leader,*» Pixit said, and then he knocked Chauda sideways in order to nab the next potato that Jyx tossed.

Chauda knocked him back, and Pixit sprawled against the floor, but he still ate the potato.

I don't want to be a leader! Jyx should lead.

"What should we do next, Mina?" Ferro asked.

Zek elbowed him. "She's thinking. Give her a minute."

"Looks more like she's panicking," Ferro noted.

That was close to accurate. They were all looking at her as if they expected answers. She opened her mouth to say that she didn't know, that *they* should come up with the next idea, and that all she'd done was draw a few pictures and write a few words . . . which had led to Kita standing up on a table and leading a protest against Professor Werrin . . . which was rather amazing.

Instead of a disclaimer, what came out of Mina's mouth was: "We have to spread the truth farther. We have to find a way to get the essays into the hands of the real lightning guardians, the ones who've already completed their training."

Her friends were all nodding. "Yeah," Zek said, "they're the ones who are supposed to be doing the big 'showcase' tournament in the capital with the prime minister. It's not enough to get the students to boycott. If we can get the full lightning guardians to quit, that will make a difference! Can't hold a celebration if no one's willing to celebrate."

Mina wanted to cheer. He'd heard the words she'd said and the ones she hadn't. If they could reach all the lightning guardians — or even just enough of them — within the next few days, they could really make an impact.

"But how are we going to get it to them?" Ferro asked. "We can't exactly slip the essays into their textbooks. They're not even at Mytris."

Mina considered it. There was one place they did see lightning guardians. "With the festival coming in five days, the prime minister will want extra electricity stored up. There will probably be more thunderstorms very soon."

"So?" Zek asked.

"Wait — are you saying what I think you're saying?" Jyx asked.

Mina felt herself grinning. "We give them to guardians *inside* the next storm."

TWENTY-TWO

MINA was right: the very next day, another thunderstorm was scheduled for harvesting electricity for the festival. Professor Dano posted news on the bulletin board at breakfast. Staring at the posting, Mina tried not to feel full of nerves and doubts. On either side of her, Ferro and Zek jostled for a better view.

"You're sure you want to do this?" Mina asked the boys. "We could get in trouble. Spreading 'false propaganda,' the prime minister will call it. This is bigger than just convincing a bunch of students."

Ferro looked at her as if she'd suddenly turned a weird shade of orange. "Are you kidding? We met the outsiders. Drank their tea. Talked to them. Zek, back me up here."

"You know why we wanted to be storm guardians?" Zek asked Mina.

She shook her head. She'd always known she wanted to be a storm guardian — Papa had been one, and then Gaton had

had his egg, and she'd dreamed about it from a young age. Her family had thought it was because she wanted to help out with the farm, but it was so much more than that. She'd wanted to help the world!

"Well, my parents said I had to, because I was a little kid and they knew best," Ferro said. "But after that, I wanted Brindle to hatch because I wanted to be like the guardians in the stories — you know, a hero."

She knew exactly what he meant.

Zek jumped in. "Yeah! We want to do something important."

"Right, important!" Ferro said. "We want to be like those lightning guardians who make people's lives more awesome. The ones people talk about and remember."

Yes, yes, and yes.

"That's why we follow you," Zek said.

Ferro nodded. "You have big ideas. Not just about lightning relay. You want to change the world. Make it better, and stuff."

Mina stared at them both. She'd never imagined herself as someone anyone else would follow. Weren't leaders supposed to be loud, barking orders into speaking tubes? Or at least giving rousing speeches?

«*Told you so*,» Pixit thought smugly.

Wordlessly, she handed Zek and Ferro more copies of her essay. Zek tucked them inside his jacket, between his cotton shirt and the weatherproof leather. Ferro slid them into a pouch.

Everyone watched the gray mass of clouds boil over the blackened hills. The beautiful blue sky looked as if it were being eaten by an amorphous monster. Mina wondered how this storm had affected the outpost and hoped it hadn't been bad. She thought of the gravestones.

We have to stop it.

«*We will.*»

She felt Pixit's confidence flow through her — it tasted like warm syrup.

On Professor Werrin's whistle, all the storm beasts thundered across the practice field and took to the sky. They flew toward the storm.

The graduated guardians were already there ahead of them. Mina saw flashes of lightning as they dove into the storm. Again the students were supposed to keep to the edges of the chaos and let the real guardians gather the lightning from the heart. But Mina had no intention of following those orders. *This time we disobey on purpose, instead of by accident.* Hopefully that meant there would be a better outcome.

«*Less crashing would be nice.*»

She urged Pixit faster, and he flew like an arrow toward the storm. She entered it at the same time as the other students, plunging into the rain, wind, and fury. It whipped around her. She yanked her hood up over her face and pulled it closed — it would both protect her from the rain and keep anyone from being able to identify her later.

Mina and her friends had wrapped each essay in a bit of blanket — that stuff repelled water as well as fire. Insisting she didn't like sleeping with a blanket anyway, Jyx had cut hers up. Mina reached inside her jacket for the first essay.

Up ahead she saw a flash of light and a silhouette of a boy on a beast. She leaned over, flat against Pixit's neck, as Pixit aimed straight for the boy.

The guardian didn't see them, but his beast dodged sideways. Pixit banked hard, so they came up beside the guardian. Mina pressed the wrapped essay into the boy's hand, which was open, ready to catch electricity.

He flinched, surprised, but his hand instinctively closed around it.

And then Pixit wheeled away, disappearing into the storm, for Mina to deliver the next one.

⚡

Mina ate quickly, determined to flee back to her room and copy more essays. She'd had the idea of using the message balloons — they could send the essay out to their friends at other storm-guardian schools. Nearly everyone knew at least a few other guardians. *Maybe we can reach more than just lightning guardians.* She imagined what would happen if all guardians of every type refused to participate in the festival.

«*It would have to end.*»

Finished, she headed for the door, flush with their success and excited about all the possibilities. But before she could leave,

Professor Werrin entered the dining hall. Her cane thumped with her, and Mina felt rooted to the spot. Professor Werrin nodded pleasantly at her, but Mina couldn't do anything but stare as the headmistress crossed the dining hall and climbed onto the platform for the second time that week.

Everyone fell silent.

The headmistress didn't even have to thump her cane again for attention.

"Students, I am afraid I have some rather disappointing news," Professor Werrin said. She sighed heavily as if she didn't want to say the words. Mina watched the faces of her friends, and of the students who weren't her friends — everyone looked just as anxious as she suddenly felt. She felt Pixit shift closer to her. "Due to recent 'activity' here in the school, the prime minister and her advisors have determined that, for the safety of all, Mytris Lightning School will be sealed until the conclusion of the festival."

Frantic conversations broke out around the hall.

«"Sealed"? What does she mean?»

I don't know.

Judging by the frenzy of babble, the other students didn't know either. A few of the beasts shifted uneasily, and Mina saw that they were sparking more than usual.

Professor Werrin held up a hand. "This means that no student or teacher from Mytris will be allowed to either participate in or view the festival."

Gasps of outrage echoed from half the hall.

Moans from the other half.

She didn't say the festival was stopped, Mina thought. *Just that it will be going on without us.* Some of the students and a few of the teachers, including Vira, began to shout — not at Professor Werrin, but at Jyx and Kila and the others who had been vocal about believing the essays. *Oh no.*

Professor Werrin thumped her cane forcefully, and the shouts stopped, subsiding into loud rumbles. "Communication both into and out of the school will also be severed." She held up a hand as more yells greeted that pronouncement. "I know all of you have family beyond these walls. Rest assured that important messages, such as those concerning the health and well-being of your loved ones and other related emergencies, will be allowed through, but those communications will be screened by professors and doled out as needed. Nonemergency communication will be suspended until further notice. No balloons will be sent or received. No river ships will dock."

More shouts.

"This ban is only in place until the end of the festival, and the prime minister has decreed that the date for the festival will be moved up by four days, to prevent any interference. It will be occurring tomorrow. I know these measures sound extreme to some of you, but the festival is important to the morale of all Alorrians."

Tomorrow! Mina thought. But they hadn't reached all the guardians!

"Many people have worked long and hard to create an event designed to delight and inspire, and the prime minister won't allow their efforts to be in vain to satisfy the whims of a handful of misinformed radicals." Professor Werrin fixed her gaze on Jyx and Mina's friends, frowning especially at Kita. "I hope those of you who have made these extreme measures necessary think long and hard about what you have done. Actions have consequences. Ideas — flawed, wrong-headed, hurtful, and hateful ideas — can be just as damaging as fists. I am only sorry that the few have ruined things for the many." She then swept out of the dining hall.

Three seconds after the headmistress left, everyone exploded into shouting. Vira, screaming at Kita, Jyx, and their friends about how they'd ruined everything, launched herself across the tables, and dozens of her friends joined her. Screaming back at them about how hateful and selfish and shortsighted and stupid they were, Kita, Jyx, and dozens of other students threw themselves into battle. Sparking, their storm beasts slammed into one another.

A few teachers yelled at them to stop, but other teachers, like Vira, were in the thick of it. Mina, unable to run, unable to move, stared as students and beasts fought in front of her, over the tables, and up on the metal ladders, chains, and other obstacles.

I did this, she thought in horror. *This is my fault.*

Beside her, Pixit was growling and sparking. «*I want to help!*»

No! Mina thought sharply. *This isn't helping!*

«*Those are our friends!*» Pixit howled, and then he charged into the fray. She felt pain shoot through her arm as another beast bit into him.

Pixit! She took a step forward — and saw, across the dining hall, Professor Dano. He was backed against the massive sculpture of a lightning beast. Looking at him, she thought the metal umbrella-cane that the professors carried didn't seem like enough protection. If lightning bolts began to fly, he'd be in danger. *He needs to get out of here!*

But he wasn't trying to run. Instead he beckoned her over.

Keeping to the edges of the hall, Mina hurried to him.

"You and I are both too quiet to catch this mob's attention," Professor Dano said, "but if you could ask your beast to fly to the top of the statue and roar as loudly as he can, that might do the trick. There's a speaking tube within the statue's head, installed by the school's last headmistress. It should amplify him sufficiently."

Pixit? Mina called with her mind.

«*Mina, they're throwing potatoes!*» He sounded both pleased and outraged. She tasted his excitement, sweet and tangy. He'd never been in a fight before. Neither of them had.

She repeated Professor Dano's request and added, *Can you roar loud enough?*

«*Let's find out!*»

She watched Pixit flap up to the top of the lightning-beast statue and perch on its head, just above its golden eyes. Rearing back, he opened his mouth and let out a roar. The speaking tube magnified it, louder than any of the shouting, shrieking, and howling.

For a brief instant, there was shocked silence.

Into the silence, Professor Dano said, "Now that I have your attention, you will all return to your rooms. We are the protectors of Alorria. We do not fight among ourselves. Go!"

Everyone scattered. Some ran. Some skulked. But all of them left, until it was only Mina, Pixit, and Professor Dano remaining in the dining hall.

That was amazing, she told Pixit.

He purred.

"You don't need to be loud," Professor Dano said, a bit of smugness in his voice. "But sometimes it's good to have loud friends."

TWENTY-THREE

"COME to my library," Professor Dano said. "We need to talk."

Check on Jyx, please? Mina asked Pixit silently. *You can't fit up the stairs anyway.*

«*I'll make sure she's okay,*» Pixit promised. «*And the others, too.*» He flew off the statue, while Mina followed the professor out of the dining hall and up the narrow winding stairs to his library.

With each step, she grew more nervous. He knew what she'd done. How much trouble was she in?

She waited while he unlocked the door, and then he switched on a single electric bulb. He held the door open for her while she entered, and closed it after they were both inside. It made her think of a jail-cell door swinging shut. Inside, the tiny library was full of shadows.

She wondered if he was disappointed in her for failing. She

thought of how she'd promised her family to behave. Yet she still didn't regret anything. *I only regret that I didn't succeed.*

Professor Dano sank into his desk chair, put his face in his hands, and sighed heavily. She didn't know whether she was supposed to keep standing or sit, whether he expected her to speak or he planned to just sigh into the silence for a while. After a moment, she sat in the chair opposite his desk.

"You did well," Professor Dano said, looking up at her.

That was . . . good? *So I'm not here to be yelled at for getting the whole school "sealed" and failing to stop the festival?* She still didn't relax. She knew she'd failed. In fact, she'd made things worse.

He gave her a half smile, though there was little humor in it. "My friends don't believe that children have learned empathy yet. You have at least proved them wrong in that."

She wasn't sure if he expected a thank-you or not. It was a backwards kind of compliment. "Don't they remember being my age?"

Another half smile. "Just the bad parts. Children can be selfish creatures."

"Adults can be worse," Mina dared point out. The prime minister and her advisors, after all, were adults. They knew the truth and had the power to do something to help, yet they refused to.

He sighed again, and the smile vanished. "I can't argue with that." He drummed his fingers on his desk. "You must understand that this is about more than one celebration. If the prime minister acknowledges that the festival causes deadly storms beyond the mountains, then it opens the door to change."

What does he mean? All she wanted to do was stop the festival. Stop the festival, and you stop the killer storms.

"The prime minister would need to reevaluate every use of storm beasts. If the festival causes harm, what else does? How does keeping our fields perfectly watered affect the outsiders? How does controlling the wind on the sea affect the rest of the ocean? Examining the effects of our actions could have ramifications throughout the entire economy. Alorria has been prosperous because of its carefully cultivated selfishness. What happens when that crumbles?"

Mina hadn't thought about any of that. *But the prime minister must have.*

"People fear change," Professor Dano said. "And that is what stopping the festival represents: change to our way of life. That is why the prime minister is taking steps to silence the 'rumors' you and your friends have been spreading. She doesn't want to go down in history as the prime minister who destroyed our prosperity."

Mina swallowed. "Am I . . . are we . . . in trouble?" She couldn't bring herself to say the word "expelled."

"The prime minister and her advisors hope this action will be sufficient to punish everyone who spoke up, and will deter others from doing the same. She'd rather not resort to more extreme measures — she still hopes to have your loyalty, or at least your service, after you graduate. So long as you behave yourselves from here on in." His lips quirked on the word "behave."

"We gave my essay to guardians inside the storm," Mina blurted out.

His eyes widened, then crinkled, as if he was amused. "Nicely done. Still, though, it won't have a far enough reach to have an impact. Not before tomorrow. If we had more time . . . but we don't."

"What are we supposed to do? Sit back and let people die?" She jumped to her feet. Mina then clapped her hands over her mouth and sat abruptly. She'd never dreamed of shouting at a professor before. "Sorry," she said between her fingers.

He chuckled. "Just because you're quiet doesn't mean you have nothing to say, does it? We've been funneling emergency supplies across the border for months now, at risk to ourselves." He gestured to his right arm, which she remembered had been bandaged. She had wondered how he'd hurt himself — she'd never have guessed he'd been off helping outsiders. "And we have been doing all we can to spread the word beyond the border of the exact date and time, and predict the location, of the worst of the storms, so people can prepare. Now we'll have to spread word of the new date."

Mina froze as a sudden thought hit her. "The people in the Dern outpost aren't going to have time to reach their city's storm bunkers." They wouldn't be expecting the ten-year storm to come tomorrow! They thought they had four more days.

Professor Dano sighed. "I know. But we have limited time

and resources. Every storm guardian who believes in our cause is out warning as many as they can. Hundreds of thousands of people live in their cities. We have to focus our efforts there."

But that's not enough! She pictured Neela, Eione, and Varli. "We can help. There must be something we can do for Dern —"

He shook his head. "You've risked enough. It's time for you to go back to being a student: learn as much as you can, and bide your time until you get another chance to help. I know it's difficult: sometimes we have to accept that we've done our best but it wasn't enough."

Tears pricked her eyes. She blinked them back. She was *not* going to cry. It couldn't be over! There had to be more she could do! People's lives were on the line!

His voice was gentle, even kind. "I know this isn't much consolation, or perhaps not any consolation at all in light of the seriousness of the situation, but I will be giving you an A on your essay. Though you veered from the assigned topic, you did write a persuasive piece."

Mina nodded. Her throat was too clogged to thank him, and she didn't feel like there was anything to be thankful for. She'd failed. There would be more graves in Dern — if anyone was left to bury the dead.

⚡

Mina trudged back to her dorm room. There was no one in the halls. Every door was shut, which was good. She didn't want to see or talk to anyone. She'd nearly made it to her door when Vira suddenly came out of the bathroom.

Vira was sporting a black eye, and her hair was half up in braids and half dangling over her cheek. She brushed hard against Mina's shoulder as she walked past. Mina flinched away, opened her mouth to say something, and then shut it.

"What?" Vira snarled. "Oh, I forgot — you didn't join in the fight. Too scared to choose a side? Coward." She stalked away.

Mina watched her go, and a half-dozen retorts jumped into her mind. She didn't say any of them. *I did* choose a side, she thought at Vira's back. *And I'm not a coward. I just don't fight the way you fight.*

I also am not going to lose the way you're going to lose.

She felt her hands curl into fists. It felt good.

"I'm not giving up," she said. Quietly, but out loud. She wasn't going to quit, and she was not going to abandon the people of the Dern outpost to their fate. She didn't care anymore if she failed her training or was expelled from Mytris, if there was a way to help save the people who had helped her. *Some things are more important.* She couldn't just wait for another chance to help, not when she could *make* a chance. She marched over to Ferro and Zek's door and knocked on it.

A few seconds later, it cracked open. Ferro poked his nose into the gap. "Oh, it's you. Thought I heard Vira. Didn't want to get pounded on again." He opened the door wider.

"My room," Mina said quietly. "Bring everyone you can, but leave your beasts — they'll be too conspicuous. You can fill them in through your mind." She moved down the hall and knocked on Kita and Saril's door. She continued, choosing the doors of the students who had fought the hardest in the dining hall. She knew who they were — she'd watched it all. She introduced herself to each of them, even though her voice was shaking and her heart was pounding hard.

Most of them already knew who she was, which surprised her. She'd accidentally made more friends than she'd been aware of. If things hadn't been so serious, she would have stopped and marveled at that. They all accepted her as a fellow lightning guardian, and they were willing to follow her to hear what she had to say.

Her gang of about a dozen filed after her, into her room, where Pixit and Chauda were curled around Jyx, comforting her. Jyx dashed the tears away from her eyes and jumped to her feet. "Mina!"

Mina put her finger to her lips and herded everyone inside.

Jyx's eyes grew wider as she saw so many kids crowding into their room, but she didn't say another word. Mina closed the door behind her and leaned against it. She met the eyes of each person in the room. To her surprise, they were all waiting for her to speak, expectant looks on their faces.

"I am the one who wrote the words and drew the pictures," Mina said. "I crossed the border, by accident at first and on purpose later. I've met outsiders from an outpost on the other side of the mountains. They bandaged Pixit when he was hurt and helped me get home."

"They fed us tea," Ferro piped up.

Jyx shushed him. "Mina's speaking."

He shut up.

"And they're going to die if we don't help them. They aren't expecting the festival to happen tomorrow, and they won't have time to evacuate. They'll try to ride it out, but the outpost's storm bunkers aren't strong enough to withstand a ten-year storm."

"But Mina, we can't stop the festival," Kita said. "We tried. Really, really tried. But the school is sealed. We can't even send balloons."

"But we can still fly," Mina said.

"Not everywhere," Zek said. "Even if we flew as far as we could and talked to as many guardians as we could reach, it wouldn't be enough."

"Plus we'd be caught," Ferro said.

Mina shook her head as everyone began talking at once.

Jyx shushed them again, and they fell silent.

"It's too late to stop the festival," Mina said. "And you're right — we can't fly to enough places in Alorria to convince enough people of the truth before the festival. But we *can* fly to Dern. And we can save those people from the storm."

She saw disbelief on their faces. "But we can't stop a storm!" Kita scoffed.

Mina noticed that Jyx, out of all of them, was smiling. "You have another plan," Jyx said. "I'm in."

"You didn't hear what my plan is yet," Mina said.

"Don't care," Jyx said. "I'm in."

Mina smiled at her friend. «*Chauda says to tell you she's in too,*» Pixit told her. «*Obviously I'm in. But then, I can read your mind, and you're thinking very clearly and loudly right now.*»

Ferro raised his hand. "I kind of care what the plan is."

"When I fell in that first storm, Jyx's beast, Chauda, wasn't strong enough to carry the two of us. But our beasts have grown. A lot."

Zek nodded. "It's all the potatoes."

A few laughed, nervously.

"Yes. They're strong enough to carry more than one," Mina said. She saw understanding begin to bloom on her friends' faces. "We save the people of Dern by carrying them away from the storm. By bringing them across the border, into Alorria."

TWENTY-FOUR

JUST before dawn, Mina slipped out of bed and pulled on her clothes. Across the room, Jyx was silently doing the same.

Outside, the sky was pale gray. A few stars still clung to it, and the early-morning birds had started to call to one another across the blackened hills. Opening the window, Mina saw a few clouds brewing far away, obscuring the peaks of the mountains. *It's starting.* She knew many guardians were in the capital already, preparing the marvels and wonders, most likely setting off countless smaller storms that would lead to the deadly ten-year storms.

«*It's okay. We can fly through rain.*»

She felt Pixit's nervousness, like bubbles in her veins. Usually they met their beasts outside and mounted them on the ground, but it was too risky to sneak through the school. They'd have to go out the window. Unfortunately, the storm beasts had grown so much that they couldn't fit with riders on their backs.

But Jyx had a solution to that: beasts first, then guardians jump out onto them. It had seemed like a good idea at the time. Now it seemed less simple.

You're sure you can catch me?

Pixit hopped up onto the windowsill. «*Absolutely.*» He launched himself out the window, then circled back to just beneath it. She climbed onto the sill. «*And if I miss, you bounce, right?*»

She smothered a laugh and leaped. Biting back a scream — *must be quiet!* — Mina fell and then thumped onto the back of her storm beast. Pixit peeled away from the school, and Mina twisted to look behind her. Chauda squeezed herself out the window, followed by Jyx, who leaped onto her back. They flew silently north.

One by one, the others joined them, until they were over a dozen strong.

Ahead the clouds were streaked with gray so dark it was nearly black. It looked as if morning wouldn't touch the mountains. *We have until dawn.* At sunrise, the festivities would begin with a flourish, and that, Mina believed, was when the storm would begin in earnest.

«*Unless you're wrong. Unless the prime minister is starting before dawn.*»

Thanks, Pixit. Really didn't need that worry. She didn't remember the last festival — she'd been two — but she'd read records of the last few for one of Vira's assignments: Mytris's main library was stocked with gushing accounts, praising the splendor of the festivals. Every festival tried to top the last, so it was *possible* that this time it would start before dawn. *It can't have started yet. Those must be the seeds of storms.*

Still, as they flew closer, Mina thought the clouds looked darker than they should. Streaks of silver flowed at a slant through them. «*The rain has begun.*»

I see that. She repeated his own words back to him: *We can fly through rain.*

«*It's sideways rain.*»

Diagonal. It just means there's some wind. We can fly through wind. She tried to sound confident in her head but knew Pixit could feel her worrying. *Maybe fly faster?*

He increased speed, and the others matched his pace.

Did everyone bring ropes?

«*Yes.*»

That had been her idea too. If this was to be a storm beyond anything any of them had ever seen, then they were bringing safety harnesses, never mind how "reckless" guardians liked to be. To her surprise, no one had argued with her.

For the first time, she had really felt like a leader.

Ferro and Zek had been in charge of gathering nets — the people from Dern would ride in them while the beasts absorbed any lightning in the area, deflecting it from them. If the storm got too dangerous, the guardians would catch the bolts before they could strike the nets.

Get in; get the people; get out, she told herself. *No time for tea.*

And then there was no time for anything, because they

were there, at the border. The mountains loomed in front of them, their peaks shrouded in storm clouds. Thunder rumbled, and Mina counted the seconds between the clap and the strike.

«*Mina . . .*»

I know.

The storm was already here.

"On three!" Jyx shouted to everyone. "One, two . . . three!"

They flew into the storm, over the mountains, and across the border.

Rain smashed into Mina's face. She blinked through it, trying to see, but there was nothing to see — they were within the storm cloud, thick gray above, below, and on all sides. She looked to her left and right and saw flashes that could be the other storm beasts. She hoped so.

Stay with the others!

If they were separated, they wouldn't all make it to the outpost — only Mina, Jyx, Ferro, and Zek and their beasts had ever been there.

"Down!" Jyx ordered.

Her word was swallowed by the rain, and Mina hoped the others heard as she and Pixit zoomed down. Rain fell with them, and wind battered at them. Another crack of thunder.

She saw — *Ground!*

Pixit pulled up, and they skimmed over the rocks.

She exhaled and twisted in her seat to see if the others had reacted in time. Jyx, Ferro, and Kita were right behind her, close to Pixit's tail. She thought she saw sparks that could be the others.

She turned back around and peered ahead of them. The outpost should be near . . .

«I see it.»

Mina squinted and tried to wipe the rain from her eyes. *Where?*

«There.» He circled once, and Mina saw the structures, shadows against the mountain. He flew over the houses, low, skimming above their roofs as the rain pounded down.

He landed beside the buildings, and Mina jumped off his back. Mud splattered. "Neela! Varli! Eione!" She ran to Neela's house and flung the door open. "Neela?"

No one answered.

The house was empty.

She ran to the next building and pounded on the door. "Hello? Anyone?"

Joining her, her friends shouted at the top of their lungs and thumped on other doors. The rain was falling harder now, slapping the ground, and she heard a sound in the distance like a howl.

She looked west — the clouds looked as if they'd been twisted around a giant's finger. They swirled like black cotton candy. Deadly candy. She'd seen pictures of such cloud formations and heard stories.

«Oh no. Mina!»

Tornado.

We can't stay!

"Neela! Eione —"

Maybe they'd escaped. Maybe —

Pixit roared, as loud as he had when he'd stopped the fight in the dining hall.

And Mina heard a voice, faint, from beside Neela's house: "Mina? Pixit!"

"Neela!" Mina ran across the mud toward the voice. She saw a hatch in the ground — this must be their storm bunker. *We found them,* she said to Pixit. *Tell the others!*

"You shouldn't be here!" Neela cried, climbing out of the hatch.

"We came to evacuate you," Mina told her, "to bring you back to Alorria, all of you!" *Crack* — more thunder. And then another *crack,* right on its heels.

In a flash of lightning, Mina saw Neela's face, wonder etched plainly on it. Neela grasped Mina's hand and squeezed. "You risk yourselves."

Jyx was just behind Mina. "Not if we leave right now. Come on. You know that bunker won't keep you safe — it will flood if the storm is bad enough. And this — it looks bad. You've got to come with us!"

At Neela's order, men, women, and children began to clamber out of the bunker.

Mina shot a look over her shoulder and felt as if her eyes had failed her. *Pixit, please tell me you don't see what I see.*

He looked.

«*I could tell you that, but it would be a lie.*»

Bearing down on the tiny outpost, only at most a mile beyond, was not one tornado but *two*. They seemed to be dancing with the sky. Lightning crackled between them.

"Faster!" Mina called. She ran between the beasts, helping people climb into the nets, helping secure the nets around the beasts' legs — also her idea. The storm beasts could have held the nets in their claws, the way Ragit, Brindle, and Chauda had when they'd carried her and the wounded Pixit back to the school, but with the storms, none of them wanted to take any unnecessary risks. All nets were tied on.

The wind and rain were so loud she couldn't hear the children screaming, though she saw their open mouths and pinched faces as they were tossed into the nets. It sounded as if the entire world were screaming in Mina's ears. She was crying, but she didn't care — her face was already slick with rain and mud.

All the streams around the town had swelled, overflowing their banks. Mina ran through six inches of water. It seeped into her boots.

"Is that everyone?" she yelled to Neela.

"Yes!" Neela yelled back.

"Then let's fly!" Mina shouted as she mounted Pixit. Eione helped Neela into Chauda's net; then Eione climbed into Pixit's.

"Don't drop me," Eione warned.

"We won't," Mina promised. *Can you carry both of us?* she asked Pixit silently.

«*I don't know if I can. But I will.*»

Lifting the net, he flapped his wings hard, rising up, and then he was sailing forward. Immediately the wind slapped into them. *Turn!* Mina cried in her mind. Below her, Eione screamed.

Directly ahead was the first tornado.

Flying still higher, Pixit veered back toward the mountains. Mina tried to look to see if the others had gotten airborne — she saw some. She couldn't see them all.

The rain was no longer drops. It had amassed into a solid wall of water. It felt as if a bucket were being poured directly onto her head. She didn't know how Pixit could see. She wiped at her eyes again and again, frantically trying to tell which way the mountains were.

All around them, lightning flashed — bolts spread out like veins in a leaf ahead of them. The gray clouds were bleached white. Again and again, lightning streaked the sky. Pixit flew between the strikes.

«*Mina, there's too much! I can't avoid it all!*»

You can do it! Keep flying!

«*You'll have to catch the electricity before the bolts strike the net!*»

But if I fail . . .

«*Catch it! You need to do it! I know you can!*»

Mina flattened against Pixit's neck and hoped that none came too close. She'd caught bolts that she'd drawn to her, within tame practice clouds, but these were another thing altogether. Electricity scurried across the clouds.

«*Mina!*»

Again, across the mountain range, she saw a web of white light, as lightning struck over and over at the peaks. "Curl up as much as you can!" Mina warned Eione. "And hang on!"

Putting all her trust in the rope to hold her, Mina rose in her seat, and she reached her arms up, hands high over her head, fingers spread. *I'm ready! Go!*

Roaring, Pixit flew into the lightning.

Mina felt it hit her fingers and rattle down her arms. She brought her hands together, holding the lightning steady above her, high above the net with their passenger. She screamed as they burst through the white light and through a wall of wind.

And then they were over and out.

Sunlight poured onto them.

Blue sky above.

Dawn had risen, and Alorria looked beautiful.

Mina opened her hands and released the electricity. Some of it sped through the air and slammed down, harmlessly, on the blackened hills below. But most of the energy was absorbed into Pixit, causing him to glow an even more brilliant yellow.

«*We did it!*»

She twisted, leaning over to see Eione beneath them.

"I'm okay!" Eione called up from the net. She lifted her face toward the sun.

Looking farther back, Mina saw Chauda and Jyx carrying Neela; Ferro and Brindle with Varli; Zek and Ragit with their passenger; Kita and Uma with theirs; Saril and Quil with theirs . . . She counted beasts and riders as they came bursting through the storm and into the blue. All the beasts glowed brilliant yellow with the lightning they'd absorbed, and all the passengers were alive and unharmed.

We all made it, Mina thought. *We did it!*

⬥CHAPTER⬥
TWENTY-FIVE

$\mathbf{A}$S soon as Pixit's paws touched the ground, Mina face-planted on his neck.

«*Are you okay?*»

We're alive. And you're amazing. She heard Eione climbing out of the net, but Mina didn't want to move, ever. She turned her head sideways, her cheek still pressed against Pixit's soaked scales, so she could see the others.

Beasts touched down on the charred hill, lowering their nets gently onto the ground. She watched as the evacuees shrugged away the nets and fell into one another's arms, hugging and crying and laughing and talking all at once. They clutched their children to them, then looked at the mountains, which swarmed with storms, held back by a wall of wind, threaded by lightning, that ran along the peaks.

Neela touched Mina's shoulder. "Shouldn't we get farther away?"

Zek answered for her. "The storms won't cross the mountains — they never do, unless deliberately directed here. Wind guardians will drive them back. You felt that wall of wind, right?"

"Yeah," Ferro agreed. "Throughout the day, they'll fly along the ridge, reinforcing that wall. Kind of cool, if it weren't for the horrificness of the storm on the other side."

Mina raised her head higher at that. *If wind guardians come along the mountains, driving away the storms . . .*

Saril asked, "Won't they see us?"

"That would be bad," Ferro said.

Jyx snorted. "At least then they'd see there are people who we're hurting, not nameless, scary outsiders. They'd see a handful of scared people, with kids."

Mina felt the tickle of an idea. She replayed for herself what Jyx had said, thinking through her idea, twisting it back and forth in her mind.

"Yes!" Kita said. "If the guardians see them and stop right now —"

Zek interrupted her. "A few wind guardians can't stop the entire festival. We already tried giving the essays to lightning guardians. You can see how much good that did."

Pixit saw the idea in her mind before she said it. «*Yes.*»

Really? You think it's a good idea?

«*I think it's an excellent idea.*»

Around her, everyone was talking: the guardians arguing about whether to stay or go, and the evacuees worrying about the storm on the mountain and beyond the mountain, destroying the outpost and their homes, ravaging the towns and cities. Some of the kids were crying. Some of the adults, too. Eione was arguing loudly that they wouldn't be able to go home — there wasn't going to be a home left, thanks to the Alorrians. Varli was saying the children needed fresh clothes and food, and beds to sleep in. They were scared and exhausted. Neela agreed they all wanted to be cleaned up, if that was possible, but if not, they were grateful at least to be alive. Ferro was saying to bring them to Mytris, and Zek was telling him that that would never work — they'd be caught. Kita was saying she didn't care if they were caught, because this was the right thing to do.

"I have an idea," Mina said.

No one heard her.

"I have an idea!" she said, louder.

Still, they were all talking at once. *Can you ask Chauda to ask Jyx to get their attention?* Pixit did. Jyx whistled loudly, and everyone shut up. "Mina has an idea," Jyx said.

They turned to look at her. All of them, guardians and evacuees alike, were a bedraggled mess. They were mud-spattered and soaked through, filthy and pathetic. Looking at them, no one could deny they'd been through a disaster.

"There's still a chance to stop the storms," Mina said. "But we need to fly."

"Where?" Ferro asked.

"To the heart of Alorria. To the capital city. To the prime minister herself."

Saril sputtered. "But we can't go to the prime minister

looking like this! And we can't bring outsiders with us! Do you know how many people will be around her? How many will see?"

Mina nodded. "Yes. I do. And they all have to see us, exactly as we look now. They have to see what our storms do. And they have to see who they hurt. They need to see that the rumors have faces and voices and names and lives."

Necla was nodding. Fione too.

Jyx. Ferro. Kita. All of them.

"Mount up," Mina said.

"You heard her!" Jyx called. "Everyone, back to your beasts! We fly!"

⚡

«The best part of this plan,» Pixit said as they flew, «is that the prime minister and her people won't see us coming. It's completely unpredictable.»

That's because I didn't think of it until just now.

«Precisely! It's brilliant!»

He had a point.

Unlike Mytris, which would be impossible to sneak into — by now, someone had to have noticed they were all missing — the capital wouldn't be closed. In fact, everyone all across Alorria was welcome. People would have been streaming into the city ever since the new festival date was announced. A few bedraggled additions wouldn't be stopped as suspicious. *And we aren't actually trying to sneak in, anyway,* Mina thought. *That helps.* They were going to the same place as everyone else: the center of the city, as close as possible to the people with the power to stop the festival.

«*And then we say hello!*»

And hope they listen.

Flying straight from the barren lands, it was still a long journey. Plenty of time for Mina to think through all the things that could go wrong, and all the ways this could fail. She couldn't help worrying that she was bringing the evacuees out of one storm and into another.

But it *felt* right.

We have to try.

She saw the capital in the distance. If Mina had thought the city looked impressive before, it was nothing compared to what lay spread before them now.

Each building looked clad in rainbows and diamonds — they sparkled in the sunlight, and only when Mina and the others flew closer could they tell it was because every building was encased in its own waterfall. Rain beasts flew between them, with guardians leading streams of water in soaring arcs above the city. Sun beasts lined the street, beaming rays of light at the water, creating even more rainbows out of the droplets. In the air, rain guardians shaped clouds into animals: deer that pranced across the sky, little cats that played hide-and-seek behind the towers, dolphins that dove through the blue.

Music poured out of the city, and the musicians were carried on platforms propelled on the wind directed by wind guardians. Violinists and singers flew through the air, between rainbows created by rain and sun beasts. Dancers swung on ribbons that were held by more flying storm beasts.

And then the snow guardians came, and in their wake, the streams of water were frozen in midair. Skaters emerged from the windows of buildings and sped across the ice, high above the street. Cheers echoed so loudly through the city that Mina could hear them even from outside.

As Mina and her friends flew into the city, the cheers and music became nearly deafening. The sound swallowed them, until it sank into their bodies. Mina felt the singing inside her bones. Everywhere she looked there was another wonder.

The breeze carried the scent of flowers, and undercutting it, Mina smelled the hint of char. She watched the tops of the buildings, looking for the lightning guardians. Every skyscraper had a metal rod that rose from it.

She heard a crack.

There!

A ball of lightning shimmered around the top of one of the rods, and a lightning beast swooped past it. Leaning sideways, its guardian scooped up the ball and tossed it to the next skyscraper, where another guardian caught it.

And then the sky suddenly darkened, as the wind guardians swept thickening clouds in front of the sun and the sun guardians dimmed their lights.

"Whoa, the tournament!" Jyx said from beside her. "It's started!"

As if her words had ignited them, the lightning guardians burst into action. There were dozens of simultaneous matches played between dozens of teams, all over the city, using the lightning rods on the tops of skyscrapers as their goalposts. Zipping between the rods, the players tossed bolts, they blocked, they dodged, they ducked, and they soared. Lightning zapped through the air, zigzagging between the skyscrapers in a game that was faster, more dangerous, and more extraordinary than Mina could have imagined.

«*Mina.*»

This is amazing!

«*Mina! We're here. The heart of Alorria.*»

Ahead was the bridge, and the capitol building itself. The roof had been peeled back so that the beautiful hall was open to the sky. Bleachers had been built all around and bedecked in every flower imaginable: sunflowers from the farmlands, tropical blossoms from the rainforests, cherry and apple blossoms from the orchards, white sprays of snowdrops from the mountains, rushes from the lake district, and what looked like black roses to represent the barren lands. She saw the section that held the prime minister, beside the archway.

Mina wanted to turn Pixit around and flee.

She felt so small compared to all this. How could she ever capture the attention of an entire nation? Or even just one person in it? *This was a mistake. It will never work. They'll never notice us. They'll never hear us!*

«*I'll fly us as close as I can.*»

And then Mina spotted a device that looked familiar. A projector with a speaking tube. She remembered it from her short-lived trip to the capitol. Jyx had been amazed to see it. She'd babbled about it — what had she said?

«*It's powered by lightning,*» Pixit supplied. «*It puts someone's image on a wall, and it can make someone's voice twice as big. Three times. A hundred times, if you have enough lightning.*»

Mina began to grin.

Tell the others. We need every spark they've got.

Gliding down, Pixit gently lowered the net, then landed next to the unused projector. Mina dismounted and helped Eione climb out. Then she helped Neela. No one was paying any attention to them — all eyes were on the sky, watching the extraordinary game of lightning relay.

"It's a projector with a speaking tube," Mina said. "We're going to power it so everyone can see and hear."

"And then you're going to tell them about us? As if you know what it's like to be us?" Eione asked, crossing her arms. She was glaring at the richly dressed people with undisguised disgust. "You can't know, living here in safety and comfort. We're your props. You want to make them pity us."

Neela shot her a look. "Eione, these children are trying to help us."

"I don't want their pity," Eione said. "I want them to stop murdering our people and destroying our homes. How's she going to convince them to do that? Look at these people, smug in their wealth, blinded by their excess. What is she going to tell them that's going to compete with all this?"

Mina concentrated, spreading her fingers, drawing the lightning from the border out of Pixit. Beside her, the other students were doing the same. "That's not why I'm here. I'm the quiet one. I'm not going to tell them anything," Mina said. "You are."

Eione gawked at her.

As the lightning built between her hands, Mina felt all the hair on her body begin to stand on end. The strands of her hair rose upward. Her skin tingled. "It's not my story to tell," Mina said. "They don't need to see or hear me. But I am going to make it possible for everyone to see and hear *you*."

Now! she thought at Pixit. She heard him spread the order to the other storm beasts, and from them to their guardians. All of them hurled their lightning at the rod that rose from the projector.

It absorbed it, crackled, and then squealed a high-pitched noise.

Eione looked terrified.

And Mina knew exactly how she felt. "Go on. Just because you haven't been heard before doesn't mean you don't have something to say."

Neela placed a hand on Eione's shoulder and squeezed,

and Eione stepped up to the projector. She pushed back the hood of her jacket. "People of Alorria." The tube took her voice and amplified it, sending it across the city, echoing from the skyscrapers.

People looked up and around, searching for the source of the voice. The lightning guardians paused in their game, looking down. Eione's image rippled across the side of the capitol building.

Eione faltered. Softly she said, "I can't."

Loudly, Mina said, "You can."

The other evacuees clustered around her, supporting her — their images joining Eione's on the wall of the capitol. Eione raised her voice. "My name is Eione. I'm thirteen years old. I am from beyond the mountains, and I am here to tell you that you are killing us."

CHAPTER

TWENTY-SIX

EIONE spoke until the lightning power ran out, which wasn't long, given how much energy they were using to amplify her voice to be heard throughout the city. But it was enough.

As soon as the speaker cut out, there was chaos. All over the bleachers, everyone was out of their seats, talking and shouting. In the streets, people were swarming together, as if they were angry bees. Mina pressed closer to Pixit. *Did it work?*

Maybe.

She didn't hear any music. Didn't see any fountains streaming overhead. Didn't see any games. Didn't see any guardians and their storm beasts performing for the crowd. Just saw people, angry and upset people.

"It might be a really good time to leave," Ferro suggested.

"Take us home, Mina," Neela said. She laid her hand on Mina's still-wet-and-muddy sleeve. "Or take us back to whatever is left. We've done what we could."

"Quickly," Jyx added. She pointed across to where the prime minister sat. A few guards were pushing through the crowd, trying to get from the advisors to the speaking tube. But the crowd was thick, slowing them.

The students and the evacuees scrambled back to the storm beasts. Pixit was right — no one had expected them, and so no one was prepared to stop them. No one even knew if they *should* stop them, or what they were going to do next. Such a thing had never happened in the history of Alorria. Mina heard the excited chatter: Outsiders in the city? During the festival? And what that girl had said! Was it true? Could it be true?

Yes, she heard people say. Just because mountains surrounded them didn't mean they were separated from the rest of the world. They were part of the world. Their sky was also everyone else's sky. Eione had put a face and voice to what many people, especially other storm guardians, had suspected.

This is going to work, Mina thought.

«*Of course it will. But maybe we should hurry just in case.*»

Most of the guards had rushed to protect the prime minister and other dignitaries, expecting an attack to follow the speech, but Mina and her friends had done what they came to do.

And so they simply flew away.

No one stopped them. No one followed them. There was too much confusion in the city for anyone to decide how to act, and so Mina and her friends were able to leave without incident.

They flew north, back toward the mountains. Mina felt

Pixit faltering beneath her. He'd never flown so far or carried so much weight for so long. *Pixit, are you all right?*

«We did something that matters. Like you always said we would, back when I was in the egg. Like in the tales you read me.»

You did amazing. Absolutely beyond amazing.

«So did you.»

From Chauda's net, Neela called, "Look, the storm is dispersing! Your festival has seen an abrupt end."

Wow, Mina thought as she stared at the peaks of the mountains. Neela was correct — the gray clouds were breaking up and drifting apart. She didn't see the flat streaks of silver or the flashes of lightning.

They crossed the mountains into gentle rain.

Ahead, the outpost was at least partially standing. Several buildings had collapsed, and many roofs were ripped to shreds. But Neela's house was there, as were a few others, with broken windows but still-upright walls. They'd been spared the worst of it — Mina could see the path of destruction where the tornadoes had ripped through the trees, only a quarter mile away. A terrifyingly near miss.

After landing, the students helped the evacuees out of the nets. Mina hugged as many as she could, and they hugged her, Pixit, and the other students and beasts. And then Mina and her friends climbed back on their beasts.

With only their guardians to carry now, the storm beasts flew slowly, tiredly, back to Mytris.

Everyone assumed they had disobeyed the "sealing" in order to go watch the festival. Several students had tried that and been caught as they snuck through the school. Mina, Jyx, and her friends told no one the truth. Not yet. Not while they were still exhausted and filthy and hungry. «*And I need to pee,*» Pixit told Mina.

They trudged to their rooms after Professor Werrin finished yelling at them for irresponsibility and selfishness, and banished them to the dorm. Mina was so tired she'd barely heard any of the words. From the glassy looks in her friends' eyes, she doubted they had either. Pixit visited the bathroom and then collapsed in his bed. He was snoring instantly.

She and Jyx stripped off their muddy, wet clothes, washed themselves, dressed in their nightclothes, and fell asleep. They slept straight through dinner and through the night, only waking again for breakfast. So did the others.

Standing on a platform, Professor Werrin lectured them once more for leaving the school while it was forbidden, and she doled out punishments: no free time between training lessons for three months, a ten-page essay from each of them on the importance of obedience, plus they had to help clean the mess of mud that they and their beasts had tracked through the hallways. "You're lucky Alorria needs you, or I'd see you all expelled!"

Not a single one of the students or beasts objected to any of this. They were still too tired. And they were all very well aware that they'd actually broken the school rules and possibly a law or two in a rather spectacular way.

After breakfast, Mina met with Professor Dano in his library. To him she told the entire truth. And he put his face in his hands and began to cry. When he finished, he was smiling.

"You did beautifully," he told her. "Go rest more, and I'll find out what has come of your actions. I'll tell Vira and the other teachers that you all have been confined to your rooms as extra 'punishment' until dinnertime — no training today."

She went back to her room. Jyx, Chauda, and Pixit were already there, asleep. They woke before dinner. Mina finally felt like herself again, though she ached everywhere.

"Ugh, Chauda, Pixit, you still have mud in your scales," Jyx said. "We'd better fix that before we show up in the dining hall."

They shooed the beasts out the window, then met them outside and scrubbed them clean. Pixit sighed happily as the last of the filth was wiped away. *Feel better?*

«*Much. Do you think Neela, Eione, and the others are all right?*»

I hope so. It will take them a while to fix the outpost, but at least Dern still exists. And even more important, they won't need to dig any new graves.

«*You know, it's funny — we did something big. And yet it still feels like the world is exactly the same. It's an ordinary day. The sun is shining. Birds are chirping. Shouldn't something have changed?*»

Mina looked up at the sound of footsteps. A dozen students were running out of the school toward them — a mix of those who had handed out copies of Mina's essay and those who had fought against them in the dining hall.

They skidded to a stop in front of Mina and Jyx. The one in the lead asked breathlessly, "You have to tell us: Did you see them?"

Mina and Jyx looked at each other.

"Who?" Jyx asked.

"The agitators!" The student waved her hands in the air for emphasis. "Everyone's talking about it. A group of agitators crashed into the middle of the festival, disrupted the entire thing. The prime minister suspended the festival because of it! It was supposed to be terrifying. You were there, right? You were the ones who snuck out to watch, weren't you? Was it terrifying?"

Mina and Jyx tried hard *not* to look at each other.

"Very terrifying," Jyx said. "But also kind of exciting."

Another student pushed forward. "What happened?"

Mina stared at the students, all of whom were waiting for her to speak. She noticed that some of the teachers had come to listen too, including Vira, who, for the first time in days, was looking more curious than hostile. *They're listening to us.* Mina began to smile. "Well, as it turns out, those essays were right," she said softly, but they heard her. They were hanging on every word. "We saw the outsiders with our own eyes. And they'd clearly been through a storm. They said the worst storms come every ten years, exactly on the day of our festival. There's a connection between what we do here and what happens there."

"Whoa," several of the students breathed together.

"So what do you think the prime minister is going to do?" the first student asked, wide-eyed.

Mina's smile faded. "I don't know. But I hope she does the right thing." *We've done our best. It's up to her now.*

$$\lightning$$

They found out two days later, when the balloons began to arrive again with news. All the students were called into the front hall, where they gathered amid the lightning-blasted glass sculptures, and Professor Werrin stood before them.

"Students, I wish to update you on some unusual news, before rumors take hold, as they so often do," Professor Werrin said. She scowled at a piece of paper in her hand. "As you know, the festival was interrupted by a visit from . . . our neighbors to the north. And to our surprise, they came to plead for our assistance. Their lands have been plagued by increasingly terrible storms, and there appears to be a connection between these storms and our use of the storm beasts. While Alorrian storm experts research this connection, the prime minister has permanently canceled the remainder of the planned festival activities —"

A cheer broke out among the students.

Looking around, Mina couldn't tell who'd started it — she didn't think it was Jyx, Ferro, Zek, or any of the other students who had come with them on the rescue mission. The first cheer came from across the room, but it spread fast until the majority of students were cheering, whistling, and clapping. She joined in.

Thumping her cane on the floor, Professor Werrin caught their attention again. She read, "'Furthermore, humanitarian aid will be extended to those who were impacted by the catastrophic storms. This offer of aid is not an admission of a causal relationship between our weather control and their storms. It is basic decency.'"

Mina felt dizzy. The festival was officially stopped! Plus help would be sent to the people in the storm's path, if they needed it. Maybe the government wasn't admitting guilt, but that sounded like an apology to Mina. *We're cleaning up the mess we made.* She thought of Necla, Eione, and Varli. Maybe they'd have assistance rebuilding their outpost. *They're going to be okay,* Mina thought at Pixit.

«Yes.» He sounded smug. «*I knew it would all work out.*»

No, you didn't.

«*I believed in you, from the start. Told you that.*»

Professor Werrin rolled the message up and tapped it on the palm of her hand. "This news does not excuse you from training or lessons. I believe you all have somewhere to be?"

The students dispersed. After pausing to hug Jyx, Ferro, and Zek, then Kita and Saril, Mina ran through the hall and up the stairs. She knocked on Professor Dano's library door. "Come in," she heard from inside.

She burst in. "Did you hear?"

Professor Dano smiled. He seemed to be doing that a lot

more lately. "You forced the prime minister's hand. Faced with such a public display, she had no choice. She had to react like this, or risk appearing selfish and unethical." He stood and pulled a ledger off the shelf. "My colleagues are now maneuvering to bring the data we've secretly collected over the years to the forefront." He laid the book open in front of her. In it, she saw row after row of dates and numbers: rainfall, wind direction and speed, and severity of storms, matched with a record of storm-beast activity in Alorria. "You've given us an opening, Mina. You made people listen. Now the truth can come out."

"Then we did it!" She couldn't stop smiling.

He closed the book and placed it back on his shelf. "It's not over, of course. There will be those who don't believe the data, who challenge the truth, who will try to hide it again or obscure it or discredit it. But the door to change has been opened."

"How can I help?" she asked.

"This is where I'm supposed to say, 'You've done enough,'" he said. "'You're just a child. Go play and don't worry about the world.' But there's no point in saying that to you, is there? You won't listen."

It was the first time that anyone had ever accused Mina, of all people, of not listening. He looked confused when she laughed.

⚡

Just before lights out, after an exhausting day of extra-hard training, Mina met with Jyx, Ferro, and Zek and their beasts in her and Jyx's room. She repeated for them everything that Professor Dano had told her, and they dissected everything Professor Werrin had said, with the beasts chiming in through their guardians. They talked about what they should do next: finish training and graduate as quickly as they could, so they could help the outsiders as much as possible.

It's a good plan, Mina thought. She hoped they'd be assigned somewhere near one another after they graduated. She was going to request that.

«*And if we aren't together, we can fly, remember?*»

She laughed and then, at Jyx's demand, repeated what she and Pixit had said.

They all smiled at one another.

"Hey, speaking of flying, did you see that double loop to the goal the guardian in the red shirt did during the festival tournament?" Ferro asked.

"Yes!" Jyx pounced on it. "And did you see the fake-out throw to the second rod? Brilliant, especially if you're playing with multiple rods."

Zek nodded. "Yeah, makes it trickier to guard."

Mina leaned back against the wall and listened as her friends babbled about new relay tricks to try and strategies to win. Absently, she spread her fingers. She remembered how it had felt, catching all that energy in her hands. There had to be ways to use all their power to help people beyond Alorria.

«*We'll find ways.*»

Yes, we will. And then Mina leaned forward and said, "Since we already saved the world this week, how about we beat you at lightning relay tomorrow?" She knew how her friends would react to that — their faces lit up in smiles.

"Oh yeah!" Jyx said. She pointed at Ferro and Zek. "Prepare to lose."

"*You* prepare to lose!" Ferro cried.

Zek shook his head. "That was a terrible comeback. I'm embarrassed for you."

"You have a better one?" Ferro demanded.

"Yeah," Zek said. "Or I will. In a few hours, when I think of it."

And they kept talking and laughing, until lights out forced them to bed.

⟣ CHAPTER ⟢
TWENTY-SEVEN

MYTRIS LIGHTNING SCHOOL
GRADUATION DAY . . .

MINA brushed Pixit's feathered scales. Sparks showered around them, and Mina felt strands of her hair rise. She laughed. He was stuffed full of lightning from the last storm and was so excited that he was shimmering. "You ready?"

«Been ready since the day I hatched! Well, almost.»

He sprang up, shook himself, and sprayed more sparks around the dorm room. She laughed again as he romped to the window and launched himself outside. She followed, climbing onto the sill and then jumping out onto his back.

Soaring, she shielded her eyes from the sun as she looked for the river ship. It was docking at the station — she watched the sailors scurry over the deck, secure the ship against the dock, and lay out the plank for the passengers.

«I see them!»

Papa. Mother, holding Rinna's hand. Gaton, carrying Beon.

Excited, Beon started bouncing in Gaton's arms, pointing up at Mina. Mina waved back at them, and then Pixit flew down toward Mytris.

She joined the other students in the front hall. Eighteen of them were graduating today, or at least they would if they passed their final test. Pixit wedged himself in between Chauda and Brindle, and Mina reached over to squeeze Jyx's hand. On her opposite side, Ferro reached over to take her hand. He was already holding Zek's. The four friends stayed linked as Professor Werrin led the procession of teachers and professors through the arched doorway. All of them stood at attention as the families filed into the cathedral-like room.

Mina heard Beon and Rinna cry, "Mina, Mina, Mina!" And then Mother shushed them before she smiled and waved. Papa was beaming with pride.

"Wild guess," Jyx whispered. "Your family?"

Mina nodded. *They're here!* She wanted to run to them and hug them, but she stayed in position. Ferro released her hand to wave at his grandmother, and Zek waved at his parents and brother. "Are yours here?" Mina asked Jyx.

"Yeah, there." Jyx nodded toward a stiff-backed couple who were admiring one of the glass sculptures rather than paying attention to the students. "That's the sculpture from their graduating class."

Mina looked at them, then at Jyx. "Our sculpture will be better."

Jyx grinned. "You know it."

Professor Werrin thumped her cane on the floor. All eyes shifted to her. She'd dressed for the occasion in golden robes but carried her same cane with the black orb. "Welcome, Class of Fall 894, and welcome, families and friends! These students exemplify some of the best that Alorria has to offer. I am proud of their dedication and achievement, and I hope you are as well. During this time of change, it is more important than ever that our storm guardians be ready to face the challenges that lie ahead."

At the word "change," Mina glanced across the hall and met Professor Dano's eyes. He gave her a nod of approval.

"Now, will the students in the Mytris Lightning School Class of Fall 894 please begin?" She raised her cane, and the orb opened into a net. She stepped back. So did the audience.

Mina, Jyx, Ferro, Zek, Kita, Saril, and the other graduating students stood in a circle around a pile of sand in the center of the hall. Their beasts joined the circle, and each student laid one hand on their beast's back. They raised their other hands, fingers spread wide.

The air began to crackle.

«Ooh, this is fun!»

Mina grinned at Pixit and then at her friends. Electricity began to jump between their fingers and coat their hands up to their wrists. They let it build, as they'd practiced, until each of them held a writhing sphere of white light.

"On three!" Jyx called. "One, two, three!"

All of them hurled their lightning at the sand. And the sand sprayed up in an instant, freezing into an array of glass tubes that mimicked the shape of the lightning strikes.

For a moment, there was silence.

And then the audience burst into cheers.

"We did it!" Jyx cried.

She hugged Mina, and Mina hugged her back; then they hugged Pixit and Chauda. Everyone else started hugging one another too.

We really did it, Mina thought at Pixit. *We're real storm guardians now.*

«Told you we would be,» Pixit said smugly.

Professor Dano stepped forward, cleared his throat, and then looked to Professor Werrin, who thumped her cane again. Slowly the crowd quieted. "Your assignments are posted on the wall outside the dining hall," Professor Dano announced.

Everyone stampeded out of the front hall, cramming into the corridor. Mina hung back with Pixit, admiring the sculpture. It was, she thought, the prettiest one.

Her family clustered around her. Beon and Rinna each hugged one of her legs. Papa hugged Pixit first, then Mina. Mother and Gaton embraced both of them, reaching over the twins.

"Aren't you going to see where you're posted?" Gaton asked.

It was strange, but it felt like it didn't matter. She tried to find the right words to explain why. "Wherever I go, it will be all right. I know who I am, and that matters more than where I am."

«Besides, Jyx will tell us,» Pixit added.

Sure enough, less than thirty seconds later, Jyx and Chauda came barreling back into the front hall, skidding to a stop just short of the new glass sculpture. "Guess what?" She danced in a circle around Mina and didn't wait for Mina to guess. "We're together!"

«*Yay!*»

"And guess where? Beyond the mountains!"

Mina felt as if she'd had lightning poured into her. Beyond the mountains! *Pixit, do you know what this means?* It meant that the prime minister had really listened. It meant they'd be doing what no storm guardian had done before: using their power outside Alorria. It meant they'd have a chance to do more, fix more, *be* more. *Together, we're going to do great things!*

«*Together, we're going to have more adventures!*»

She smiled at Jyx, Chauda, and her other friends, who were all coming back into the front hall brimming with news, and at her family. And then at the glass sculpture that they'd made out of sand and lightning. *Together, we'll set the world on fire.*

ACKNOWLEDGMENTS

ALL books start with a spark. That spark could be an idea, an image, a feeling, or a wish. And if that spark is nurtured and loved (and turned upside down and shaken a few times), it grows into a book.

The spark for this book was three words:

Mina was quiet.

I wanted to write a book about a quiet girl and her lightning dragon. But I didn't want it to be the story of a quiet girl who learns how to be loud. I wanted it to be the story of a quiet girl who discovers she's strong, exactly as she is.

I was a quiet girl. And it took me a long time to discover you can be quiet *and* strong.

But stories don't grow from sparks to full-fledged books on their own. I'd like to thank my incredible agent, Andrea Somberg, and my amazing and inspiring editor, Anne Hoppe, for nurturing this spark. I'd also like to thank the fantastic team at Clarion

Books and Houghton Mifflin Harcourt: Amanda Acevedo, Dana Cuadrado, Lisa DiSarro, Candace Finn, Sharismar Rodriguez, Jackie Sassa, John Sellers, Tara Shanahan, Karen Sherman, Tara Sonin, Rachael Stein, Dinah Stevenson, Kiffin Steurer, Veronica Wasserman, and all the other awesome people who fanned the flames. Thank you to Brandon Dorman, whose gorgeous art graces the cover of this book. And love and thanks to my husband, my children, and all my family, for being my strength, my inspiration, and my joy.

ABOUT THE AUTHOR

SARAH BETH DURST's fantasy novels for children, teens, and adults include *The Stone Girl's Story*; *Drink, Slay, Love*; and *The Queen of Blood*. A threetime finalist for the Andre Norton Award for YA Science Fiction and Fantasy, Sarah has won the Mythopoeic Fantasy Award for Children's Literature and an ALA Alex Award. She lives with her family in Stony Brook, New York.